_Steven E. Petire_

9/9/98

J Pagter
9/01

Value
$30

# LETTERS
## AND
## JOURNAL
## OF A
## CIVIL WAR
## SURGEON

# LETTERS
# AND
# JOURNAL
# OF A
# CIVIL WAR
# SURGEON

Stewart J. Petrie, M.D.

Pentland Press, Inc.
England • USA• Scotland

PUBLISHED BY PENTLAND PRESS, INC.
5122 Bur Oak Circle, Raleigh, North Carolina 27612
United States of America
919-782-0281

ISBN 1-57197-095-9
Library of Congress Catalog Card Number 97-075508

Printed in the United States of America

# DEDICATION

This book is dedicated firstly to my mother, Emma Robinson Petrie. Because of her great affection for her grandfahter, Dr. Myron W. Robinson, she saved much of his memorabilla and especially his letters from the Civil War era upon which this book is based.

Dedicated also to my wife, Mary, for her great support and patience in preparation of this manuscript.

# TABLE OF CONTENTS

# CIVIL WAR TRAVELS OF
# DR. MYRON W. ROBINSON

*May, 1861*—New Haven CT to Washington, D.C.

*October, 1861*—Washington, D.C. via Newport-News to take Hilton Head and return to Fort William McHenry, Baltimore, MD

*Spring, 1862*—Leave Baltimore, capture Fort Pulaski and return

*Spring, 1863*—Leave Baltimore via Hilton Head to capture Jacksonville-Fernandina and return

*May, 1863*—Leave Baltimore for Folly Island and battle of Fort Wagner. Later to garrison at Hilton Head.

*April, 1864*—Hilton Head to James River Campaign (Bermuda Hundred)

*April 27-May 12, 1864*—Home on leave

*May through December, 1864*—Siege line Petersburg, Richmond, VA

*December, 1864 to April, 1865*—Fort Fisher Campaign and Wilmington, NC

*May to August, 1866*—Hillhouse Hospital, Wilmington, NC

Home to Hebron, CT

# FOREWORD

The enthusiasm to write this story has always been somewhere in the back of my mind. There have been so many excellent works and studies done on this strangely interesting Civil War that it seemed superfluous to try to add anything further to its cataclysmic history.

Even when I was a small boy, my mother made the annual pilgrimage to my great-grandfather's grave in Colchester, Connecticut. The tombstone records that buried there lies Major Myron Winslow Robinson, surgeon general of the Connecticut Sixth Volunteers. I remember well stopping by an old covered bridge en route, and pumping water from an old well for the flowers planted at his grave.

I grew up surrounded by the memorabilia he kept from the Civil War. My brother and I often played with his sword. It was labeled with the letters, "MS," for "Medical Service," although at one time we made believe it stood for "Miles Standish." He had many colorful medals from the Grand Army of the Republic (GAR) conventions following the war, as well as a wooden cane in which were inscribed many kindly messages from his patients at the Noroton Soldiers' Home, where he spent his last years as superintendent. The brass uniform buttons and military insignia did not make as much of an impression as his surgical instruments from the Medical Department in the Civil War. Not realizing their historical value, I used some of these instruments during dissection class in anatomy when I was in medical school.

Our most important discovery was the many letters he wrote home to Hebron, Connecticut, from his various duty stations during the bloody conflict. Since these have never been published, I thought I would build my story around the historical background of these letters. These will be introduced from time to time throughout this narrative. I have interjected an "Historical Note" (some are from little-known sources) in order to paint the background against which this tragic history is played out.

The accounts of the Connecticut Sixth Volunteers and the articles related to this epic adventure are drawn from the many excellent works noted in the bibliography. I have tried to place my great-grandfather in these scenes in the most likely way, based chiefly on the accounts in his letters, but also on the probability of his actions and deeds serving close to the point of battle and in other areas. The actions in early 1865 relating to the Fort Fisher battle are verbatim from his journal.

I apologize to the many Civil War historians if I have erred or taken too many liberties with these accounts. However, I do share with the multitude of Civil War buffs the fascinating spell that this incredibly devastating war has woven around us.

Winfield Scott envisioned a three-part strategy to defeat the Confederacy. The first part was to keep the Army of the Potomac in contact with the Army of Northern Virginia, thus neutralizing their ability to take the offensive northward. The second part was to neutralize the forces in the West (chiefly by taking control of the Mississippi and its major port cities). The last part was to choke off the supply line to the Confederacy by blockading and/or capturing the major port cities, especially along the Atlantic coast. The following true story is a part of this third stratagem.

To get a flavor of the opinion of my grandfather's friends and colleagues at the time of his death, I will also herewith reproduce this obituary:

### Myron Winslow Robinson, M.D., Noroton Heights.

Myron Winslow Robinson was born in the town of Lebanon, May 4, 1839. His father was William Robinson, descendant of John Robinson of early American history, minister of the Pilgrim Fathers. His mother was Sophia Robbins. The greater part of his life was spent among rural scenes. His early school training was at the academy at Ellington, Tolland County, the population of which town was 1,452. He began the study of medicine at Hebron in 1858, and graduated at the Berkshire Medical College in 1860. This college, among the earlier medical institutions of New England, has now passed out of existence, and among the nine hundred members of the Connecticut Medical Society there is only one remaining who received this diploma. It may be noticed that the curriculum of this institution embraced only two years. We have indeed made progress in medical education.

Dr. Robinson went back to Hebron to begin the practice of medicine, although the town at that time could not have had a population of more than one thousand, scattered over the hills. It may not seem strange, then, that with the military spirit burning at fever heat throughout the land he became fired, like all the rest and went to the war.

He gained a promotion on November 16th to the position of hospital steward and in the regular army service. Here, of course, his medical knowledge came greatly to his help, as it was his medical knowledge that had gained the position for him, and it was, too, in the direct line of his life work. But this was only the beginning of further promotions. Dr. Samuel McClellan of New Haven, the second assistant surgeon of the Sixth Regiment, was discharged from the service on January 6, 1863, and on May 11 of the same year, Dr. Robinson was commissioned to fill his place. Dr. F. L. Dibble, surgeon of the Sixth, left the army at the expiration of his term of service, and Dr. Robinson was commissioned surgeon in full on December 21. He was mustered out of the service with his regiment at Raleigh, North Carolina, August 21, 1865. His period of service in the army, therefore, embraced a period of three years and three days. He experienced hard and trying service with the Sixth Regiment. Two months after he joined the regiment, the men were called for and were engaged in the terrible night assault upon Battery Wagner on Morris Island. In that encounter, one hundred and forty-one were killed, wounded, or missing. Later the regiment landed at Bermuda Hundred and was engaged in the operations around Richmond, especially at Drury's Bluff, at Deep Bottom, and in the trenches around Petersburg until near the close of the war.

Later, it was detached and sent, under General Terry, against Fort Fisher. This, the largest earth fortification in the Confederacy, stood at the mouth of Cape Fear River and guarded the city of Wilmington, North Carolina, which had become the last port of supply for what was to be the lost cause. General Lee had said that if Fort Fisher fell, his army could not subsist. The fort had been pronounced impregnable, but it was captured by assault on January 14, 1865, but not without severe loss to our forces—110 killed, 536 wounded. So that the surgeon of such a regiment found plenty to do.

The war was nearly over. Dr. Robinson spent the summer at Goldsboro and he did not return north with his discharged men, whom he had zealously attended and to whom he was very much attached, but remained in Wilmington in charge of the Hillhouse Hospital in that town. He was not yet tired of ministering to the sick. Later, he returned to his native state and settled in Colchester, a town adjoining the one in which he was born. This was a town of three thousand souls and included the celebrated Bacon Academy and a large rubber factory. These increased the size and activities of this country town.

In 1867, Dr. Robinson married Emma J. Stewart, the daughter of Ralph Stewart of Portland. She was a congenial companion and a faithful helpmate. Three children were born to them, of whom two still survive. A son, Harry, lived but a few days. The other son and daughter are now living together in West Haven. There are three grandchildren. Mrs. Robinson went to the better land May 23, 1909, since which time the doctor has been cared for by his daughter; but he never failed to miss and to mourn for the tender care and the constant companionship of her who had so long been a partner in all his experiences.

In 1899 he was appointed surgeon in charge of the Soldiers' Home at Noroton. His entire life was thus changed by coming out of a country practice with his long tedious rides, his exposure to all weathers, and its service day and night, to the indoor life of institutional work. It was trying, too, because the majority of those with whom he had to deal were now old men of formed and often irregular habits, who expect in a home freedom from restraint; men who were often dissipated, sometimes perhaps a little ugly. His task was all the harder, because he had had for a predecessor Dr. William H. Brownson. Dr. Robinson's hard common sense, his equipoise, his tact, his sense of humor were all-sufficient and the men became very much attached to him. His army record also contributed much to the hold he had upon the men. They went to him for advice in their personal and financial affairs, and he was always ready to help them. Kindly and considerate, tactful and resourceful, he filled a trying position.The old soldiers became more attached to him and when by intrigue the scheming friend of one higher up sought to supplant him, the veterans all over the State arose in protest and the doctor remained secure in his position.

He was no man for dress parade; there was nothing of the show about him. He was full of humanity and could give reasons for the faith that was in him. He was a good companion and was fond of narrating his experiences. A good observer of symptoms, he became solicitous about himself. He came to be short of breath on exertion, and sought a specialist in New York. The specialist took his blood pressure, treated him for heart disease, and enjoined rest. One who knew him well suggested that Dr. Robinson knew his condition and preferred that his life should end in his accustomed activity, rather than as an invalid. His daughter found him dead in bed when she went to his room to call him on the morning of May 27.

"After life's fitful fever he sleeps well." He enjoyed the companionship of his fellows and held membership in many organizations. He was especially proud of his membership in the Norwalk Post G.A.R., the Connecticut State Medical Society, and the Fairfield County Medical Association. In 1895 he became president of the New London County Association, which made him one of the vice presidents of the State Medical Society. At the time of his death, he was the medical director of the G.A.R, Department of Connecticut. He was buried at Colchester.

# CHAPTER ONE:

# *Thoughts of Earlier School Days*

Growing up on a small farm with my many brothers and sisters around me did not give me much time to reflect on just where the path of life would lead me. Little did I know that the dangers, experiences and adventures I would encounter would far surpass my greatest imagination.

It is hard to believe that my eyes which have seen the snow fall gently on the haystacks, seen the first slivers of dawn creep across neatly plowed fields and seen the majestic sunsets over the mountains, would later come to witness unbelievable scenes of carnage and destruction.

I believe that is was through my kindly parents and my church that I felt a compunction to help people and improve their well being. This led to a preceptorship type training with our local Dr. Craig. He called upon me and instructed me with all matter of medical problems. These were mostly trivial, but also included fractures, burns and lacerations, mostly from farm injuries. In this way, I came to know my limitations, but this further whetted my desire to increase my medical knowledge.

[This letter is from Ellington Boarding School, Ellington, Connecticut. The envelope itself depicts Ellington Boarding School and states Rev. F. W. Chapman, A.M., principal.]

*November 13, 1859*

*Dear Father:*

*I have received yours in due time and was very glad to hear from you, although I was sorry to hear that you had lost Old Brin. It was something of a loss but small compared to some that have more to lose. I am unusually well at this time and I hope that this may find you all the same. It has been quite stormy here this afternoon, so that we have not been to church. Just before noon, I heard as dull a preacher as I have ever heard, the Rev. Mr. Pressenden.*

*I am getting along finely with my studies at present, Latin and French. Mr. Chapman gives me the use of my lamp as long as I want in the evening. I sometimes study to near short hours. Last night it was just 12 o'clock when I went to bed. It will be as late as that tonight, if I do all I intend to. I have to get up at six o'clock.*

*Sometimes when I think of how much there is to be learned, I feel I almost despair. When I think of what has been accomplished by others, I start with redoubled exertion . . . I regret exceedingly that I am not able to go to college as I intended to last spring when I came here, but I don't see any way that I can. If I did, I would be quick enough now, but if I cannot, I suppose that I must do the next best thing.*

*I suppose Orville\* has convened his school, I will send a letter in this for him which please forward to him. Thanksgiving I suppose is nearby, I would like to spend it at home, but think that I shall not unless you conclude to come after me the Wednesday before, in which case I would come. If you conclude to come, let me hear. I do not feel able to hire a horse to come or to come on the cars. For the reason I have not enough to carry me from one depot to the other. I hope I shall have enough to keep me in repairs till the close of the term when I shall have to recruit. Tell Mother I am most obliged to her for those mittens. I shall need them soon. My pantaloons, my everyday ones have worn out so I wear those with a stripe on the sides. My coat, I will hardly think will last this winter term but don't know. I will make it last as long as I can. It looks pretty rusty and fringy besides being shabby generally. But for that I don't care if it is only decently respectable. I must close for want of room. I will write soon.*

*From your son . . . Myron*

*Tell David to write, I intend to write him*

\*Orville was his half brother, born February 16, 1837.

Finding a place near school for three dollars a week was a stroke of luck, but I felt guilty for spending money when it was so hard to come by. My father wrote me that he now had to buy another plow horse to replace my favorite old "Brin." I learned to ride him bareback as a lad and was quite proud of this old horse.

I lived as inexpensively as I could. In order to make my already-worn clothes last a bit longer, I would take them off and put on a robe upon returning to my room. I studied with my old clothes on; I also wore them when I took a walk. In this way, I hoped to make my poor "wardrobe" last through the winter. (I did wish for warmer clothes in that windy, cold place.) If I had had just a little more money, then I could have tried to make it home for Thanksgiving.

My landlady near Ellington was most pleasant and seemed not to notice my embarrassment at the few, often threadbare clothes that I hung in the closet. I still remember the path through the lane to school, which led on to the church. Although some years have passed, I well remember the pleasant sound of leaves crunching under my foot in the crisp fall season. The beauty of this area of central Connecticut made me feel less lonesome on my journey to school. The church sermons on Sunday were long and boring, and thus I felt my thoughts wandering back to my beloved family in Hebron. How I wished I could be there for Thanksgiving.

The ability to study late at night was made possible by the loan of a lamp from the headmaster, Mr. Chapman. If I was to follow my dream of becoming a doctor, I felt driven to absorb information from all sources and try to excel in all studies. I thought this was difficult until I met my next challenge, namely Berkshire Medical School.

# CHAPTER TWO:

# *Berkshire Medical School*

*Pittsfield, Mass., Aug. 2nd, 1860*

Dear Father:

I now take my pen to inform you of my safe arrival here. I arrived here Tuesday Eve at about 1/2 past 6. I had a very pleasant ride but was so tired I did not enjoy it as I should otherwise have done. I do not feel entirely rested yet but am middling smart and gaining.

I had a very pleasant visit in Brooklyn, saw Charles and Theron, they were all well except the baby which is very troublesome. I had company from Andover to N.Y. which made it quite pleasant for me. Sylvester Gilbert came aboard at Middletown and we were together the rest of the time, played checquers and had a good chat—and came across the ferry together to Brooklyn. I find Austins without any difficulty at all—got there before they were up, they were somewhat surprised to see me. He lives in a very pleasant place where you can look back into the country. He is doing some business but not driving at the present time. Eliza says he is doing better this summer and I guess he is. I should not know he drank by his looks but perhaps may at times now.

Perhaps you would like to know something about this place so will give you a brief description.

Pittsfield is not a city as I supposed but only a village on the Western Railroad and being the terminus of the Housatonic RR and also of the Pittsfield & N. Adams. It contains 8 churches, about 60 stores, 3 RR depots, and 3 newspaper offices, several hotels which are crowded with visitors and 7 or 8 thousand inhabitants besides several manufactures and Young Ladies Institutes. It contains a park, a large square on which front the principal Hotels and the Berkshire Medical College. It surpasses all other places I was ever in for wealth or beauty.

*I have obtained a boarding place on Fen St.—with a Mrs. Green. It is a very good place for board but think my room does not compare with the price. I pay three dollars per week which includes washing and lights—it is 3/4 to 1 mile from the College. It is the nearest and best I can do yet I am going to try to get a cheaper place if I can. The professors directed me where to go—I tried several places—found board was from 3 to 4 dollars at them all and excluded washing at that. If I can find a better or cheaper place near the College shall do so. Quite an accident occurred here the day I arrived—a boy burst a blood vessel killing him instantly. Yesterday an Irish boy seven years old had both arms run over by the cars—he crawled under them while they were stopped and while he was backing out between the trucks they started running over both arms. Prof. Childs amputated one arm in the morning by consent of his parents, the other in the afternoon—both above the elbows.*

*I went down and saw the operation. We had our introductory lecture this evening by Prof. Seely—he gave a very good lecture of an hour's length.*

*Now Father write soon as you receive this and I will write then how I get along, cannot now for I have not fairly commenced. Please send any letter or other document addressed to me to Pittsfield without fail or breaking the wrappers will save trouble.*

*Your Affectionate Son,*
*Myron*

*Pittsfield, Mass., Sept. 19, 1860*

*Dear Father:*

*I now take my pen to answer your kind letter which was received and read with a great deal of pleasure. We have had a very pleasant day today and we are having a magnificent evening. The moon gives forth a splendid silvery light, while all the earth is wrapped in the most profound silence. "Tis as the general pulse of light stood still." It is pleasant to think that our friends are lighted by the same light that shines upon us, although they are far from us.*

*Have you heard from Warren\* lately? —and how is he getting along? I am getting along fairly at present excepting I am feeling very tired, come to sit on hard seats and listen to six or seven lectures a day and be quizzed as we have been for two or three hours evenings, besides it is very wearisome and beside the anxiety connected with the candidate for graduation. Sometimes, when I think of how much expense, how much self-sacrifice and time and hard study and care and anxiety and, after a life of the greatest responsibilities, after the thanklessness of mankind, I wonder that any one would undertake the study of Medicine.*

*But again I think of the satisfaction of knowing how fearfully and wonderfully made, and the good that can be accomplished, I wonder that so few enter the profession.*

*I have been examined by one Prof. and have got to be examined by seven more, besides I commit that time will determine the result and upon the result depends my future success. I have just come in from our evening's quiz and I am so tired I can write no more and besides it is very late. Give my regards to Mother and all the rest who inquire. Write me how the doctor gets along without fail and what the prospect is.*

*Your affectionate son . . . Myron*

*I will send you a paper . . . please preserve it for me.*

*Warren was a brother, born in 1823.

Thanks to the encouragement of my family, and to the good word (and tutelage) put in for me by my old preceptor, Dr. Craig, I was admitted to Berkshire Medical School in Pittsfield, Massachusetts. My dream of going to medical school, becoming a doctor, and helping people had finally come true!

The faculty were most friendly toward us and tried to be reassuring to us as tyros in this medical endeavor. In contrast, the local populace avoided us simply because we were medical students. In the streets and coffee shops, the "locals" almost ostracized us as a class. There was some fear that, because we deal with the sick and the dead, we might bring ill luck or ill health to them. I directed so much of each day to my medical studies that I had to remind myself to tell the family back in Hebron of the polarized political climate hereabouts.

*September 30, 1860*

*Dear Father:*

*Now I take my pen to answer your kind letter which was duly received. I should have answered it immediately but found no opportunity. I am quite well at present—I hope this may find you all enjoying the same blessing without which there is little enjoyment—we are now on our last half of the course and will soon be done. The first half seems the shortest of any time I ever saw of the same length. I am getting along finely, or at least I think so, with my studies. Three of our Profs have finished their course, two new ones commence theirs. This week I understand there are to be two or three holidays on account of the Berkshire Agricultural Fair, after which comes six lectures a day. The more I study the better I like to study medicine. Yesterday I visited "Balance" or "Rolling Rock," in Lanesboro about three miles from here. It is a large rock visited by hundreds every season. A gent there told us the estimated weight was 1,000 tons. I could jar it with my two hands and by putting under it a rock, could move it by hand near an inch. It could formerly be moved by the wind or tipped with the hand but some villain undertook to pry it off and so broke away the stone underneath. I had a pleasant afternoon. Rain fell. It is very pleasant all around here, you can see the Catskill Mountains for miles by taking a short walk. I think it is the pleasantest place in New England all things considered. But it is very cold, we have had a number of frosts, one so as to freeze water. Tonight, returning from church, the grass was all glistening with the frost by the moonlight and it was really stiff. I think it will be the coldest night of the season thus far. Fruit is quite plenty here but does me but little good. Last Sunday I went to escort some ladies visiting where I board to New Lebanon in New York, about eight miles from here, to a Shaker meeting. I was very amused and interested in their mode of worship. Today, I have been to church this afternoon. I heard a missionary from Turkey, he was quite interesting. Father, where is Mr. Knight—and who preaches in*

*Hebron? Now please write soon and tell me all the news. I love to hear from home often but do not very often think of home. I wish to be there, all are strangers here so you cannot conceive how welcome is a letter from "SWEET HOME," than which there is none like, I have a very pleasant boarding place and very nice folks. The lady of the house sends her respects to Mother. I have changed my boarding from where I first was, I found a place for $2.50 a week and could pay my way. I am obliged to practice very close economy and do not know if I shall be in arrears at that, but I shall do the best I can. There are a great number of things I was obliged to have after I got here, and never thought of, but I shall work for the rest.*

*Now, won't you answer this week? I tell you all the news, I must close for want of room. I subscribe myself,*

> *Your affectionate son—Myron*

*Give my love to all the folks. Where is Dr. Porter and how does Dr. Craig get along?*

[Dr. Craig was Myron Robinson's preceptor.]


Knowing how scarce hard cash was back home, I had to ask for more financial help. Even by skipping meals, sharing books, preserving my clothes and shoes as best possible, I had to find some way to garner a few dollars.

In the little "free time" available, I joined friends to tour interesting sites in our local environs. I would remind myself to write the folks at home about these trips.

I found it hard to sleep nights with exams near at hand. I studied by myself and with fellow students and noted that we all shared this same apprehension. We all studied up to the last minute to cram every bit of knowledge possible into our heads. But would we remember it when queried? Would my preceptors back home be proud or disappointed in my performance?

[In this letter, the envelope itself was embellished with a picture of Abraham Lincoln and was mailed in Pittsfield, Massachusetts, on October 30, 1860.]

> *October 28, 1860*

*Dear Father:*

*I now take my pen to answer your letter which should have been answered before, but I understood you in your last that you were going to write again soon so I have been waiting to hear from you.*

*Although I do not write often, yet I frequently think of home and friends but I have not seen one familiar countenance since I have been here and public prejudice is so much against medical students as a class and nearly all of them think more of their friends at home, than in this place. Yet I find no fault with my acquaintances here as extensive as they are beneficial, perhaps yet I am surprised that any one preparing for so high an honorable station in life and one that is much respected when obtained, should as a whole be dreaded by the community. But it is so, and even the very name of Medical Student strikes a sort of terror in many. But enough of this, I like it here very much. It is very pleasant and*

*I think it has been justly termed the "Garden of the Bay State." The college stands on an eminence at the South part of the village which affords a fine view of the surrounding mountains on the north and west—and of the Housatonic River on the south, and a short distance from here the Catskill Mountains can be seen here for miles along the Hudson. With such a scenery as this, anyone can't but be contented. The weather I think is colder than at home. Two weeks ago the snow fell which lasted for three days on the mountains and two here. Today, the air has felt much like snow and tonight it appears some like it, there being a circle around the moon. I have been to church three times. In the morning and the evening at the Episcopals, in the afternoon at Dr. Todd's church as I suppose you have heard of before. He is considered by his parish as very smart, I cannot think so. He is quite an old man. I received a letter from Theron last week and also from Eliza, all were well. Tell O\* to write me soon and tell Father the same and tell Mother she has not answered my letter as she agreed. I shall be at home or start for home Friday the 10th of November if nothing happens and if I do not change my mind. I would be glad to be met at Andover Depot at that time the last train of the evening, if I change my arrangement as I probably shall not, I will write again. I have yet little time to write anyway. I have letters which ought to have been answered long ago but I have little time to do anything of that kind. We have six lectures a day and expect we shall have evening lectures soon. Politics run high as the election approaches. Rep. are sure of success but I don't keep much posted in politics. I will send you a speech of Carl Schurtz which I want preserved till I come home. The Dem. had a mass meeting last night at North Adams, about 20 miles from here by railroad. I went to the depot to see the train start and surely they were the meanest looking set I have seen this long while, nearly all being Irish and some part being drunk before they started—even the D's were themselves ashamed and no wonder. The Wide Awakes parade occasionally but they are made up of intelligent working men and they look finely too. But I must close as it is late. Give my love to all and write soon.*

*This from your son Myron W. Robinson*

\* O was brother Orville.

*November 7th, 1860*

*Dear Father:*

*I take my pen to ask of you a favor and if you can grant it without too much inconvenience on your part. If you cannot, without some trouble, do not.*

*If you can send me five dollars ($5.00) by mail you will do me a favor but a greater one to the profit of B.M. Institution and I will try to find some employment, posting books or something of the kind to pay you.*

*Please write and let me know whether you sent it or not so I will know upon what to depend. I do not myself care two coppers whether or not I pay before I go home but they wish a settlement with every student before he leaves.*

*The bill to pay is for dissecting. I shall start for home Thursday the fifteenth and be at Andover on the last train. The election returns confirms Lincoln's election in every northern state except Oregon and California to be heard from. There is said to be one state for Douglass, and that is the state of DESPAIR.*

*A motion is now pending made by a wicked wag, "that the Democratic Party be patented, as they are selling out too cheap."*

*Poor Locos! They prepared a large hall in town for illumination last night, by being defeated in this town they waited for tonight about the news of Douglass' election but not hearing that, they are nowhere to be found and their lamps have gone out. Burlingame is defeated. No more news.*

*From your son*
*Myron Winslow Robinson*
*B.M. College, Pittsfield, Mass.*

On December 2nd, 1860, I returned to Berkshire Medical School after a pleasant holiday. At a church social I met a most wonderful lady (a Miss Emma Stewart). We promised to write to each other and I hoped to see her again.

# CHAPTER THREE:

# *Which Path To Choose*

The two years at Berkshire Medical School passed quickly enough. Preceptorship with Dr. Craig back in Hebron made me a bit more confident, but still I felt the overwhelming need to know much more. Although the books and lectures on medicinal plants and herbs were all new information to me, I desired to know more of anatomy and surgery.

The ever-present feeling of impending doom by way of possible failure in studies was partially offset by the beautiful countryside: the frost-covered meadows by moonlight and the "ring around the moon," signaling the impending fall of our first snow. These were all pleasant memories for me, especially because of the sweltering humidity I would endure later during the war.

During my years of military service, I would frequently be confronted with the need to make rapid and often gruesome decisions following the violent battles; it seemed like only yesterday that I received the entrance cards entitling me to lectures on "Theory and Practice of Medicine," "General and Special Anatomy." "Principles and Practice of Surgery," "Materia Medica," "Medical Jurisprudence," "Chemistry and Toxicology," "Physiology and Pathology," "Obstetrics and Diseases of Women and Children," and "Microscopic Anatomy." While some of these studies were repetitious, it made me feel proficient to have passed my tests well over the two-year period of training.

Upon finishing medical school, I pondered as to where my path should lead. I shared the great anger that part of our nation should seek so violent a course of action in order to make their point regarding secession. Firing on Fort Sumter and on our own U.S. soldiers made us all quite furious. Torchlight parades and patriotic music helped the recruiters fill the ranks of the Federal forces. Should I take the time and money to continue attempts to start a medical practice? Or should I join the army and show loyalty to our fine flag? Perhaps my medical knowledge could "pull me up by my boot straps" and move me up from a private's rank to a medical position. My folks were not overjoyed with my military decision, nor were the few patients I had garnered in my first nine months of practice.

# CHAPTER FOUR:

# *Leaving Connecticut for the Department of the South*

In the spring of 1861, we sailed out of New Haven harbor with our recently recruited and trained soldiers of the Connecticut Sixth Volunteers. As we boarded our ship, the *Elm City*, at Belle Dock, we could look over the city and understand why the early Dutch explorers called New Haven the "Place of the Red Mount." The evening sun striking the faces of the backdrop of East and West Rock gave this red appearance. Oncoming rains, however, obscured our view of the "Mounts."

Despite much hospitality by the local New Haven citizens and despite much cheering and good food, it was still depressing to spend this rainy night putting up with the usual military delays before boarding our ship. The clouds thickened and the drummer's drummed "strike tents." Despite being drenched to the skin, our hearts were lightened by two days' rations for our haversacks and by the band playing "The Gal I Left Behind Me." The coast of Connecticut slipped past our starboard side, the sun itself seemed too drenched to show itself much as it set behind the Connecticut hills. Some signs of homesickness may have been evident. We were heading with trepidation toward the war and wondered how many of us would return.

The following day was Wednesday, September 18, 1861, and our boat was tied up by the barnacle-covered pilings at a dock in Jersey City, New Jersey. Again, more delays until we boarded a train taking us through Philadelphia (where we were warmly entertained at the Union refreshment room). Our hearts were also warmed by the hospitality and loyal support of these folks. This was in contrast with the sullen and almost hostile atmosphere greeting us in Baltimore. Our soldiers actually were ordered to "fix bayonets." This was necessary because we learned a Baltimore mob had fired on the Sixth Massachusetts as it passed through the streets en route to Washington, D.C. The Sixth fired back, and nine civilians and four soldiers were killed. President Lincoln decided that no more troops would go through Maryland, for fear it might stir up the Maryland citizens to the degree that they might join the Confederacy.

The ride from Baltimore to Washington, D.C. was a low point of this trip. Although the officers fared somewhat better, we were huddled into dirty cattle cars. Crowded as it was, one couldn't relax, because the floors were covered with filth and muck from the recent cattle transport.

We arrived in Washington at 6:00 in the morning on September 19, and it found us in a better mood, especially since, after a long wait, we heard the call "fall in for rations." The food was poorly prepared but nonetheless acceptable. We were allowed sightseeing time in the city. The beautiful Capitol, with its partly finished dome, interested us so much that some of our troops enjoyed themselves by making "speeches" from the rostrum in the House of Representatives. They got great pleasure sitting in the seat formerly held by Jefferson Davis, now president of the Confederacy.

### *Historical Note*

Washington, D.C. became the most heavily fortified city in the world. The announcement of the state of war between the North and the South actually caught Washington in a state of unpreparedness should Confederate troops sud-denly move north. Twenty-two batteries and seventy-four forts ringed the city over a thirty-seven-mile area. Enemy campfires and rebel flags could even be seen across the Potomac.

Once the reality of war between the states was fully recognized, Lincoln anxiously awaited the arrival of the Federal troops. Since Washington was sur-rounded by the states of Virginia and Maryland, his unease was understandable. It was felt that Washington should be secured against any possibility of invasion. Governor Andrews of Massachusetts realized the seriousness of this problem and forwarded several regiments in readiness to move on to Washington. On April 17, the Sixth Massachusetts entrained for Washington, but there was a major problem as they pulled into Baltimore. During a transfer of troops from one rail-road station to another, they were attacked by a pro-Southern mob, and this led to shots being fired and casualties on both sides.

Lincoln's anxiety was assuaged by the arrival on April 25 of the Seventh New York Infantry. They marched up Pennsylvania Avenue, and Lincoln and his staff caught the excitement of the event and felt much more secure with this evi-dence of Northern military might making its appearance in the capital. Although this was only one division, there was great restoration of faith, and a spirit of loy-alty and almost revelry greeted them.

The national fervor spread like wildfire throughout Washington; many were heard to shout the words, "Forward to Richmond!" They did not wish the rebel congress to meet there as scheduled on July 20, and hoped that the national army would take Richmond by that time.

Lincoln immediately wished to play on this national sentiment of loyalty and support and summoned several generals to consider a campaign against the

Confederate forces encamped around Manassas Junction, only twenty-five miles west of Washington. General Winfield Scott, who was actually from Virginia but loyal to the Union, was to head up this force to inflict a once-and-for-all blow against the Confederacy at Manassas. Actually, General McDowell was empowered to direct the Union forces, with a remarkably bad outcome on July 21 at Manassas.

Although Fort Sumter surrendered in April 1861, the first real battle occurred that summer. The battle of Manassas Junction took place with a feeling that, although the Union forces lacked experience, victory would be easily attained.

Despite early success by the Union forces under General McDowell, Confederate reinforcements arrived and turned the tide of battle. Members of Congress, their families, and many other Washingtonians turned out in picnic-style fashion to witness what they felt would be and end to the secession movement in one stroke.

The Union ranks broke and the retreat turned into a rout. The war was not about to end with a single battle.

* * *

While in Washington, I was in the dark as to just where and when we would move out, but I took time to meet with the second assistant surgeon, Samuel McClellan, on Meridian Hill, just outside of Washington. We remained for twenty days, and filled these days by taking inventory of our medical supplies and reviewing our plans for effectively packing this material for whatever travels were to be arranged for us. The army was quite stringent with its accounting practices for our supplies. The surgical sets were in especially short supply, as well as many of the medications.

We took some time out from this medical planning to view the incessant drilling of the troops, as their numbers grew larger each day. We were elated by a brief visit from President Lincoln. In view of the proximity of the enemy to the capital, he was equally happy to see our troops. This was of some assurance to our president, as we came to learn that he was extremely anxious about the fate of our capital. The distant sounds of battle could be heard on a quiet evening, but this had the effect of making our troops anxious to get on with the war, not knowing what dreadful times lay ahead.

### *Historical Note*

Stocks of medicine held by Union physicians included opium, morphine, Dover's Powder, quinine, rhubarb, Rochelle's Salts, castor oil, sugar of lead, tannin, sulfate of copper, camphor, tincture of opium, sulfate of zinc, camphorated tincture of opium, tincture of iron, tincture of opii, syrup of squills, simple syrup, alcohol, whiskey, brandy, port wine, and sherry wine, among others. These were put on temporary shelves in the camps. With marching orders they were again packed into boxes. The bottles were protected with old papers stuffed in amongst them. Most treatments were in powder or liquid form; pills and tablets were rare if available at all. Surgical supplies included chloroform, ether, brandy, aromatic spirits of ammonia, bandages, adhesive plaster, needles, silk thread, catlins, artery forceps, bone forceps, scissors, scalpels, bullet probes, and tourniquets.

Gastrointestinal diseases were the bane of existence for the troops of both sides. Epidemics of jaundice, diarrhea, and related maladies swept through the campsites. There was no clear-cut understanding as to the cause of these problems, although some degree of sanitation was attempted when possible in the more permanent campsites. Twice as many soldiers died from various illnesses as were killed in battle. The frequently used treatment for these intestinal problems often did more harm than good. The treatment often included heavy doses of lead acetate, opium, aromatic sulfuric acid, tincture of opium, silver nitrate, belladonna, calomel, and ipecac. The soldiers frequently died as a result of dehydration due to worsening of the gastrointestinal problems by such purging methods. Quinine was widely used, as was alcohol in the form of brandies for almost any illness. Mercury and chalk (called blue mass) were often used for a wide variety of illnesses. So-called childhood diseases frequently raged through the various army camps.

There were two small tents for medical officers and their medications. One small tent was for the kitchen department and supplies. Chronic cases were evacuated to the rear, a mixed blessing because of the gangrene and endemic infections in the hospital. Gangrene was seldom seen in the field.

Four surgical cases were available: one for major surgery, one for minor surgery, a pocket case, and a field case, which was carried by the surgeon on his person into the battle area. The first assistant surgeon carried the twenty-pound hospital knapsack, also called the surgeon's field companion, into the battle area so there could be access to the many instruments needed there. These were used to stop bleeding, bandage, and then evacuate beyond musket range (but not beyond artillery range). To get to a field hospital, the ambulances had four wheels but still gave one a rough ride, so much so that many injured people held their arms or legs up off the floor to prevent the severe pain caused by bouncing over the rough roads. A hinged rear door allowed access to remove stretchers. The instruments were washed with water and wiped dry to avoid rust.

The field tents were often staked down using swords or guns to hold the tent fly open. Near the operative tents, many soldiers died while waiting, and the call could often be heard, "Oh Lord," "Mother," "Father," or "Doctor."

Washington issued a general order on June 6, 1862: "Surgeons should be considered non-combatants and should not be taken prisoners." This was accepted by General Lee on June 17, 1862. Nonetheless many were taken prisoner and many died. Thirty-two were killed during the war; ninety-nine were injured in accidents; and eighty-three were wounded, ten of whom later died. Four doctors died in rebel prisons, seven died from yellow fever, three from cholera, two hundred and seventy-one from other diseases.

Not wanting the war, they did not prepare for it; not wanting heavy casualties, they did not prepare for them, either. Hospital attendants were either poorly trained or untrained. Convalescent care was rarely provided. When there was a great inflow of casualties, the convalescents were pushed out. In the end, however, good hospital care came about.

In the troop supply train, the ammunition was first in line followed by the rations, and finally by the medical supplies.

* * *

# CHAPTER FIVE:

# *Rough Seas on the Way to Battle*

A short train ride took us from Washington to Annapolis. There we exercised, drilled, and regrouped before boarding for the campaign at Port Royal, South Carolina.

On October 19, our regiment boarded ship with sealed orders under General Sherman. As a medical steward, my quarters were small but a great improvement over the crowded hold that housed the troops. Seventeen regiments boarded thirty-three steam transports for the sail southward. Several gunboats accompanied the transports. Because of Connecticut's proximity to the sea, our troops felt quite at home and enjoyed relaxing in the warm fall sunshine of this day at sea.

After a layover at Hampton Roads, Virginia, we had a pleasant sail south for two more days with no foreboding of the frightening storm about to engulf us. The wind imperceptibly increased and the minor rolling of the ship turned into shuddering crashes through the surf. The bow shook off each wave much like a horse might rear and throw his head back. Maintaining headway seemed difficult, if not impossible. I was invited to view this from the pilot house; from there I could see the waves sweeping across the decks and sailors having trouble keeping their footing while lashing down the hatches and securing items on the deck. We were able to make headway with the steam up, but another ship was not quite so lucky. It wallowed and broached in the heavy sea and finally dropped from sight. Any effort to save any personnel on the doomed ship was out of the question because of the captain's wish to avoid the same fate. He was skillful and successful in his efforts to keep his bow into the sea, even though this worsened the anxiety and seasickness of our brethren troops.

The storm scattered the fleet over a wide area of the sea with some losses. (Two ships were sunk, with horses, cannons, and military equipment gone overboard.) We thanked the Lord for having been spared. As if to accept our thanks, the pale evening sun suddenly broke out with broken shards of dark clouds riding off to our stern. The fleet reassembled with no other problems for the remainder of our trip to Port Royal.

Port Royal is on an island north of Hilton Head near Beaufort, South Carolina. Sailing among these off-shore islands and narrow channels near Port Royal and toward Laurel Bay took great knowledge and seamanship on the part of the skipper.

A fleet under Flag Officer Francis Samuel Dupont, with twelve thousand troops commanded by General Thomas W. Sherman, captured Fort Beauregard and Fort Walker in Port Royal Sound, South Carolina. This victory on November 7, 1861 secured this area as a base for future operations for the indefinite future. The base was obtained with minimal skirmishing and loss of life.

Thanks to good fortune and leadership, we were able to establish Hilton Head as a more-or-less permanent base for our Southern campaigns. The taking and holding of this land by our troops proved to be easier than expected. Admiral Dupont, by a series of figure-of-eight maneuvers, was able to use the heavy fire of his ships against the defenses of Hilton Head and its surrounding fortifications. Sailing in this pattern in front of the fortifications at Port Royal allowed him to give broadsides even though these were from a moving platform, with the desired effect of routing the rebels. There is a traditional belief that one cannon on shore equals four on a boat, but Admiral Dupont's accuracy while shelling the Port Royal area seemed to contradict this otherwise well-held tenet.

The Sixth Volunteers entered into this first campaign four months after sailing out of New Haven harbor. Although the troops pretty much had their "sea legs" by that time, I noted a combination of anxiety over the impending battle for Hilton Head and an eagerness to get on with what they had drilled and trained for. In light marching order, they scrambled into the small boats and made their way toward shore. The ominous rifle and cannon fire slowed and finally ceased. A big crew of the Wabash raced ashore and hoisted the stars and stripes, where but moments before the rebel flag flew.

In the great national spirit of our time, bands struck up patriotic tunes while the men cheered with a thousand voices to celebrate this first great sea battle of the war. Port Royal and Hilton Head thus became a permanent encampment for our troops in this part of the war. Again, our aim was to prevent blockade running of supplies to the Confederacy. Beaufort was formally occupied December 15, 1861.

November in South Carolina was not so very cold, but wading ashore in chest-high water was not to be recommended. I saw the soldiers with arms and ammunition held over their heads, but not a complaint was heard; their spirits were heightened by the victory. The medical section came ashore at dawn's first light and immediately set up tents in order to make preparation for what might come next. Lieutenant Colonel Ely was in command and took charge of preparing defenses and picket lines, in order to avoid a counterattack.

Our resting soldiers devoted themselves to a new task that they had never considered back on the farms of Connecticut: how to open a coconut with their bayonets. Even the sight of palm trees was most unusual to all of us, to say nothing over our awe at the ghostly hangings of Spanish moss.

As our medical personnel came ashore, we had the first opportunity to use our medical skills. The medical section was overwhelmed with the degree of savageness of the battles and with the resultant injuries. They also viewed and cared for the serious injuries to enemy soldiers; sad moans and groans and requests for water by the rebel soldiers were all one could hear. "Battlefield medicine" was a self-taught profession, as we rapidly learned. Injuries to arms and legs could be attended to (often by amputation, since there was usually not enough bone left to splint or set—this was the effect of Minie balls and canisters and shrapnel.) Some attempts were made at saving shattered bones, but this resulted, at best, in limbs shorter than the extremity preserved. The danger was that with the circulation limited, gangrene would set in, with fever and death a frequent result. We also found, disgusting though it seemed at first, maggots cleaned up the wounds; soldiers often did better through lack of attention, which allowed maggots to grow.

Things we never heard or learned of in medical school have become second nature to us. If we survive this war, such knowledge could be of great help to us back home. Perforating wounds of the chest and abdomen were most discouraging to us, as all we could do is provide pain medicine and fluids, and support them as best possible, knowing full well that most would be dead by morning. Traditionally, many were laid aside under a so-called "dying tree."

Of the many things we learned, a "spoke" arrangement of beds with a central dispensing station proved practical in situations when we were not on the move. Anesthesia was not always available, but free use was made of chloroform and morphine, especially to those who couldn't otherwise be helped. It actually seemed absurd to me the amount of time spent learning about herbal medicine and other frippery when rapid surgical decisions and treatment were now so necessary.

We knew even then that amputations were done too readily, but often the alternatives were worse. The wound would suppurate and infection would spread. A late amputation was fraught with the dangers of suppurating wounds followed by fever and death; it seemed that this suppuration was easily transmitted to newer cases that we operated on.

Another significant problem with amputations was the fact that we worked often into the evening and night hours. It was quite hazardous to use chloroform with the open flames nearby, especially with our lanterns. We needed all the light we could get in probing bullet wounds and trying to restore as much as we could to the wounded bodies, but I was ever fearful of the flammable chloroform so close to open flames.

[Excerpt from *The Civil War In Song and Story* by Frank Moore (a humorous poem from an invalid soldier in a New Haven hospital, who was wounded at the battle of Fair Oaks)]

How An Amputation Is Performed: Imagine yourself in the hospital of the Sixth Corps after a battle. There lies a soldier, whose thigh has been mangled by a shell; and, although he may not know it, the limb will have to be amputated to save his life. Two surgeons have already pronounced this decision; but according to the present formation of the hospital in this camp, no one surgeon nor two, can order an amputation, even of a finger. The opinion of five, at least, and sometimes more, including the Division Surgeon, always a man of superior skill and experience, must first be consulted, and then, if there is an agreement, depend upon it, the operation is necessary. This did not used to be, in the early months of the war; but it is now. Suppose that the amputation has been decided upon; the man who is a rebel and an Irishman, with strong nerve and frame, is approached by one of the surgeons, and told he would now be attended to, and whatever is best would be done for him. They cannot examine his wound thoroughly where he lies, so he is tenderly lifted on to a rough table. A rebel surgeon is among the number present, the man as I have said has a strong nerve and it is not reduced because of loss of blood. So, then, the decision is communicated to him that he must lose his leg. While the operating surgeon is examining, and they are talking to the poor fellow, chloroform is being administered to him through a sponge. The first sensation of this sovereign balm, like those pleasant ones produced by a few glasses of whiskey, and our patient begins that he is on a spree and throws out his arms and legs and talks funnily. The inhalation goes on and the beating of the pulse is watched; and when it is ascertained that he is slowly oblivious to all feeling, the instruments are produced and the operation commences. Down goes the knife into the flesh and there is no tremor or indication of pain. The patient is dreaming of the battle from which he has just come. Hear him, for he's got his rifle pointed over the earthworks at our advancing line of battle; and always shows an admiration of thought brought on by his anesthesia. The leg is off, and carried away; the arteries are tied up, and the skin is neatly sutured over the stump. The effect of the chloroform is relaxed; and when the patient opens his eyes, a short time afterward, he sees a clean white bandage where his ghastly wound had been, and his lost limb is removed. He feels much easier, and drinks an ounce and one-half of good whiskey with gusto. This is a real incident of amputation, and the chief characteristic of the description will answer to everyone.

### *Historical Note*

It has been noted that three out of four soldiers were hit in the extremities; at that time, the only proper treatment for a compound fracture was amputation. Indeed, amputations constituted 75 percent of all operations performed by Civil War doctors. Experienced surgeons performed an amputation in a very brief period of time; it was noted that those amputations performed within forty-eight hours of injury had a significantly better outcome than those done after a longer delay. Many discoveries of aseptic technique had not yet been made, and thus the onset of severe infections at the site, septicemias, and gangrene, all contributed to the mortality of delayed amputations.

Bacterial cause of disease was not known at that time and it is easy to see how spread of infection from the post-operative infected wounds to the instruments and to new casualties came about. Sharpening the scalpel on the boot heel, not using gloves, and other unsanitary procedures led to a high morbidity and mortality rate. It was felt that the relatively few cases of tetanus (lock-jaw) were a result of the fact that this was "new" ground that was fought over. Tetanus spores, horses, and other causes had not been over this land much before, although there were many other factors of infection present. Yellow fever in the seaports was brought there by transport ships from southern climes. Poor field sanitation and water supply led to widespread dysentery and hepatitis-type infections with jaundice.

A medical observation was made regarding the excellent wound healing of some rebel soldiers who were taken prisoner. There was little or no redness, infection, or induration around the sutures closing the lacerations. By questioning these troops, it was learned that in the absence of regular suture material, horsehair was used. Horsehair being quite stiff, it was boiled in water first, with a resulting sterilization of this suture material, with good results for the wound.

Casualty accounts made after the war revealed that one in sixty-five died in combat, one in ten were wounded, and one in thirteen died of disease. Military field sanitation and evacuation of the wounded were some of the good things to come out of this ghastly war.

* * *

# CHAPTER SIX:

# My First Fort McHenry Experience

The days following the major assault on Fort Walker and Hilton Head were unexpectedly pleasant. Because of heavy casualties from military action of the Army of the Potomac, I was sent on temporary duty to Fort McHenry to care for the wounded from the recent battles further north. I both gave and received more military medical training; I had the great chance to live like a human being, having spent a considerable length of time living in encampments. My time in Fort McHenry was thus pleasant.

> *Post Hospital; Ft. McHenry, MD.*
> *January 11th, 1862*
>
> *Dear Brother and Sister;*
> *I suppose you have been wondering where I am and why I have not written before, but I have been so busy, or rather so lazy, that I have not written yet but intend to today. I arrived here the 20th of December and have been here since. I spent Christmas in New York state (not in the city) and a very fine time I had.*
> *I do not expect to stay here for long so you may address your letters to me like this:*
> *Hospital Steward*
> *USA, Baltimore, Md.*
> *and then I will get them as they are advertised every week and I am not sure where I will go to.*
> *After I left home and I arrived at Caroline's, she had received news that David was killed in the Fredericksburg battle, but not being published in the paper, she thought it could not be so but that he was taken prisoner, or more probably wounded and sent to some hospital besides that of his Reg't so I wrote*

*to a friend of his in the same company and yesterday received an answer. He said all he could find out about David is that he was wounded in the loins and was carried off the field to this side of the River where he died and was buried, that he had tried to find the spot and could not. He had written his parents concerning him. He said he was with the Flag when he received his wound—that he bore a high reputation both with the officers and men in the regiment as a soldier.*

*I think Caroline must feel dreadfully, she did when I saw her, and so did A. and the children, still they were in hopes to hear that he was alive. But such are the fortunes of war.*

*I have seen Charles once since I have returned. I believe the Co. were gone a few days to Stuart's Woods but have returned. With my love to all and especially to the "little corporal"*

*I will close hoping to hear from you soon.*

 *Your Aff. Brother, Myron*

[He refers to the "little corporal" in many of his letters—he was one of his nephews.]

I indeed was reluctant to leave the troops; I had become so fond of caring for them under serious and bloody battle conditions. I had a sense of guilt brought on by the fact that, with our troops needing more medical help, I was a long ways from being with my regiment, although I accompanied many of our wounded north to Fort McHenry.

At Fort McHenry, my position improved somewhat since my appointment as hospital steward. I would be promptly awakened at dawn by an orderly who came to my room each morning. I would don my "hospital clothing" and set off for a brief breakfast. Making rounds on the sick and wounded with the surgeons taught me much about not only the care of battle injuries, but also the even greater number of other illnesses. Gastrointestinal problems, jaundice, and typhoid seemed to be most prominent.

In the course of events, I contracted some of the same maladies as afflicted our patients. Despite the generally good food at the hospital, I actually lost weight, probably due to poor appetite. It accompanied my continuous low-grade fever and chills.

When I felt better, I would get some stamps to send out some overdue letters. I carried and reread my received letters very often; this may have worsened my homesickness. I looked forward to some time off so I could visit Charles and George, who were nearby in the general Baltimore area.

When I fell asleep at night, I often heard cannons in the distance. At first, I thought it was thunder, but this "thunder" was man-made and at a regular cadence. I hoped it might portend an early end to the war. Though the newspapers sounded quite optimistic, I tended to doubt that this was the case.

January, 1862 was very cold, and the war news remained grim. Sadly, David was killed outside Fredericksburg. I came to learn that this ill-fated expedition of Union forces under the newly appointed General Burnside had moved rapidly toward the Confederate defenses outside Richmond and still again, a lesser Confederate force turned back the Army of the Potomac. Through newspapers and general comments by our officers, we learned that McClellan, through a combination of illness and indecisiveness, was replaced by General Burnside in this campaign. Burnside himself seemed reluctant to take over a large army although he felt quite competent in managing smaller military groups. One of the higher ranking officers of General Lee's inner circle reported that, as General Lee viewed the slaughter of Union troops outside Fredericksburg, he made the comment, "It is well that war is so terrible, otherwise we should grow too fond of it."

The actuality of this war was brought to my attention much distant cannonading in September. We received a flood of casualties following this, from the distant battle site of Antietam. These soldiers had been badly mangled from the encounter, and although our losses were high, it was felt to be some sort of victory for our forces. At least we kept the rebel forces at bay and thwarted further incursions. In any case, the fall season was now upon us and it seemed that the war would not go on much further. I learned at this time that should the war continue, I would be transferred from the more pleasant duty at Fort McHenry to rejoin the Connecticut Sixth on the coast of South Carolina.

*September 18th, 1862*
*Fort McHenry, Md.*

*Dear Father and Mother:*

*I now take my pen to write you a few lines, although my time is limited for it is quite late and I ought to be in bed. I suppose you know that I am now out of the ranks and am acting Hospital Steward in the Hospital at this Post and not in the Reg't. I have a good place and am well suited with this good living, a good bed and good accommodations as I can wish.*

*I have plenty of practice in the Hospital. I think it the most instructive school by far that I have ever attended. I am very well suited with my place, my pay I suppose is somewhat increased but I do not know how much. I see Charles nearly every day, am about as far from him as to you from Lucius*. He is well I believe, as is also George and the rest of the boys.*

*I have had a touch of the Fever and ague as what they call here the Shakes yesterday. I had ague, chills and some fever, but am better today only I am very weak. I think I have broken them up entirely.*

*We have glorious news tonight from the war but I am afraid it is too good to be true but it does seem to me as though the time has come for this rebellion to be crushed and now may be the time. Last Sunday we could hear the firing distinctly in the western part of the State. We heard it till after sundown. Please write soon all the news. My love to all Charles & Lucius & families and all friends. Write all the news and send me a paper occasionally if you can. Please send me one dollar in postage stamps and charge to me as I am nearly out and cannot get one here, do not fail to send them soon. Goodnight*

*From Your Son*
*Myron*

* Lucius Watterman was his brother-in-law born December 7, 1817

The first signs of winter gradually became evident at Fort McHenry. The days became shorter and the weather often very severe. The waves roared up Patapsco Bay, and lashed against old Fort McHenry. Even the short distance to the hospital was a challenge, with freezing ruts in the mud and slippery footing. And it was only October!

My hometown finally saw fit to pay me my "bounty" for enlisting. I sorely needed some money to properly attire myself in a nice uniform. I enjoyed having a closet, a proper bed, and furnishings since I had been moved out of my drafty and often leaking tent. Sunday inspections took away some of the precious little time I had for myself, but I hoped that my small "medical contribution" was helping to shorten the war, at least a little bit. In my small bit of free time, I tried my hand at writing poetry.

*Headquarters, Cripple Brigade*
*Convalescent Camp*
*Fort McHenry Oct.1st 1862*

*Dear Father:*

*Prelude*

*1st*
*From old New England's rugged hills,*
*Along her sunny vales.*
*From pleasant farm house and from shops,*
*The stalwart soldier hailed.*

*2nd*
*Leaving his home and friends behind,*
*And all he holds most dear,*
*He grasps his gun-springs to the helm*
*The ship of state to steer.*

*Part I*
*Within McHenry's stately walls*
*There is a little band,*
*Who left their home so cheerfully,*
*To save their Father land,*
*From shame disgrace and tyranny.*
*That they forever might be free.*

*II*
*The 18th is a noble band*
*As everyone might know,*
*From cheers and praises long and loud*
*Wherever they may go;*
*To save their flag from traitors hands,*
*These men have left their native lands.*

*III*

*We now have been here near five weeks,*
*The men are well and strong,*
*The time to me has seemed quite short,*
*To some, it has seemed long*
*But long or short tis naught to me,*
*For our years are numbered one, two, three*

### IV
*Very many are the summoned here,*
*As to when we'll have to go,*
*So many and so various they,*
*That not a man can know,*
*But where'er we go, we're bound to fight,*
*Yes, that we will with all our might.*

### V
*Our pleasures surely are more fun*
*Than when we were at home,*
*But this we care for not at all*
*As through the camp we roam,*
*For we are a going to fight some day*
*Because!-we cannot get away.*

### VI
*If you would sell all that thou hast,*
*And be a "soldier boy"*
*And sleep on the soft side of boards*
*O'er run you'd be with joy*
*To eat hard bread and meat so tough,*
*Perhaps you'd say "it is enough."*

### VII
*And then so nice it is dark night*
*To go and stand on guard,*
*And pace your beat for two long hours*
*Around this dismal yard;*
*But now we do not care a bit,*
*The reason why-we can't help it.*

### VIII
*For inspection today they have been out*
*For load they did not lack,*
*For several hours they had to stand*
*With their knapsacks on their back,*
*But O!! to them 'tis mighty fun*
*To stand with knapsacks in the sun.*

### IX
*The Reg't won the greatest praise*
*From our gallant Brigadier*

*From everything that I have heard*
*It is the best that's here,*
*The reason why, is plain, dear Father,*
*It is—because there is no other.*

    *X*

*But now I'll close this wild harangue*
*For I think that t'would be better,*
*But here I'll say Sir many thanks,*
*That I'm no longer in the ranks.*

                                 *Part II  October 2nd, 1862*
                                 *Thursday night*

*Dear Father:*

*My machine with which I grind out poetry has run down and I cannot start it so I will have to wind off without giving the moral or anything of the kind but that I can give just as well when I get home and when that will be is a problem that I cannot find anyone wise enough to solve. This afternoon I suppose they are at it again as cannonading has been heard plainly to the southwest which sounded as though they were at it right smart again.*

*It is rumored that peace commissioners from the Confederate states have arrived in Washington but it is not thought it will avail anything without giving up all their arms and their leaders which I do not think they will ever do, we have not whipped them enough yet nor is that all. I am better than when I wrote but am still weak. Charles is well, think he would like to have you write him. Tell O I will answer his letter soon, when I receive the stamps. I am very thankful and my love to Mother and all the rest. Did Harlow\* get my coat at Camp Aiken, please let me know.*

*Your Aff. Son*
*Myron*

\* Harlow was another brother born March 26, 1820, to William Robinson's first wife. Myron was one of three children born to his second wife.

# CHAPTER SEVEN:

# The Star-Spangled Banner and Naval Considerations

Within eyesight of our small hospital, one could usually see not only the tents of our rebel prisoners, but also the looming walls of Fort McHenry. Although some of the walls were moldering, vine covered, and in general showed their age, they still looked formidable. Some of the permanent staff at the fort filled me in on some details that I vaguely remembered from my history books. One of the permanent party group gave me quite a tour of the fortifications, along with a healthy dose of history. While this tour and its interesting history was still fresh in my mind, I decided I should jot it all down in my journal.

As my tour guide explained, because the English were commandeering American ships at sea and impressing the seamen into service for the British ships, we declared war in June, 1812. "Free trade and sailors rights" was the battle cry of the day.

Having defeated the Americans at Bladensberg, and burned Washington, D.C., the British next aimed to destroy Baltimore by a combined land and sea attack. They landed at Northpoint in a skirting maneuver toward the northeast side of Baltimore. The well-organized attack force scattered the American defenders at the battle of Northpoint. The British halted just short of the city to await the destruction of the defending Fort McHenry by the British gunboats (previous shelling of Fort McHenry by gunboats had proven to the British navy that a naval attack alone would not take the city).

A disorganized attack by a second landing force of British troops in an inlet west of Baltimore went awry, and they withdrew. These British ships were especially rigged to allow heavy mortars to be used on their foredecks. A large flotilla of British ships with long range cannons bombarded the fort beginning at seven A.M., September 14, 1812.

The Fort McHenry guns did not have a high enough trajectory or enough range to hit the British ships. The British also used a new attack weapon, (the Congreve rocket) on board the H.M.S. *Erebus*. The inaccuracy of this and other naval cannons led to the failure to take this fort—despite the intensity of the cannonading.

Several U.S. infantry units and a special organization put together by the War Department (called the U.S. Sea Fencibles) were well trained in muskets and cannons and did an excellent job against the British flotilla—once within their range.

With the failure of the British ground troops and with the obstinate resistance of Fort McHenry despite thunderous cannonading, the British fleet finally withdrew. The last act of this part of history was the use of the British fleet (with reinforcements) in the attack on New Orleans. In January, 1815, this force was repelled by Andrew Jackson's famous battle of New Orleans. Sadly, the armistice had been declared prior to this battle, but the news did not arrive in time to forestall this battle.

I was already aware that an inspiring poem had been written regarding the thrilling tenacity of our defenders at Fort McHenry in the face of this prolonged bombardment. I always had questions in my mind as to how it came to be that a highly regarded Washington lawyer, Francis Scott Key, happened to be on board a British ship at this time. A superior officer of the permanent staff was kind enough to explain the background of this situation to me.

A man named Dr. Beanes had been arrested by the British for allegedly breaking a pact made with the British, in order to spare the countryside around Baltimore from destruction by the British forces as long as no hostile actions would be brought to bear upon the British ground forces.

General Skinner, commissioner general of prisoners, along with attorney Francis Scott Key, had won their point in gaining a reprieve for Dr. Beanes. However, the British command officers thought that these three might have been privy to some British plans regarding the assault on Baltimore. For these reasons, Key, Skinner, and Beanes were detained on the British ship during the bombardment. Francis Scott Key jotted down notes as to how thrilled he was that "our flag was still there." This was polished up, set into a poem format and later put to the music of an air (unknown to me) called "Anacreon in Heaven."

We now had many Confederate prisoners in custody and in clear sight of our hospital. I guess that part of their penance was that day after day they were forced to look at our grand flag flying over their heads.

The naval officers on the ships that brought us here from our recent battles further south told us of the major adventures they had at sea while trying to stop the resupply of the Confederacy. One such story was of the Fingal. This ship was carrying arms, and in October, 1861 was in the cotton trade with England by way of Bermuda. The pilot who was to bring them into Savannah Harbor was a drunkard and ran aground off Fort Pulaski, but because he was under the cover of the Fort Pulaski guns, the cargo was secured and later freed itself and docked in Savannah. It was reported the cargo found its way to Tennessee and even to Richmond.

# CHAPTER EIGHT:

# *Savannah—Fort Pulaski Campaign*

All good things come to an end and I left Fort McHenry on this early March day of 1862, to go south again to take up my position with the medical section of the Sixth Volunteers for the Fort Pulaski campaign. I found the troops to be in good humor and good health. Dietary problems were ever a source of concern for us, especially when trying to keep soldiers in the best possible health under these rugged conditions. Scurvy was a debilitating and recurring problem, but this was avoided in the past because the nearby plantations furnished our regiment with a quantity of good things to eat. Pigs, chickens, and geese as well as sweet potatoes, sugar cane, and other fruits and vegetables were available. Not much fighting of any great amount seemed to go on and I found the Sixth Regiment working unloading transport ships.

The doctors on board could do little but treat the symptoms of bowel and stomach upset caused by the water and food. Water and storage containers had previously housed kerosene; this, along with a poor diet composed largely of hardtack, saltpork, and no vegetables led to serious health problems at this time. Poor sleep associated with a bad lice problem led to decreasing morale in this recently proud outfit—no more practicing scrambling into small assault boats, but only trying to get through each day as best as possible. Being anchored offshore in this condition seemed worse than any prison. Later, "spotted fever" broke out, and many said that they wished for the decisiveness of battle rather than this grueling day by day descent into illness and disability. Lice problems, lack of general cleanliness, and ever-present illnesses made life quite miserable, as one might expect. Fumigation of the transports and barracks ashore did not do much for the illnesses, but they did minimize the lice and rat problems on board the ships. As the medical person responsible for this brigade, I ordered the troops ashore to bathe and exercise. Smallpox vaccinations had been done at Port Royal; this helped somewhat, but I later learned that repeat vaccinations were often needed but very often not given. Thus recovery was short lived and things worsened again.

A torrential rain unfortunately started the troops off with soaking wet field-packs and rations. I came ashore at daybreak as the troops were resting. Smoking was allowed for those few who had dry tobacco. The troops always had an eye out for foraging possibilities and thus saw the chance of improving their meager diet with fresh fruit in bloom.

The battle plan seemed to be to reconnoiter up the Savannah River and prevent any "blockade running" from that port. Our regiment occupied Jones Island, about halfway between Fort Pulaski and Savannah. This island was merely a tidal flat with no shrubs or trees, only seagrass. Much of it was under a few inches of water at high tide. Despite the blazing sun, vicious insect attacks, and poor sleep due to mud and tidal washing, the troops did amazingly well at constructing a foundation for the heavy guns. With use of shale, mud, and sand brought up from the river, a good foundation was set in place. The sun baked this hard enough to allow the mounting of heavy guns, but such guns had to be manually dragged across the island under cover of night. A few soldiers were required on each wheel to move them forward to these prepared positions. The soldiers were not at full strength because of the recent problems with fever, dysentery, and poor diet. To the credit of our "Connecticut Yankees" this was completed quite successfully.

This initial campaign to take Fort Pulaski did not end well. The hard working troops of the Sixth had indeed turned some mud flats on the Savannah river into satisfactory gun platforms. I was told that this should suffice to bombard Fort Pulaski and also to keep the Confederate ship *Atlanta* bottled up in Savannah. Our sick and ailing troops were not in battle ready condition and were temporarily transferred a short distance back to Hilton Head to recover.

Although the Sixth was ostracized by other troops during our short convalescent period on Hilton Head, recovery was fast and so we rejoined the assaulting forces against Fort Pulaski.

We improved in health so much that by late March we received our orders to embark for Dawfuskie Island, only a short distance south of Hilton Head, and just north of the harbor entrance to Savannah. We landed at ten in the morning. The battle of Fort Pulaski was about to begin.

On the tenth of April, the battle began. Colonel Olmstead was the commander of Fort Pulaski, and he refused surrender terms. He felt that the huge five-sided fort with seven-foot-thick walls and massive guns could be well defended. Ironically, its construction was engineered by a Connecticut Yankee in the past. Our marshy island battery gave a good account of itself with very accurate demolition of Fort Pulaski. The exchange of artillery lasted into the evening of the tenth and resumed again the following morning. A large breach of the fortress walls made its powder magazines vulnerable. At that point, the rebels recognized the wisdom of surrendering rather than being blown up.

I well remember going back and forth between Fort Vulcan on Jones Island and our base at Tybee to minister to the wounded. An anxious moment came when a tactical error led to withdrawal of our gunboats, which thus exposed our position on Jones Island to attack by the rebels. Colonel Chatfield of Oxford, Connecticut, proved his cleverness by floating the ten-inch Columbiad (a long chambered, muzzle loading cannon) to Fort Pulaski and using the ruse of a "Quaker Gun" (a large log made to resemble a cannon) in its place. Therefore, no counterattack occurred and we were to leave this area in the hands of a holding force with offshore gunboats.

General Terry and Colonel Olmstead met following the surrender of Fort Pulaski. Major Gardner, of the Seventh Connecticut Regiment tells us this characteristic story of General Terry, the late colonel of his regiment.

After Fort Pulaski had been placed in General Terry's charge, and as rebel commander, Colonel Olmstead was about to be sent north as a prisoner of war, General Terry, appreciating the embarrassment to which Olmstead might be subjected, told him that it was not probable, that he was supplied with current money, and as Confederate money was valueless except as a curiosity, he desired that he would accept a sum that might free him from temporary inconvenience. He then gave him fifty dollars in good money. Colonel Olmstead gratefully accepted the offer, of course, with suitable acknowledgments of the generosity that prompted it.

Our regiment then withdrew back to Dawfuskie Island. Morale improved to a fair degree. I could note this because of the story-telling, singing, and the playing of a new game I had not seen before. This was used with a wooden bat and ball and was called "baseball;" it drew much attention from many soldiers. This game was invented by one of our officers named Abner Doubleday. He was second in command at Fort Sumter where he was captured with its surrender, to be released later and given safe conduct back to Union lines.

As the water was not too cold, the troops took the occasion to wash themselves and their clothing in the somewhat brackish water. Scrambling in and out of the cold water would prove to be helpful practice for the undertaking that would occur later off Morris Island.

The troops were elated, surprisingly, because of their success in winning Fort Pulaski. I say, "surprisingly," because their general health was not good. Fevers, skin infections, and dysentery had debilitated these soldiers to a large degree. Once back at Hilton Head, they began to recover. Knowing this, I was again transferred back to Fort McHenry, in this pleasant spring of 1862.

Word trickled down to me that, by the spring of 1862, Union forces controlled the port of Beaufort, Hilton Head, South Carolina, and Savannah, Georgia. Although I wondered at the importance of our expedition later to Jacksonville and Fernandina (I was having difficulty in seeing the justification of the hazards to our gallant men of the "Old Sixth"), I came to understand that it was also necessary to cut off these port areas to the Confederacy.

It is hard to express the very warm feeling of brotherhood that existed amongst the men of our unit. I shared very warmly in this brotherhood and personally felt the mental anguish that these troops suffered, knowing that they would again go into the "meat-grinder" of still another bloody battle. It is hard to think that many of these fine Connecticut boys whom I grew to know so well will not be returning home.

# CHAPTER NINE:

# *Return to Fort McHenry*

I had mixed feelings about again returning to Fort McHenry. In many ways, I preferred staying with the regiment, but since I was on temporary duty with the Sixth during the campaign, I fully expected it. It was quite convenient that I was able to accompany the wounded. By returning to Fort McHenry, I felt that I could further upgrade my training in battlefield medicine. There were several books available to us; in particular I appreciated the book entitled *Handbook For The Military Surgeon* by Dr. Tripler and Dr. Blackman, as well as *A Manual Of Military Surgery* by Dr. Samuel Gross.

I was welcomed by my colleagues when I returned to Fort McHenry. They plied me with many questions regarding specifics of the Savannah campaign, but they were especially interested in the medical aspects of the care of our troops. My quarters, while Spartan, were quite nice and a big improvement over those I had while in the field. Out my window I could see the fort itself and the growing number of tents of our Confederate prisoners.

Although my duties at Fort McHenry were mostly routine, I learned much in accompanying the more experienced surgeons on their rounds on our soldiers. After such rounds, I was given a lengthy list of procedures, dressing changes, and medications required by my recently inspected patients.

[Letter from Dr. Robinson to his sister, Sophronia Abell, who was married to Silas Abell, March 22, 1846.]

*Direct Acting Hospital Steward*
*U.S. Army Convalescent Hospital*
*Fort McHenry, Baltimore, Md.*
*October 28th, 1862*

*Dear Sister Fronia:*

*Your letter this day a week was duly received. I was very glad to hear from you as I always am from any of my friends. I am glad if anyone takes interest in me enough to write.*

*I am far from home and relatives and you cannot imagine how much pleasure I take in perusing letters from home. I sometimes almost wear them out reading them, and papers too. I received one last night for which I was truly thankful. When I get engaged reading the news from one's own state I forget but that I am not at home enjoying all its comforts and blessings but when I look up and see our cotton house\*, step out and see the central ground and hear the sound of martial music and the measured tread of the soldiers, I almost sigh to find it an illusion, a dream.*

*Today, it is very windy and rainy, the tents a whipping in the wind and it is so slippery outside one has to be constantly on his guard to avoid a collision with the earth. This is on account of the clayey soil I never saw anything like.*

*The bay is very rough today, the waves are reaching and dashing against the shore (which I am only about 40 feet from) with great fury. To see the tossing waves as they swell to and fro, foaming, and dashing is a majestic sight reminding one of "Him who holdeth the waves as in his hand." It makes me think how much it is like the voyage of life, ever changing one day, calm and placid not even a ripple to break the perfect quiet that pervades: the next one perfect tumult, thus passing on to the wide wide ocean. Thus it is even with this life, with one day all happiness, the next filled with sorrow and gloom. But with a few more partings some joy, much sorrow and this poor life's play is "played out" and we pass over the swelling tide to the boundless ocean of eternity "Unwept unhonored and unknown." Sundays here are not much as they are at home. It is not a day of rest, often my work is increased as inspection is always on Sunday. I do not know why it is so, but it is.*

*I wrote Silas in reply to his letter, did he receive it or not, you did not mention it, tell him to answer it and I will write another if he did not receive that one.*

*Sunday night—*

*The wind is blowing very hard, I fear some of the tents will blow down if it continues to blow. It is a bad night for soldiers but I think much more for sailors. I do not mean it is a bad night for me for I am fortunate enough to have good quarters, have a tent 14 x 16 feet in size with 4 iron bedsteads with mattresses and a good warm fire and another tent the same size attached. You wrote as though you thought I was with the Reg't, I am not. I'm in the garrison but not in the Reg't. I see Charlie nearly every day. I have given him both my blankets so with his own I think he is comfortable. I suppose I am liable to be called to the Reg't when it leaves, if I am, I think I shall enlist in the Regular Army. I might speak of the officers but I will wait until we are disbanded. I am sorry Father has had such poor times, he has the heart disease and should avoid much hard exercise and excitement.*

*I often think I have seen him for the last time. It will be a long while before I see him again, if I ever do. Not that I do not expect to return home, for I cer-*

*tainly do if I have a home to return to, if I have not, I may do as many men around me have done, join the Army and spend my life there. I like it if I can stay where I am although with the present Army I am disgusted.*

*Each days paper has an editorial to this effect "The Grand Army of the Potomac is about to move," or, "an early forward movement is expected," or something of a kind. Then again as battle news comes "that the rebels are in full retreat and our army is in hot pursuit." "They are about to be bagged the next day; they are not bagged but are perfectly demoralized." There is certainly mismanagement somewhere and thousands of precious lives are being sacrificed for nothing. McClellan has been waiting for the Potomac to rise, I expect he will wait for the muddy roads to become passable. Your cakes were received it seemed as like if we were in your pantry.*

*Charles and I pronounced them the best that were sent. I must close. My love to all. Please write soon*

*Your brother*
*Myron*

\* "cotton house" refers to their tents.

# CHAPTER TEN:

# Jacksonville—Fernandina Campaign

November of 1862 came along and I wished that I could look forward to the holiday season. It had been quite some time since our "adventures" further south at Dawfuskie Island and the great success at the battle of Fort Pulaski. Since there wasn't any intense need for my services at that time with the sixth, I was again shipped back to Fort McHenry. I indeed thought I could do some good. I considered myself experienced enough to see great flaws in some of my senior officers. These officers seemed much more interested in protocol and laborious paperwork than they did in the practical care of the sick and wounded. The most outstanding example of this was the fact that sometimes detailed accounts of medical instruments were not always possible under active field conditions. Nonetheless, these martinets demanded this. Comfortable as my situation and my quarters were at Fort McHenry, I longed to get back to the "fellowship of battle" and help all that I could with the members of the good old Sixth.

During the last weeks of 1862, I hoped and prayed that I would be home for the holiday season, but the war showed no sign of ending. As I fell asleep at night my thoughts drifted off toward home and just how wonderful it would be to see family and friends, especially my nephew, the "little corporal," and my dear Emma. My quarters were so nice that I had a feeling of guilt when I thought of the primitive conditions that the regiment lived under in their encampment in South Carolina at that time. I would be in the regular army for the next three years, but I suspected that some advancement from my hospital steward's job would occur long before this time would be up.

[Letter to his brother-in-law and sister, Sophronia P. Abell, of Colchester, New London County, Connecticut.]

*Post Hospital, Fort McHenry, Md.*
*November 29th, 1862*

Dear Brother

*Your letter mailed the 24th came to hand the 27th. It found me once more back home at Fort McHenry serving no more among, or rather under any self conceited volunteer officers but in the Army of the U.S. I can tell now how long I have got to serve. I have been reckoning and find that I have but 153 weeks and 3 days longer to serve. When if I choose, I can once more become a citizen and live like other beings, enjoy a home, if I ever have one, can breath freer, wander again over the broad green earth, visit my friends & all without permission or restraint.*

*I can take my nieces and nephews and my little namesake the "Corporal" on my knee and point to the stars and stripes and tell them how nobly I fought and what privations I endured to sustain that good old flag (if it is sustained?). How in every battle I escaped unhurt, because I was miles away and not within hearing of the guns. But I will ridicule no more, For the fortunes of war may, before the close of another week, bring me where I will not only hear the sound of guns but the whistle of death messengers as they one by one select their victims. But I have learned "in whatever state I am in therewith to be content for it does no good to be any other way in the Army."*

*It seems you did not get my other letter. I answered yours next to the last as soon as I received it and I hope you have received it, but fearing you have not, I will repeat the substance of it now, I sent you a receipt like the one you wanted me to send you, in order for the town of Hebron for my bounty.*

*But what is of more importance to me I asked you to send me $25 as I was entirely out of money having expended it for a uniform and have not yet a complete outfit. If you can possibly borrow it I will return it at the next payday if you request me to or will credit it to you. If you send it, you had better have the letter registered at the P.O. Please write me as soon as you receive this as I want to know on what to depend as regards to the $200 or whatever is right. You had better carry the receipt enough to file it before court. Write as soon as you get this—*
Myron

*December 1st, 1862*

Dear Sister

*I thought that I would not be partial but would enclose in this a few lines to you.*

*It may not be disinteresting to know just how I am situated so I will tell you, but, by the way I do not suppose I will not stay here very long but do not know if I will stay till spring but do not think that I will. I think that perhaps before many months I may be in the Army of the Potomac. Well I am in a house and it does not hardly seem as though a house made to live in as I have lived outdoors for so long. I have a room as large as a good sized bedroom, the wall and ceilings are papered, a good carpet on the floor, a good fireplace in which I have a fire night and day, have a secretary and library and in fact have things as nice as I could anywhere. I am now in the regular Army for three years as a Hospital*

*Steward. I should like it were it not for one thing, no society at all, no friends, all strangers, all that is what I do not like to be deprived of comforts of home and society of friends I am willing to do.*

*I was glad to hear you had been recruiting for the infantry and had done so well. There is a great need for Corporals in the service and if you chooze to name him after me and he wishes to I will find a situation for him in the Army, which I think would suit him if he is much like his uncle Myron (I mean over the left). But I do hope you will name him after me for I shall feel honored and if I live, some day I will give him occasion to be proud too.*

*But it is getting late, I must close, should have finished this and sent it yesterday but Sunday is the busiest day of the week here and so I had no time. Give my love to the girls and tell them I will write them when I get time. Write or tell L.P. too and direct to*

    *Your Aff. Brother*
    *Myron W. Robinson*
    *Hospital Steward U.S. Army*
    *Fort McHenry, Md.*

As time went on, my duties at Fort McHenry become quite perfunctory—almost boring. The steady flow of casualties kept me quite busy, but I must admit it was with a sense of relief that, for the second time, I received temporary orders to return to Hilton Head in preparation for the attack on Jacksonville—Fernandina.

*April 27, 1863*

    *Dear Father*

*I start this afternoon for Fortress Monroe and from there for S.C. I will send my trunk by express to Andover depot and the key is in this letter. I will send it unpaid as I have not money enough now I do not think to get there, charge it to me and let me know how much it is. I will send the receipt of the Co, in this.*

*When you receive it, please take out the clothes and see to them and also the books. All well, when I get there I will write again.*

    *This from your Son*
    *Myron*
    *P.S. The key is tied to the handle of the trunk.*

At first I thought I would be going to the Army of the Potomac, but instead I was dispatched on a packet boat to Hilton Head. I happily rejoined my many friends and soldiers of the Connecticut Sixth. Our command learned that the ports of Fernandina and Jacksonville had been used by the blockade runners since the fall of Fort Pulaski and Savannah a year ago. Not as important strategically as Savannah, the port was still a thorn in our side.

While I missed the easier duty at Fort McHenry, I understood that the Sixth and others in the area certainly might need our help. They seemed to be meeting with minimal resistance. A large rebel gun mounted on a railroad car had been a nuisance, but was later driven away by our gunboats. The climate was so nice that it was easy to see why northerners had come here in the past during the winter months to avoid the cold northern climate.

March at Fort McHenry, in Baltimore, was still quite cool to cold—especially at night and in the early morning. I was doubly pleased therefore to be in Florida. The balmy weather and the light number of casualties, for once, made me happy with my situation. I was, however, sure this pleasantness would not last for long. After this all too brief sojourn, I would be going back still again to Fort McHenry to finish up my training and duties there. The port of Jacksonville-Fernandina was secured and a small garrison left in control of the area.

As we departed, we could see major fires breaking out in Jacksonville. It was said that this was caused by the retreating rebel troops, but ours had something to do with it as well. This success led to orders returning us to Hilton Head.

### *Historical Note*

Certainly Florida was a state of the Confederacy, but it did not play an important part in the campaigns of the war. Cattle raising, both for the Confederacy and for sale to Cuba and elsewhere, bolstered the food supply for the Confederate army. Again, blockading ships worked to prevent some of this cattle trade, especially off the west coast of Florida.

Fort Zachary Taylor and Key West remained in Union hands throughout the war; they served as a great deterrent to Confederate blockade runners. Constructed in 1845, the fort was named after President Zachary Taylor, who died in office earlier that year. Building this fort was a slow process, taking more than twenty-one years, due to hurricanes, shortages of men and material, and the ever-present yellow fever. Captain John Brannon assumed control of the fort for the Union in coordination with our blockading fleet. Its armament included 198 cannons, a ten-inch Rodman, and Columbiads with a range of three miles. It boasted unique features, including sanitary facilities flushed by the tide and a desalination plant.

Paradoxically, Richard Taylor, the son of Zachary Taylor, fought on the Confederate side. He learned military strategy under Stonewall Jackson in 1862. He took command of fifteen thousand men after the loss of southern Louisiana to the Union. He attacked Union forces under General Banks and defeated them near Shreveport, Louisiana. The irony of this event was that General Banks had previously been humiliated in battle by Stonewall Jackson—now Jackson's protégé also defeated Banks. The only consolation for the North was that the Union forces in southern Louisiana later defeated the rebels.

\* \* \*

As I did a year before, after the Fort Pulaski battle, I bid farewell to my comrades of the Sixth (as well as to other medical staff of nearby commands). I again returned by packet boat to the luxury of my Spartan but otherwise comfortable quarters at Fort McHenry. I was being quizzed daily during my hospital duties as to just what a hospital steward does on the battlefield. At least the Florida campaign was brief and my services not often called upon.

CHAPTER ELEVEN:

# Spring, 1863 Arrives; The Battle of Charleston Begins

While I was performing my duties as a hospital steward at Fort McHenry, and also attending to the sick and wounded on our recent campaigns, the Sixth was skirmishing in the island/wetland area just south of Charleston. These forays ended as the fall of 1862 gradually turned into winter.

In the spring of 1863, having had two short tours of temporary duty (the campaigns to Fort Pulaski and to Jacksonville), I prepared once again to bid farewell to my many comrades and even my many patients at Fort McHenry. By that time, we had a large contingent of Confederate soldiers under our care as well. On my last day, I found myself feeling a bit nostalgic about leaving such good friends, to say nothing of leaving my very satisfactory environment for the conditions in the field with the Connecticut Sixth. I did however feel much more confident over my capabilities and was prepared to help all that I could with the sick and injured. That spring, it seemed that our commanders decided to do something about the Confederate supply port of Charleston and thus I again was shipped south to Hilton Head to organize further our programs for the new battles that were sure to occur.

Traveling south along the coastal waters would have seemed pleasant that spring except that I was going to rejoin the wartime actions which were sure to heat up. It was a very warm feeling to be back amongst my comrades and they certainly welcomed me very sincerely. After much drilling and preparation we moved up from Hilton Head to Folly Island. I could only think of the fact that May 1863 marked another birthday for myself, as I reached the "old age" of twenty-four!

One of the few pleasant moments of the entire war occurred to me on April 11, 1863. Our company commander, Captain Isaac Bromley, called me to his quarters and I was sworn in as an officer in the U.S. Army and was given the title of assistant surgeon of the Connecticut Sixth Volunteers. As I looked forward to the full-scale attack to begin shortly thereafter, I could only hope that I would be up to the bigger job and bigger responsibility now mine. My days as a hospital steward were over.

*Hilton Head, S.C.*
*May 12th, 1863*

*Dear Father:*

*I now take my pen to inform you of my whereabouts and you see by this that I am in the old Palmetto state. Yes I am here and I think will stay here for some time by the appearance—still do not know. I arrived here last Friday after a sea-sick voyage.*

*I went to Beaufort the night I got here and stayed. Saw the Hebron boys and came back here the next day. 2 Co's of my Reg't are here, the rest are in Charleston but I think are coming back soon.*

*I am here on a plantation, sand about as deep as one would desire. Fleas and mosquitoes in abundance, it is a low marshy place the poorest place for a camp I ever saw. I saw a few cases last year of Yellow Fever, shall wonder if there is not a good many this year as the ground is full of buried sinks. Did you get my trunk O.K.? Let me know. I think I will send for it here, I ought to have taken it. I am going to send you Dan Lewis' bill get $10 if you can and send it to me. I am fearfully short of money, tell him he must let me have $10 if possible. Tell him you will take off 5 dollars. Take half off his bill if you can get it, if not get what you can. There is no prospect of pay soon and I am very short. I cannot write any-more for I am shaking enough to drop my pen. My love to all, answer as soon as you get this so I will hear from you. Write about war news, send me a paper will you? I have never had one from you, and I want to see a Conn. paper.*

*Your Unworthy Son*
*Myron*
*Asst Surg 6th Reg't C.V.*
*Hilton Head, S.C.*
*Love to all*

[Letter to his sister Sophronia Abell, Colchester, CT from Folly Island S.C.]

*Folly Island, S.C.*
*May 24th, 1863*

*Dear Sister*

*You will see by the date that I am now in "Rebeldom," not nominally, but in reality. Imagine a small island—for I do not think it of enough importance to have a place on any map you have—about ten miles southeast of Charleston and in plain sight of Fort Sumter, Moultrie & Beauregard and Morris and James Island lying near both and on the southern end of this island amid bushes and briars and heaps of sand and weeds—upon a beach continually mashed by the restless ocean waves ever roaring and tumbling chanting its rude requiems to*

*"Him" who alone can stay its restless power—in a small tent well furnished with ammunition boxes which serve as table seats and writing desks and at night time for a bed—and there you will find your brother on this fine Sunday morning laboring to collect these few roving thoughts to send to his sister "Frona" who I suppose at this moment is fixing the girls for church or combing "Papa's" hair or perhaps training the "Little Corporal" so that some day he can be a Surgeon in the Army like his illustrious predecessor or more probably a Brigadier or Major General.*

*But I do not think I will go to church today for there is no church here. There is one in plain sight of here but it belongs to the "Rebs" so I do not think I will go there with the "Stars and Stripes" proudly waving about and above me.*

*We are building fortifications as fast as we can and mounting guns. We sometimes give the rebels a few shells to start them up and they return the compliment.*

*They do not harm us nor do I think ours do them or frighten them either. We are in plain sight of the Charleston "Blockading Fleet" and often enjoy the sight of the chase and the capture of a "Runner." They are firing at something nearly every night. It is very warm here. It is as warm here today as it is north in July and August. Mosquitoes gnats and wood ticks abound. There is but one house on the island and the owner of that has "done and gone and left it before the inhuman Yankees came here." We have plenty of raw pork and hard tack to eat. The greatest loss I experience is that of getting news as we are 50 or 60 miles from the P.O. at Hilton Head. I sometimes get an old newspaper and when I do I read it advertisements and all, Theron said in a Norwich paper, the "Bulletin" I think, was a notice of my promotion with remarks and I wish I could get a copy. I would like it much if I could. There is a rumor that we are to be to Florida and I do not know if it is so. I must tell you I had peas and some blackberries for supper, the first supper in S.C.—was a guest of Lieut. Metcalf of the 1st Conn. Battery at Beaufort, S.C. He is from Hartford, native of Lebanon and I must close, Grandpa Gramma, S.P., Julia, Cally, Delia, Little Corp., and yourself. Please write very soon and direct to:*

*M.W. Robinson*
*Asst. Surg 6th Reg't C.V.*
*Hilton Head, S.C.*
*As ever*
*Your brother Myron*
*Sister Frona—P.S. Tell the girls to come down here and we will go blackberrying for they are real thick around here and if they cannot come to be sure and write me and I will try hard to answer their letters.*
*Myron*

Despite the somewhat rigid conditions that we lived under on Folly Island, there were many good aspects. The climate was favorable and much good food was available. Fish, clams, and berries were easily obtained to augment our meals.

Sailing on board the *Cosmopolitan* again was not as arduous as on our previous trip, chiefly because it was a short trip to Hilton Head. From there we went to North Edisto Island and again foraged for the many fruits and vegetables that gave some relief to the diet, which was otherwise limited to saltpork (also called salt horse) and hardtack. Potatoes in the diet prevented much scurvy. The great use of saltpork was a problem because it was often fatty and spoiled easily in hot climates. "Pickled" beef was noted to be too salty. Soaking it required much water, which was not always available. Thus saltpork was better when troops were in the field.

Confederate units harassed the Sixth as we marched across Johns Island. We were joined by the Forty-seventh of New York, and by the Fifty-fifth and Ninety-seventh of Pennsylvania. The rebels had quite an advantage, knowing the lay of the land. They could hide behind hillocks, boulders, and ravines while firing upon our troops. Most of the injuries were minor, however, and very few were evacuated to the rear. This campaign was actually more a skirmish and did not advance our cause. Supplies were cut off and lack of food and supplies was an omen of the outcome, although the little village of Legareville on the Stono River was taken despite resistance there.

Our misery was slightly relieved by then being able to use cook fires. Heretofore, these were not allowed, to keep our size and position unknown to the enemy. It brought to my mind the origin of the word "curfew," from the French couvrir feu, "to cover fire." It was now the beginning of the lengthy campaign to permanently seal off Charleston as a supply port for the Confederacy.

On June 8, the Sixth rode across the river to James Island, only a short distance from Charleston. They eventually were forced to withdraw despite support from heavy shelling from our Connecticut batteries and from the gunboats off shore. Sharpshooters and rapid rebel forays into our ranks made life miserable to the point that withdrawal became necessary. Working with the medical section, I was kept busy stopping bleeding and helping other surgeons to probe for and remove bullets that came from the sharpshooters who were defending James Island.

I recall being given the privilege of reading a recent and rare army bulletin that indicated that regular army units had better sanitation and lower sickness rates simply by keeping latrines further from cooking areas (and attempts at fly control helped.) The newer recruits and conscripts would not take orders well, especially regarding sanitation. This was reflected in the fact that their camps were dirtier, rifles were rusty, and equipment poor. Many presumed that these soldiers were used to having their mothers do the cooking and cleaning for them; they didn't do well on their own with such chores.

Secessionville was just west of the main part of James Island. Taking it would seal the fate of all Confederate troops on James Island, especially Fort Wagner. The Battle of Secessionville began June 16, 1863, and it had a bad outcome. Bad planning seemed to be at the root of the problem. It was to be a five-day operation, but ten thousand men were sent in with only two days ration, and the battle site was poorly chosen. To put the best face on it, it was called "a successful reconnaissance." After several days of heavy shelling, we were spared further agony by virtue of General Hunter's recent arrival from the north. He ordered an evacuation to Edisto Island. Thus James Island and its proximity to Charleston persisted in thwarting our efforts.

CHAPTER TWELVE:

# Military Considerations Regarding Fort Wagner

### *Historical Note*

The 1860 cotton crop was so large, that much of this still over hung the cotton market in the early war years. The south actually put an embargo on exporting cotton at first thus to use this as a bargaining chip with Britain and others. The cotton needs of the British cotton industry were met by new sources from India, Egypt, etc. and some from the blockade runners that got through. Evidence did show that England's cotton mills were one by one running out of cotton supplies. Because England could carry on at a lesser degree and that it was swayed by the fact it had already fostered a strong abolitionist sentiment, recognition of the Confederacy never came about, although much other help to the Jefferson Davis government was given.

Presaging the end of the New England whaling fleets, the government bought up a large number of whaling vessels. They were sailed to the Charleston harbor area, filled with stones and scuttled. This was in hopes they would blockade part of the channels into Charleston harbor and thus be an obstacle to resupplying Confederacy. I learned this from letters from home as well as from some of our troops who came from the Mystic and New London areas.

The Confederacy offset some of this naval advantage by virtue of commissioning two warships, the *Alabama*, and the *Florida*. They both served the Confederacy well as a scourge of the sea by sinking many federal vessels.

Not satisfied with a largely defensive role, the limited Confederate Navy developed a manually operated submarine. On February 17th, 1864, this submarine (named the C.S.S, *Hunley*) steered toward the ever present picket line of blockading Union ships off Charleston. By means of an explosive charge at the end of a long spar, it was able to blow up the U.S. ship *Housatonic* For years it was felt that the *Hunley* perished in the same explosion. However, the author Clive Cussler, reported that on May 11th, 1995, after a prolonged under sea search, it was located some distance away in about twenty feet of water. The *Hunley* was forty feet long with a six foot beam. It was intact but covered with silt. Perhaps it developed leaks at its seams after the explosion and could not get back to its berth. The *Hunley* was a true submarine with an eight man crew, however the *Hunley* drowned three crews (seventeen men totally) in trial runs before she sunk the federal ship *Housatonic*. Both the *Housatonic* and the *Hunley* were lost in this episode.

* * *

## *Historical Note*

The Confederacy was quite determined to maintain Charleston as a seaport to maintain supplies needed for continuing the war. Its approaches were well guarded by Fort Moultrie to the north on Sullivan's Island, Fort Sumter in the middle of the harbor and Battery Gregg and Fort Wagner (actually a battery but called Fort Wagner) on the northern end of Morris Island, on the south side of Charleston harbor entrance. Fort Johnson further up the harbor was also to be contended with. The narrow channel allowed some "controlled" blockages to be left in place, as well as "torpedoes" (actually a type of mine that was, of course, deadly to any ship striking one).

Generals Seymour and Duane tried to convince Commodore Dupont of the importance of a joint action with a planned assault on Morris Island. Dupont refused because of fear of losing his ironclads, but he did promise a heavy bombardment. Therefore General Seymour established a base on Folly Island for future action against Morris Island. Brigadier General Vogdes, with the One Hundredth New York, and Brigadier General Stevenson, with a company of artillery and engineers, left Seabrook Island and took the men to Port Royal. General Hunter was later removed and General Seymour and his Morris Island plan took over.

President Lincoln, as well as a large group of senior naval and army officers, realized that capturing Charleston was of major importance in defeating the Confederacy. The Union forces amassed a significant number of troops in the Hilton Head area. The major supply ports of the South had already been taken, as well as the areas around Hilton Head. Beaufort was taken after only a brief struggle, and Port Royal then served as a good port but also even as a postal office for letters to and from the North.

To take the heavily fortified city of Charleston, an obvious strategy was to move up the barrier islands south of Charleston and neutralize the batteries and defenses on James and Morris Islands. A key area of the rebel defense of Charleston was Fort Wagner; the secondary defenses included nearby Battery Gregg, near Cummings Point; James Island batteries; and several smaller batteries on the southern part of Morris Island.

Fort Wagner was one of the most strongly defended outposts; it contained "splinter proof" protection for its gunnery crews. It was surrounded by a fifty-foot moat, which was five feet deep and often flooded with sea water. If the attacking forces could stand the withering fire while advancing up this narrow beach to cross this moat, they would still have to scale a thirty-five-foot wall of sloping sand. It was from Fort Moultrie that Union Major Anderson evacuated his troops and family to Fort Sumter in the early winter of 1861, feeling that Fort Moultrie would be more difficult to defend. It was heartbreaking for him to lower the U.S. flag and surrender Fort Sumter in April 12, 1861.

In regard to Fort Moultrie, the advent of amphibious attacks made coastal defense forts obsolete. However, in 1776, the original Fort Moultrie fought off a fleet of eleven British warships under Sir Peter Parker. Because of the strategic difficulties of defending Fort Moultrie from any South Carolina forces, Major Anderson left Fort Moultrie for the presumably safer Fort Sumter. Later, the Confederates at Fort Moultrie withstood a twenty-month siege, commencing in 1863. The rifled cannons of the Union forces destroyed major portions of the brick and stone sections of the fort. It was abandoned (as was all of the Charleston area) in 1865. This withdrawal was done to avoid being cut off and captured by General W. T. Sherman as he swept northward following his prior march to the sea that ended at Savannah.

Fort Sumter was a man-made island guarding the channel entrance to Charleston. In 1861, Major Anderson had provisions in the fort for no more than thirty days. If he did not receive additional supplies within a month, he would have to surrender. Lincoln had been aware, of course, that the Buchanan administration two months earlier had sent an unarmed merchant ship (the Star of the West) to Sumter with provisions and additional troops; she had turned back when fired upon by the shore batteries. He had not suspected, however, that the situation was as critical as he later discovered it to be.

Could Sumter have been reinforced? Lincoln's military advisors answered that it could not be relieved or even provisioned without an army of twenty thousand, and a bloody battle. There were not twenty thousand men in the regular army of the United States, and if there had been, they could not have been assembled or transported to the danger point in time. Although the Federal naval officers felt that the shore batteries could be defeated in a naval assault, it was felt that an attempt to relieve the fort would be almost certain to precipitate war.

Southern "commissioners" were even then in Washington attempting to negotiate the transfer of the forts still in the possession of the Union to the Confederacy. Lincoln resisted this, but wanted time to consider other options. His other option was to send a letter to Francis W. Pickens, governor of South Carolina, with the message that Fort Sumter would be supplied with provisions only, but no new troops. Pickens, not knowing which way to turn, relayed this message to the president of the Confederacy, Jefferson Davis, in Montgomery, Alabama. The outcome was that General P. G. T. Beauregard, in command of Charleston, demanded the evacuation of the fort; if this were not done, he would take it by force. At 4:30 A.M., on April 12, 1861, a thirty-four-hour bombardment of the fort began. They surrendered the fort with, surprisingly, no casualties except a horse. The surrendering force under Major Robert Anderson was granted amnesty and returned to Union lines.

In 1863, the key barrier island in the advance of the Union forces was Folly Island. It was separated from Morris Island by the strong tidal inlet called Lighthouse Inlet. Folly Island was just over six miles in length and as narrow as one-half mile in places. The mid portion of the island was much wider, but it tapered off to sandy low-lying areas toward the southern end. Tidal marshes characterized much of the entire area west of the barrier islands, although some small rivers flowed through areas, such as the Folly River just to the west of Folly Island.

The other chief barrier islands below this were Kiawah (separated from Folly by the Stono Inlet); Seabrook Island just south of Kiawah; and, across the Edisto River, Edisto Island. South of Edisto were a group of smaller islands, St. Helena being the largest. Just inland from St. Helena were the important towns of Beaufort and Port Royal, and of course just below this was Hilton Head, which had become a major base from which to assault the areas to the north. All of these islands were easily viewed from the troop transports bringing the Union soldiers into position to attack Fort Wagner and Morris Island as mentioned before.

Folly Island may well have remained a desolate barrier island but for the strategic needs noted above. An otherwise obscure deserted island, its name became well known in the Union states and even overseas through the newspapers. It rapidly became quite a large military base for the operations aimed at Charleston.

While General Beauregard and the valor of the Confederate forces deserve much credit for the defense of Charleston, the geography was also a great attribute. The Cooper and Ashley Rivers on each side of Charleston, the ever-shifting sandy shoals, and barrier islands off shore were detriments to capture, as were the great defensive fortifications on the approaches to Charleston Harbor: Fort Moultrie to the north; Sullivan's Island, Castle Pinckney, and Fort Sumter in the harbor itself; Fort Johnson on James Island and Fort Wagner and Battery Gregg on Morris Island to the south and the southwest .

A large battery of cannons was aligned all along the shoreline on the lower tip of Charleston. Castle Pinckney, a small island just offshore, was not as formidable a deterrent, as it was a prison also for the Union forces later on.

Before the fateful "final assault" on Fort Wagner, there were earlier attempts to take Charleston. In November 1861, Commander Samuel Frances Dupont used his naval power to subdue the area of Port Royal Sound (Port Royal, Beaufort, and in particular, Hilton Head, which was to serve throughout the war as a base for federal troops in this area).

Under pressure from the authorities in Washington, D.C., several plans were considered to conquer Charleston. Charleston was a particular thorn in the side of the federal administration—not only because of its posture as a hotbed of seccessionism, but also because of its effrontery in firing on and capturing Fort Sumter, April 12, 1861.

An attack on Charleston in June 1862 was planned, not from the barrier islands but instead across James Island in order to take Fort Lamar and Secessionville, and finally Fort Johnson in the inner harbor.

With the failure of the Battle of Secessionville, Admiral Dupont was requested to save face with Washington authorities by taking Charleston by naval bombardment. His advisors felt a prolonged bombardment and destruction of the city and its ports, along with local civilian pressure, would bring Charleston to sue for peace. Dupont felt that this was probably foolhardy, despite the addition of several ironclads to his fleet in early 1863.

## *Historical Note*

The federal navy was comprised of 427 ships by the end of 1862. This was most important since, despite the increased number of blockade runners, these ports could be effectively blocked off. Some of the blockade runners found it more important financially to bring luxury items which would occupy little space in the holds of their ships and gave much greater financial returns. The Confederacy badly needed ammunition, powder and salt. A Gideon Welles, exaggerated only slightly when he stated December 1st, 1862, "that in no previous war had the ports of an enemy's country been so effectually closed by an enemy."

\* \* \*

Some interservice rivalry went on (over who would get credit for the subjugation of the Charleston forces). Much finger pointing occurred when joint efforts of various units failed in their missions. This was definitely proving to be a harder nut to crack than the areas subjugated earlier toward the south.

Bombardments of Fort Sumter, Fort Wagner, and Battery Gregg occurred in April, 1863, but no cohesive battle plan to involve army groups on shore was carried out. Having learned that naval bombardment (with but little planned shore assault) would not lead to the surrender of Charleston, Dupont withdrew to the Hilton Head area. Some skirmishing occurred at Folly Island, but the irresoluteness of the officer in charge, General Vogdes, resulted in a stalemate. Even the troops under General Vogdes did not seem to have much confidence in his ability to command a significant assaulting force. General Vogdes set up defensive positions around Stono Inlet and Folly River. Thus ended the spring campaign against Charleston.

Two long years after Fort Sumter was taken, President Lincoln was frustrated and unhappy that Charleston had not been taken. He accepted the advice of his counselors and appointed General Quincy A. Gilmore to command the troops. Gilmore was the top cadet at West Point and was considered a good engineer; in 1861 he had seized Port Royal Sound, and built Hilton Head defenses. He had been successful in the earlier campaign at Fort Pulaski and had a promising strategy to take Charleston. Dupont's reluctance to mount a more aggressive attack led to his replacement by Foote, who gave the charge of the ironclads to Admiral Dahlgren, who was already well known because of his innovations in the use of artillery.

After thorough reconnaissance, General Gilmore proposed a plan of a joint naval bombardment and army assault from Folly Island up Morris Island to capture Fort Wagner. From there, shelling would neutralize Fort Sumter and other rebel batteries, thus allowing Dahlgren to enter Charleston Harbor and demand surrender of the city.

Fort Wagner was an irregular fortification built of earth, revetted with palmettos. and defended by significant cannons. A ten-inch Columbiad was a rifled thirty-two pounder. There were also thirty-two pound smooth bore cannons as well. Built into the surface was a huge thirty-foot by one-hundred-foot bombproof capable of housing nine hundred men. The moat in front of the fortifications and a long, sloping thirty-five-foot parapet took much construction work but gave a great sense of security to the fort.

General Gilmore worked well with Admiral Dahlgren in this campaign, but Gilmore proved to have greater engineering knowledge than military expertise. He sent a large part of his force, which had landed on Folly Island, toward the end that they would disrupt the railroad between Savannah and Charleston and to spearhead an attack across James Island. Neither of these preliminary attacks achieved their goal. General Terry made great progress sweeping northward towards James Island, but he was given strict orders by General Gilmore not to continue with this attack. This led to a counterattack by the Confederates, who were also able to reinforce their troops all along the James Island portion as well as at Fort Wagner.

The attack on Fort Wagner was preceded by the heaviest bombardment of the entire Civil War. Not only was the attack force weakened by the diversionary tactics noted above, but a heavy rain came along and interfered with proper rest and feeding of the troops before they went into this major battle.

Foote, Dahlgren, and Gilmore agreed on a plan; it was mostly Seymour's strategy: take over Morris Island, eliminate Sumter, and clear the harbor of obstructions. Foote's wounds from the action in the Mississippi River campaign became infected and he turned the full command over to Dahlgren. On June 26, 1863, Foote died, leaving a gap in their planning.

Gilmore arrived at Hilton Head June 11, 1863 and went to inspect Folly Island. He described this as a "dreary, worthless collection of sandhills—properly called 'Folly Island.'" There was an existing brigade there under the artillery man General Vogdes. He had set up a good defensive position. Because of the long, close contact of the opposing forces, the soldiers often fraternized to some degree with the rebels. They exchanged goods, newspapers, and stories, but all this changed when Gilmore arrived.

On July 7, the cook prepared three days' rations for the forthcoming move toward James Island. A surgeon, John J. Craven, established a field hospital on Folly Island, only a half-mile from the batteries. Clara Barton arrived on Hilton Head aboard the steamer *Cannicus* to visit her brother David. She deplored the small numbers of men assembled for the attack, but she wrote poetry and rode around the island noting the activity for this assault to the north. She felt General Gilmore "seemed to talk more than he acts." She later went to Folly Island.

* * *

# CHAPTER THIRTEEN:

# *Regarding Clara Barton*

Many changes in care of the wounded were made under the direction of Doctors Tripler and Letterman. Some army bulletins filtered down to us indicating some aspects of this care that would apply to our campaign, although the information came chiefly from the Army of the Potomac. After the battle of Bull Run, a good evacuation system that used ambulances was developed. This battle exposed the shortcomings of previous methods, wherein the wounded lay dying and in misery for many, many days after the battle. The Army of the Potomac solved some of these evacuation problems by designating at least some trained personnel to remove casualties from the field to station hospitals far behind the lines. Instances occasionally were noted wherein entire hospitals and their supplies were captured because of proximity to the front lines.

I became aware on Morris Island that a Miss Clara Barton and some of her staff were quite interested in the medical care of our troops. Although she seemed to be gallivanting around with our officers, nonetheless she made some permanent contributions to the medical welfare of our multitude of injured.

The following is an extract from a Report of the Sanitary Commission:

The Sanitary Commission, together with three or four noble, self-sacrificing women, have furnished everything that could be required. I will tell you one of these women, is a Miss Barton, the daughter of Judge Barton, of Boston, Massachusetts. I first met her at the battle of Cedar Mountain, where she appeared in front of the hospital at ten o'clock at night with her four mule team loaded with everything needed, in a time when we were entirely out of dressings of every kind; she supplied us with everything; and while the shells were bursting in every direction, her course to the hospital was on the right, where she found everything wanting again. After doing everything she could on the field, she returned to Culpepper, where she staid dealing out shirts to the needy wounded, and preparing soup, and seeing it prepared in all the hospitals. I thought that night that if heaven ever sent out an angel, she must be one, her assistance was so timely. Well, we began our retreat up the Rappahanock. I thought no more of our lady friend only that she had gone back to Washington. We arrived on the disastrous field of Bull Run; and while the battle was raging the fiercest on Friday, who should drive up in front of our hospital but the same woman, with the mules almost dead, having made forced marches from Washington, to the Army. She was again a welcome visitor to both the wounded and the surgeons.

The battle was over, our wounded removed on Sunday, and we were ordered to leave Fairfax Station; we had hardly got there before the battle of Chantilly commenced, and soon the wounded began to come in. Here, we had nothing but our instruments—not even a bottle of wine. When the cars whistled up to the station, the first person on the platform was Miss Barton, to again supply us with bandages, brandy, wine, prepared soup, jellies, meals, and every article that could be thought of. She stayed there until the last wounded soldier was placed on the cars and then bade us good-bye and left.

I wrote you at the time how we got to Alexandria that night and next morning our soldiers had no time to rest after reaching Washington, but were ordered to Maryland, by forced marches. Several days of hard marching brought us to Frederick, and the battle of South Mountain followed. The next day our army stood face to face with the whole force. The rattle of 150,000 muskets and the fearful thunder of over two hundred cannons told us that the great battle of Antietam had commenced. I was in a hospital in the afternoon, for it was then only that the wounded began to come in.

We expended every bandage, torn up every sheet in the house, and everything we could find, and who should drive up but our old friend Miss Barton, with a team loaded down with dressings of every kind, and everything we could ask for. She distributed her articles to different hospitals, worked all night making soup, all the next day and night; and when I left, four days after the battle, I left her there administering to the wounded and dying. When I returned to the field hospital last week, she was still at work supplying the delicacies of every kind, and administering to their wants—all of which she does out of her own private fortune. Now, what do you think of Miss Barton? In my feeble estimation, General McClellan, with all his laurels, sinks into insignificance beside the true heroine of the age—the angel of the battlefield.

Poem from *The Civil War in Song and Story*:

Narrow beds by one another—
White and low!
Through them softly as in church aisles,
Nurses go—
For the hot lips ice drops bring,
Cold and clear;
Or white eyelids gently closing
For the bier.
Strong men in a moment smitten
Down from strength,
Brave men, now in anguish praying—
Death at length
Burns the night lamp where the watchers,
By the bed,
Write for many a loved one,
 "He is dead!"
One lies there in utter weakness—
Shattered, faint—
But its brow wears calm befitting, martyred saints;
And although the lips must quiver,
They can smile,
As he says, "This will be over
In a while."
"As the old crusaders, weeping
In delight, knelt when Zion's holy city
Rose in sight,
So I fling aside my weapon,
From the din
To the quietness of heaven
Entering in.
"Standing in the solemn shadow
Of God's hand,
Love of glory fading from me,
Love of land
Thank God that he has let me
Strike one blow
For this poor and helpless people,
Ere I go."
White and whiter grows the glory
On his brow;
Does he see the towers of Zion
Rising now?

Stands the doctor, weary, hurried,
By his bed; "Here is room for one more wounded—
He is dead."

# CHAPTER FOURTEEN:

# *An Overview of Army Planning*

## *Historical Note*

Commodore Dupont's lack of action earned him much criticism from the secretary of the Navy, and he was replaced by Commodore Dahlgren. Dahlgren proved to be much more cooperative with General Gilmore in developing a joint aggressive plan to take Fort Wagner.

General Gilmore thought he could break the tenacious hold of the rebel troops on Fort Wagner by bombardment and so he had guns moved in from Folly Island. The soldiers alternated between heavy duty with construction of the batteries and duty in the rifle pits. Dahlgren "peppered" Fort Wagner intermittently, but nonetheless it was noted that the longer Fort Wagner held, the greater the inner harbor defenses strengthened. Beauregard assumed that Fort Wagner would ultimately be lost, as well as Fort Sumter, but the inner forts of Fort Johnson on the north edge of James Island, Fort Moultrie on Sullivan's Island, and possibly Castle Pinckney could hold on indefinitely. (Castle Pinckney at that time housed large numbers of northern prisoners, many from the battle of Bull Run.)

From July 10 to July 15, General Terry improved his position on James Island, but much skirmishing and a gradual yielding to progressively heavier forces was required. The Fifty-fourth Massachusetts colored regiment did very well here, but with very little rest and heavy casualties they were transferred to Folly Island, where they were shortly afterwards thrown into the "grand assault."

General Gilmore's plan for this final assault on Fort Wagner was to use land-based and navy artillery on July 17, in the hope of blasting the fort into some position of weakness prior to the assault. At sunset the infantry was to rush the battery, but heavy rain postponed this entire plan to the next day. The all-day barrage seemed to do great damage to the fort, but it was noted that the earthworks absorbed the shells better than stone; in addition, General Gilmore learned to his dismay that the estimated three hundred existing troops inside the fort were actually at least twelve hundred. In a prior assault on Charleston Harbor, the gunboat Keokuk went aground. Some excellent cannons were removed from it, as well as the code book revealing much of the Union plans. The Fifty-fourth Massachusetts, despite its recent losses and fatigue, was still strong. Other regiments indicated long sick rolls but the Fifty-fourth was able to field a very large force. They were rushed by the rebels in an attack on James Island immediately before this attack of July 16. However, they were saved by a holding action of the Tenth Connecticut, and the Union forces were allowed to reorganize to repel a greater enemy force as they withdrew in order on James Island. Some of the wounded started back by boat. They were most fearful that their bleeding wounds would attract the alligators that lurked nearby and could be heard splashing into the shallow waters.

By Gilmore's orders, three Union brigades were held back, but they could have exploited the breakthrough made by the Fifty-fourth Massachusetts and Sixth Connecticut if so allowed. By one o'clock in the morning of July 19, the battle had ceased. The Confederate forces often stripped the bodies of the Union soldiers, especially for shoes, but other loot also. The tide came in on this narrow battlefield and some of the wounded actually drowned.

Several factors were considered of importance in the failure of the "grand assault": overconfidence from their recent victories in overcoming batteries as they moved up the island; too much space in time between units, which prevented a concentrated attack after the initial successful assault; and finally, the confusion of a night assault. Thus Fort Wagner, although initially taken in the first rush, was never to be taken by arms. It fell into Union hands when the rebel garrison joined the general withdrawal from Charleston to avoid entrapment by General Sherman's forces moving north after his grand campaign through Atlanta and Savannah.

Of 5,000 Union troops attacking Wagner, 1,115 became casualties. Two-hundred and forty-six were killed, 890 were wounded, and 391 were captured. Later an exchange of prisoners took place in the city. Negroes were not exchanged, and it was learned that they were to be tried and possibly executed. President Lincoln intervened by issuing general order one hundred, which stated that one Confederate soldier would be killed for any black killed. Imprisonment at hard labor was the fate of many, however.

After the battle, General Gilmore was worried about a counterattack that might extend further south, especially against the main Union base at Hilton Head. He therefore sent survivors of the Sixth Connecticut back to Port Royal on garrison duty in order to recover their strength.

The ultimate outcome was that Charleston and its surrounding forts were not taken by force of arms, but by a prolonged siege. Many units in this attack were later moved north for the battles outside Richmond and Petersburg.

With the holding force remaining on Folly Island, and the blockading gunboats offshore, resupply of the Confederacy was greatly reduced. However, there was some degree of elation in Charleston because the fortifications were not overwhelmed. It was later learned that Jefferson Davis visited Charleston in the fall of 1863 for the funeral of John C. Calhoun. He also wished to learn of the willingness of the Charlestonians to put up with a possible long siege. He found the morale so high that he predicted that if the city were to fall to Union forces, they would leave their lovely city in ruins before surrendering it.

\* \* \*

The Army (and state organizations) learned to use new personnel as replacements rather than making up whole new regiments with newcomers. Such raw regiments could do poorly in combat with no trained sustaining power and self-confidence. While at Hilton Head, I learned that Wisconsin had developed this replacement concept to good effect. Earlier on, I had some misgivings about my own qualifications to care for so many casualties under life-and-death conditions. Licensing of doctors by states was not standardized and quite problematic. If the doctors' exams were too difficult, not enough doctors would be produced; if too lax, inadequate doctors would be licensed, to the detriment of the army (and society). The army often counted on practical field experience, ideally under the tutelage of seasoned doctors, to bring them up to snuff. Many of us were surprised to note that even with lax medical exams, such doctors did well eventually, and most had diplomas. In the second quarter of the nineteenth century, most doctors were preceptorship trained. Deficiencies were often in operative surgery, but many learned quickly and came to appreciate the importance of applied field sanitation. While I was happy with and confident of the preceptor training I received with Dr. Craig long ago in Hebron, I felt better because of the academic knowledge I acquired at Berkshire Medical School. Most medical schools were for two years (but are often repetitive in course material). Other physicians told me that many states prohibited anatomic dissection as part of the training.

### *Historical Note*

The physicians themselves had a significant casualty rate: some were captured and imprisoned (4 died in Confederate prisons), 42 officers were killed in action, 83 were wounded, and 290 were lost by death, disease, or accident.

\* \* \*

# CHAPTER FIFTEEN:

# *Into the Fray*

The dryness in my mouth and my rapid heartbeat I was sure were the result of my concern about the great assault on Fort Wagner, which was about to begin. I was bone tired from attending the many dying and wounded from our recent battle at James Island. With no rest or resupply, how could it be that we were about to take on the formidable fortification of Fort Wagner? As a major defender of Charleston and its lifeline to the Confederate forces, it seemed to be of great importance to the Union forces to deny this supply line.

The breeze from the nearby ocean dispelled some of the heat of the day. I therefore loosened my collar to begin a tour of the tents of the sick and wounded, hoping the evening breeze would make the tour more tenable, except for a few more moments to contemplate how I would manage the next crop of wounded this grim reaper of war would bring me. The recently bloody operating table and instruments were washed to the best degree possible under these poor conditions. A depressingly large stack of amputated extremities was buried, along with those not surviving their injuries from our recent struggle. Perhaps this would reduce the fly population on the hot July evening of 1863. The summer sun seemed to be sizzling into the wetland as it descended toward the west, giving me time to reflect on how such a tumultuous set of events had come to pass.

As I sat under the "fly" of my tent at water's edge on Morris Island, it was open to the now-setting sun while I rested a few minutes following rounds in the hospital tents. I felt the uneasiness shared by all our Connecticut Sixth Volunteer Troops on the evening of what might prove to be our greatest battle yet. The singing around the campfires seemed somewhat muted as the troops cleaned their firearms, sharpened their bayonets, and prepared their cartridge cases. I saw some of them sewing their names into their clothing toward the end that their bodies would be more easily identified in the case of their death.

In preparation for this night battle, they were also ordered to sew a white patch of cloth to identify them as members of the Union force. It seemed ghoulish to me that civilian undertakers appeared on the battle scene shortly after battles to embalm bodies and send them on their way back north. The truth of this became known to me through a newspaper that fell into my hands at that time. In it, an advertisement stated that "persons at a distance, desiring to have the bodies of their deceased friends disinterred, embalmed, disinfected or prepared to send home and have it properly attended to by application to the office of Simon Garland, 35 Thirteenth Street, Philadelphia, PA. No zinc, arsenic or alcohol is used, perfect satisfaction is guaranteed." The newspaper also made it clear that our Army of the Potomac was somewhat stalemated and not making any significant progress that would make me feel the war would end anytime soon.

Although my thoughts were preoccupied with the dangers of this Fort Wagner attack, I felt better when I thought of our previous successes: the taking of Hilton Head and Port Royal Sound when we first came down from the North, and the attack and capture of the seaport at Jacksonville two months earlier. As dusk enshrouded our departing attacking force in their assault on Fort Wagner, my thoughts also wandered back to the time just over a year ago when we attacked Fort Pulaski, in our quest to blockade Savannah. The troops of the sixth C.V. proved their tenacity in making sites available and ready for our artillery on the tidal flats just below Fort Pulaski. Their illnesses and poor living conditions (trying to sleep when even their rubber ponchos got wet with the rising tides, for example) did not deter them from attaining the destruction of Fort Pulaski.

Our job presently was to deny Charleston as an entrance point for supplies to the Confederacy, as well as to pin down a significant number of Confederate troops. It seemed that thus far the Confederacy had been quite successful in exchanging its cotton and other goods for armament, food, and medicine from overseas. However, we had reason to be quite proud of our offshore gunboats for fighting off blockade runners and for providing general support for our troops along this coastline.

By the time of the assault on Fort Wagner, our troops were quite experienced in amphibious landings. On our way to James Island we passed deserted plantations, some with farm equipment visible in the barns. It was a time of apprehension; we knew the enemy lay in wait somewhere ahead. Each ditch and forest glen might hold a death-dealing welcome.

The enemy had selected a position with a good field of fire—marshy wetlands in front and woods on each side. Even though they were falling back, the rebels gave a blistering fire (by rifle and howitzer with canister). The guns from the supporting ships were off-loaded in support of our advance through the briars and underbrush. Our valorous troops of the Sixth were enraged because of the wounding last spring of our commander, Colonel Chatfield; they made a headlong attack that surprised the rebels in its ferocity. This drove them back across the Pocotaligo River into the town. Although it would have been a proper tactic to follow after the rebels, they solved that problem for us by burning the bridges over the converging rivers, which we would have done anyway; this saved them temporarily, but it took away their route to Savannah. Because of strong rebel reinforcements, we were obliged to return to Mackeys Point. Our embarkation was as orderly as our debarkation, care being given to retain our equipment and care for the wounded. The dead were buried along our return route with as much honor as our situation allowed.

I was very proud of our Sixth Connecticut Volunteers in that they became so well trained in small boat assaults through the Fort Pulaski and the Savannah Campaign of the spring of 1862. This greatly minimized the confusion and allowed for better care of the injured. In past times, members of the band served as stretcher bearers to bring the wounded back to our medical tents. Since they had no specific medical training, this was a mixed advantage. We needed all the fighting men on the front line as we could, and thus could not have them fall back carrying the wounded to our aid stations.

[A letter to his parents describing six days of fighting and winning while under fire from Fort Sumter. It is in a special envelope stamped in Port Royal, South Carolina with an unusual "target type" postmark.]

*Morris Island, S.C.*
*July 15th, 1863*

*Dear Father and Mother:*

*This is the sixth day after the commencement of the fight and I am safe but hardly able to sit up. Am now under the range of fire of Sumter and shall be there soon. We have met with a glorious victory. My Reg't (6th) was in the advance and took twelve batteries, (nine cannon and 3 Mortar Batteries). The 6th captured 2 flags and several prisoners.*

*Think of me sometimes down upon the sandy beaches of S.C. with the sun directly over my head, pouring down its rays with the most severe heat. I must close*

*Good Night*
*From Your Son*
*Myron*

On the northern end of Folly Island there was a great problem with insects, largely, I believe, because of marshy wetlands and swamp lying just inland. The mosquitoes were especially bad at night, and that was when the soldiers worked secretly and tried to avoid detection by the rebel forces in planning the great assault. The smoke from campfires might have reduced the insect problem, but the plan was to keep the size of our assault force a secret until the time of attack; therefore, use of fire was limited. Despite sweltering days and stormy nights, I moved to several outposts to give medical help for the (mostly minor) injuries that accompanied the movement of heavy cannons, ammunition, and supplies by dark. Although we had much success in overwhelming and capturing rebel batteries in our gradual movement up Morris Island, several lesser assaults were made on Fort Wagner, all to no avail. I was concerned with just how evacuation of the wounded would work out with such a narrow strip of land on northern Morris Island, with the Atlantic Ocean to the east and swamps toward the west. Assaulting troops and reserves and cannons need much elbow room. What about evacuation of my wounded?

I could easily see that evacuation of the wounded would be a problem but I was encouraged by the efficiency with which the mass of men in arms had gotten here from our areas on and near Hilton Head. I was especially anxious that the ambulances, hospital tents, and medical supplies be available as far forward as practical. We left on our "favorite" old transport, *Cosmopolitan*, that we embarked upon long ago. This ship stood by to help evacuate the wounded back to Hilton Head. This I could see was a logistics nightmare. To move across shallow entrances with shifting sandbars, unload vast amounts of equipment, and move secretly in the dark was a Herculean task but it was done in quite a short time.

Our brigade was under Brigadier General George C. Strong, and included the Sixth and Seventh Connecticut, Third New Hampshire, Sixty-sixth Pennsylvania, Ninth Maine, and Forty-eighth New York. The preliminary attack on July 8 was called off because of high seas, poor coordination, strong tides, and even some seasickness.

I knew the next twenty-four hours would tell us whether our preliminary attacks had made enough damage to the enemy that we could finish this off in one major final assault. A sergeant with a leg injury reported to me as to how a recent preliminary battle was progressing. He described how difficult it was to keep the eighty small boats of this flotilla together and maintain silence. They kept out of sight close to shore under the tall sea oats and sea grass until five A.M. At that time, forty-eight Union guns, so painfully hidden and emplaced, opened fire on Fort Wagner. He went on to say that it became apparent that cannonading alone would not cause the rebels to leave the well-fortified base, and thus the Connecticut Sixth left their launches to bear on to the approaches to Fort Wagner directly. The firefight continued all day as the battle line surged back and forth on this hot day off the South Carolina coast. The sergeant told me that after skirmishing all day, the Sixth pulled back at sunset, and that he required help to get back here for medical attention. After attending to him and sewing up many lacerations and other injuries from the grape and canister injuries, I went to learn the battle plans for the next day's all-out assault.

While we were still further south at Hilton Head, ironclads under Dupont had moved against Charleston. They apparently were outgunned with fusillades from Sullivan's Island, Fort Sumter, and Battery Gregg.

I had hoped there might be some respite in the few days preceding this final assault. This was not to be. It was planned that the Seventh Connecticut, the Ninth Maine, and the Pennsylvania Seventy-sixth were to make a bayonet charge the morning of July 11, 1863. This began with a charge against great odds. The Seventh rushed across the moat and up the inclined parapet, where they sustained severe casualties. Their unit was essentially decimated by canister immediately overhead and rifle fire directly in their faces. The Ninth Maine wavered back but the Sixth and some of the Pennsylvania Seventy-sixth returned fire from entrenchments close to the fort. There they remained all night under a drenching rainfall. This stalemate existed for the next several days. I wondered at what great inner strength and courage these men had in order to keep going. Even with very little rest, poor food if any, and covered with sand and insect bites, they strove to get back into the struggle. I too was tiring badly because of the long hours of trying to save lives and keep up my morale, as well as that of the injured soldiers.

The few weeks prior to the grand assault on Fort Wagner were filled with many events and much planning. Sensing the imminent attack on Fort Wagner, we learned that Beauregard made many plans to strengthen this fort. Slaves were supposed to be lent by their owners to help in such fortifications, but the local gentry didn't furnish many. Therefore, soldiers were used for much of this heavy work. Confusion over the command of the fortifications was also a factor for the Confederate Army to consider. The infantry was senior in many respects, but the engineers had the "know how."

General Gilmore threw a diversionary force into an attack on James Island (5,260 men under Colonel Higgenson). Also a group went up the Edisto River to cut the Charleston and Savannah railroad (to prevent any reinforcement once the assault on Wagner began). In all, this committed more than half of his forces to these diversions.

A two-pronged attack was planned so that one force would land between Battery Gregg and Wagner, while the other assaulted the south end of Morris Island. Gilmore assembled barges on the Folly River on the north side of Folly Island, just south of Morris Island and Fort Wagner, while at Port Royal, Dahlgren had ready a flotilla of launches and cutters. The Morris Island attack was deferred but the other prong under General Terry did well. With naval back-up he went up Stono Inlet and fired shells into James Island and John's Island.

The One Hundred Fourth and Fifty-second Pennsylvania divisions waded into Legere's landing and moved on to take over Sol Legere Island and thus seized the causeways to James Island, which was just inland from Morris Island. Terry could and should have gone ahead and taken James Island, but Gilmore told him not to commit beyond this point and therefore no more troops were landed on that day, July 9. This gave time to Beauregard to further reinforce his fortifications. Rather than coming through the "backwaters" of Morris Island, Gilmore planned an attempt along the south coast and up the Atlantic side.

In preparation for all of this, by mid-June, Folly Island was almost "weighted down," as one soldier put it, by the amount of men and war material stationed there. There were nearly two hundred officers, and several thousand infantry troops with supporting artillery. Units assigned there were the Connecticut Sixth, the Thirty-ninth Illinois, the Fourth New Hampshire, the One Hundredth New York, the Sixty-second and Sixty-seventh Ohio, and the Eighty-fifth Pennsylvania. With these reinforcements, Folly Island changed from a defensive situation to one geared for a major offense. Besides the two-pronged diversionary probing attack, a secret attack on the inland side of Morris Island was to be a major thrust following the previously mentioned heavy naval bombardment. Due to excellent planning and secrecy, the rebel forces remained essentially unaware of the large amount of men and artillery being emplaced (especially during the night) on this southwest edge of Morris Island.

On the evening of July 9, the Sixth and Seventh Connecticut went by river to Lighthouse Inlet, such action going on into the early morning of July 10. The troops were worried about being attacked while in open boats (under the command of Strong). Early in the morning of July 10, the batteries began surprise firing on the rebel positions. An artillery duel took place and a standoff occurred until the naval monitors joined in. The Union guns gradually gained the upper hand, but a few Confederate shells landed in boats with devastating effect. The air was very hot with no breeze, contributing to the fatigue of the soldiers. Getting these badly wounded troops back across Lighthouse Inlet and to our medical area was fraught with both danger. I remained hot, tired and very busy.

Because of the monitors, the Confederate cannons began to lose effect. The bombardment was so long and loud it was heard all the way to Port Royal, more than fifty miles away. The Confederate batteries on southern Morris Island were taken and the Sixth got above these batteries, forcing the Confederate troops to retreat rapidly. In pursuit, the Sixth obtained newspapers from the rebels telling of Union victories at Gettysburg and Vicksburg. The advance was greatly slowed because Fort Sumter was able to fire directly into the Union lines, despite the fact that the monitors kept pounding away at Wagner. Contributing to the Union's initial success was the fact that the Confederate guns couldn't be depressed to a low enough angle, enabling the attacking forces to make their way. Rather than stay in a holding position, the Sixth went still further down Lighthouse Inlet, then turned north up the Atlantic side of Morris Island. At the end of July 10, Gilmore thought it best to rest up after "a good days work." He failed to follow through with fresh troops and the rebel forces regrouped still again.

The two-pronged diversion failed. The railroad lines were not cut and General Beauregard was able to reinforce both James Island and Fort Wagner.

# CHAPTER SIXTEEN:

# *A Terrible Night of Battle*

At two thirty in the morning on July 11, the Connecticut Seventh planned a bayonet charge on the rifle pits in front of Wagner. The heavy fire of this attack caused the rebels to withdraw into Fort Wagner. Soldiers of Maine and Pennsylvania supporting the attack did not keep a proper interval, as they were too far behind and got hit with a much heavier barrage. The Seventh Connecticut was decimated on Fort Wagner's wall at this time. In this skirmish the Union lost 339 men while the Confederates lost only six dead and six wounded. Overconfidence caused by the recent successful attacks up the island led to lack of close support and ultimate loss, I believe.

The final great assault on Fort Wagner was about to begin. I had deeply wished that our troops would get more rest and recovery from the recent battle action. The long summer evening could have been beautiful and calm under the setting sun, however this was not to be. The earsplitting cannonade after cannonade boomed forth from our ironclads offshore. It didn't seem possible that anyone or anything could survive this pounding holocaust. It was thought that only three hundred Confederate soldiers remained at the most, following this entire day of heavy cannonading (unfortunately, it later proved that twelve hundred able troops came to the parapets). I felt guilty over the fact that I found this great death-dealing blow uplifting to my spirits. In any case, it might have been the way to success and an end to this campaign if all went well. The soldiers, with their white strips of cloth tied or sewn to their uniform, moved forward. The guns aimed at Fort Wagner seemed to finally be silent after the extremely heavy all day barrage.

The two units to make the initial charge were the Massachusetts Fifty-fourth and the Connecticut Sixth. The Fifty-fourth was the first colored regiment to be given the honor in leading an attack. Colonel Chatfield's aide was pleased to give me such information before major battles, allowing me to make casualty preparations as far in advance as possible. The hospital tents were ready and hospital stewards had prepared bandages and other needful supplies. I wondered in the back of my mind about recent thoughts given at a higher level to a proposal for a War Department Medical School. This idea had been defeated earlier in 1863. However, Surgeon General Hammond had prepared a textbook on military hygiene and sanitation. Developed for hospital stewards, it was most helpful to me, yet I couldn't get over the great apprehension as to what lay before the Sixth in this daring attack. In a "set piece" type battle, surgeons could prepare their tents, personnel, and medical equipment in anticipation of arriving casualties. Not so here.

An ominous silence came over Fort Wagner, with only a rare shot fired from the fort. You could sense the lessening of apprehension amongst the troops. Lighthearted laughter and joking was noted even amongst the Massachusetts Fifty-fourth. They were designated to lead the attack under the command of Colonel Shaw, who was previously thought to be some type of social dilettante. He properly received great credit for training these colored troops and building them into an excellent fighting outfit. I was told that his mother had a history of strong abolitionist sentiments and that he was considered somewhat of a "mama's boy." He was obviously pampered and even did some training in Europe. He had earlier turned down the offer of leading the Fifty-fourth, but he gradually came to respect the Negroes and in deference to his mother, he took over the command of this unit. The soldiers forming the Fifty-fourth were mostly literate men and included many from other states. It included a doctor, a pharmacist, an engineer, and others (they were not runaway slaves as purported by others.) They were therefore definitely more educated than most soldiers of the Confederate Army. In their free time they were noted to observe white soldiers drilling, and did considerable drilling on their own to emulate them.

They left for South Carolina on May 28, 1863, and were given many accolades as they marched through Boston on their departure. Their morale was high despite past problems with their supplies, uniforms, and pay status. They showed their impatience to get on with this assault as the sun set over the mainland on the fateful evening of July 18. I fully understood the quandary my superiors were in regarding just how to use this regiment in battle. They had not had sufficient rest since the campaign a few days ago just inland. If they were to succeed in this attack, other officers might complain that they were denied the honor of leading this important assault on this very important target. If the attack should fail, the responsible officers would be accused of using them as cannon fodder.

To their great credit, and also to the credit of Colonel Shaw, they were very anxious to lead the assault. They knew full well that colored troops were often not taken captive, but were frequently shot in trying to surrender. It was well known that the rebel forces were taught to "kill the nigger, take the white man." I guess it was considered the height of insult to be taken prisoner, wounded, or killed by a member of the black race when the rebels had suppressed the Negroes all these many years. In the skirmishing prior to this battle, the Fifty-fourth was rushed by the rebels and they fought off this attack quite well, allowing the Union time to regroup, especially the Tenth Connecticut.

### *Historical Note*

It was known that even a bit later in the war, the South also tried to raise colored outfits, but there was great apprehension that arming Negroes might backfire upon them and this program never became a major factor.

* * *

The ominous silence was broken only by a few raucous but plaintive seagull cries that could barely be heard, but nowhere near the usual loud cacophony from the wheeling and diving birds.

With the help of some of the soldiers from the regiment, I came to learn much about what to expect with incoming artillery shells. A correspondent writing from Morris Island said:

> At night we can see the path of a shell through its journey, lighted as it is a burning fuse. When the range is two miles, the track of a shell from a mortar describes very near the half-arc of a circle. On leaving the mortar, it gracefully moves on, climbing up and up into the heavens till it is nearly a mile above the earth, and then it glides along for a moment, apparently in a horizontal line; but quickly you see the fiery orb is on the same home stretch, describing the other segment of the circle.
>
> A shell from a Parrott rifled gun, in going two and one half miles, deviates from a straight line not quite as much as a shell from a mortar. But, in passing over this space, considerable time is required. The report travels faster than the shot. A shell from a mortar makes the distance of two miles in about thirty seconds, and from a Parrott gun in about half that time. The flash of a gun at night, white smoke by day, indicate the moment of discharge and fifteen or twenty seconds gives an abundance of time to find a cover in a splinter proof, behind a trench, or something else. It is wise and soldierly to do so, but many pay no attention to these hissing screaming, flying, in the daytime invisible devils, except to crack jokes at their expense and occasionally one pays with his life for this foolhardiness.

The last rays of the sun left the ocean darker and gave a final brilliance to the clouds hanging over the ocean to the east. This vista seemed to be in sharp contrast to the large bloody military operation about to begin on a sandy strip of an island off the South Carolina coast.

Following the muffled drum roll, I could see my fine troops wheel into line and march off to the north with great determination. A thousand footprints in the still-warm sands and the glimmer of the white patches sewn to their uniforms were all I could make out to indicate the ever-fading blue line of soldiers of the gallant Sixth. My prayers went with them.

I don't know what affected me the most—the chronic fatigue, the unbearable heat, or a low grade stomach upset. In any case, I was not up to the vigorous duties that lay before me. My stomach growled from upset and emptiness, but I was eager to get on with the preparations for this "final" grand assault at Wagner.

During this horrible night (which I thought would never end), I ventured as far up the beach toward the fort as I dared. Despite warning from at least two sergeants, I took my field medical kit and twelve corpsmen along the beach with me. We actually pulled a few wounded from the lapping ocean waves as the Sixth proceeded up the ocean side of Morris Island toward the fort. I tried to set up some priorities of getting our wounded to the rear where the corpsmen and stewards would give some initial care to their wounds—especially to stop bleeding.

The agonizing screams and calls for help kept me moving forward, but I could easily sense the worsening danger even though the darkness protected my small medical group from rebel sharpshooters. I finally accompanied the evacuation of some of the worst wounded cases. My attention was called to a most tragic scene. Even though the firing died down later and the issue was still in doubt, I was kept quite busy to the point of exhaustion. While attending to our badly wounded troops, we worked through dawn and into the heat of still another day. We came to learn that despite our initial success and great losses, the fort was not taken.

We were within range of enemy guns and our medical attention was ofttimes abbreviated because of this. The night attack indeed gave us the advantage of surprise but I had to be careful with the lantern light. Some of my medical team joked that the light was attracting some "stings" that weren't insects. Thus we shielded our lanterns and kept behind the sand dunes as best possible.

The rising tide still further limited the approach to Fort Wagner and this was a hindrance both in the assault and in the evacuation of the wounded. Some wounded had to be pulled from the surf—others fell dead and their bodies were lost to the tides. I was satisfied that we were able to use our small boats to send our wounded across Lighthouse Inlet back to Folly Island. It was surprising that only one of our small boats in our amphibious fleet was hit. I remember the tangy smell in my nostrils of the salty wetlands admixed with gun powder smells as I crossed Lighthouse Inlet to give medical care at the lower end of Morris Island.

My heart was proud but filled with great trepidation as I could see the Fifty-fourth moving on the left and the Sixth on the ocean's edge on the right. This was, of course, most difficult to discern except by the tremendous flashes of cannon and musket fire. Once the massive bombardment from sea and land ceased, the rebels apparently came out of their "splinter proofs" and manned the parapets with deadly effect on our attacking forces. The Fifty-fourth surged across the sands under heavy rifle fire and crossed the moat partially filled with water. Colonel Shaw led them up the inclined parapet despite withering fire that depleted ranks on either side of them. They wavered momentarily, but Colonel Shaw rallied them on past the moat again. But when he reached the top of the parapet he was shot through the heart by a North Carolina soldier. Sergeant Carney (he became famous because he was the first Negro soldier to receive the Congressional Medal of Honor) caught the flag and saved it. I had occasion to treat him for a serious wound shortly afterwards, when he related much of this to me. Unfortunately his wounds were too serious and he died in our surgical treatment area only a few hours later.

In the meantime, the Sixth was attacking on the ocean side of the parapet. The Connecticut flag was truly the first flag to fly over Fort Wagner. They drove the rebels back from this position and from all of the accounts I received later, they held this fort for nearly three hours while waiting for reinforcements to come and cement our position. The Second brigade did not advance; even to withdraw from this battle was difficult for our troops since the rebels had regrouped and were now coming back to man the parapets.

Despite the fighting at close quarters, I was again impressed with how relatively few bayonet and sword injuries showed up in our hospital tents. The night attack was confusing to both sides and injuries seemed to have been inflicted in a willy-nilly fashion on both sides. Although we took many prisoners as well as two flags, great sadness filled our hearts upon learning that Colonel Chatfield was seriously wounded and would probably not survive. Lieutenants West and Kost were taken prisoners and Color Sergeant Gustave DeBonge and six others were killed in quick succession as they bore the Union standards in the air. The cause in question was captured by the enemy and recaptured by Captain F. B. Osborne. The Sixth took four hundred men into the battle of Fort Wagner and lost one hundred and forty, 35 percent of its men.

A shudder ran through me as I saw the flashes of hundreds of guns and heard the distant screams of the attackers, defenders, and dying. Later, when this died down, an ominous silence took over. I briefly saw the Connecticut flag flying over the fort but my optimism at seeing this was short lived, as gun flashes shortly thereafter showed that it was gone.

As we had seen in past battles, one measure of success in the conflict was the preservation of your own battle flag and capture of enemy flags. Although such flags were often helpful in indicating the "high-water mark" of your advance, at night total confusion reigned, with hand-to-hand fighting being the rule.

The remnants of the Fifty-fourth who ultimately returned were justly proud of their flag bearer despite losses of about 50 percent of their attacking force. Notwithstanding the terrible casualty rate of the Fifty-fourth, their hearts were made lighter by many compliments given them for their conduct in battle. This could not help but lead to the formation of still more colored regiments.

Without reinforcements, the Sixth also retreated, bringing as many wounded as possible with them as they scrambled back to our defenses on lower Morris Island. Our medical-surgical group was already tired before the main body of casualties arrived. By flickering lantern light, we did the best we could to decide which soldiers could be helped the most and which were beyond hope. Unfortunately, Colonel Chatfield belonged to the latter group.

The rebel troops at Fort Wagner were infuriated by the ferocity of the attack by these colored troops of the Fifty-fourth. On the other hand, the level of anger was more than matched by the troops of the Fifty-fourth when they learned of the treatment of their captured comrades and the fate of their trustworthy Colonel

Shaw. During a brief truce, one of our officers confirmed the ill treatment of our captured colored troops, and especially the desecration of the body of Colonel Shaw. He described the grisly scene wherein the body of Colonel Shaw was dragged through the fort and ultimately thrown into the bottom of the mass grave with his colored troops.

We were running low on chloroform but ultimately were resupplied. As the patients took in the chloroform, many soldiers fixed me with their eyes—looking like wounded animals and praying for release from their pain—one way or another. My medical corpsmen were of great help in getting the most urgent cases to me, in addition to preparing bandages, splinting, and generally supporting our vast number of injured as best possible. As the sun rose to come out of the ocean to the east and the heat of the day began, I tried to put this bloody scene behind me for a short while as I lit my pipe and sat down on a cartridge box. I could only think that, while this battle weakened the Confederate cause, it in effect put the Sixth out of contention until it could be recruited. The Fifty-fourth had been in the islands off Charleston for two months, while the Sixth had been in significant battles to the south, with both skirmishing and battles all the way from Jacksonville-Fernandina, Fort Pulaski, and areas between our present position and Savannah for some time now.

The only good news was that a large group of surgeons was arriving from the North, and even though the battle had been over for a few days, we urgently needed as much help as we could get. While most were anxious to learn, it seemed to me that a slight wound in a limb was sufficient for many of them to amputate. While many a victim protested against this outrage, they were told it was the only thing that would prolong life. Unfortunately, many of them died post-operatively.

### *Historical Note*

War experience turned a large number of rural doctors into operating surgeons; in the past, these doctors referred most surgical cases to city specialists.

In regard to anesthesia, records show that chloroform was used 76 percent of the time, ether 14 percent, and a mixture of these 9 percent, with very few anesthetic deaths.

\*\*\*

Colonel Chatfield was born in Oxford, Connecticut, in 1826. He was apprenticed into the carpenter business in Derby, where he served four years, after which he worked as a journeyman. He moved to Waterbury in 1855. Many felt he was a "born soldier." He served as a private in the Derby Blues and was active in raising the Waterbury City Guard, of which he became captain.

He infused a sense of loyalty and valor in his troops, and despite his injury at Pocotaligo he still spearheaded the attack of the Sixth on Fort Wagner. He was wounded in the leg as he rose to the parapet at this fort. While dragging himself down the parapet, he was hit a second time in his right hand, which knocked his sword out of his grasp. He saved his scabbard and body belt. He was carried to the rear by Private Andrew H. Grogan of Company I and was brought to our medical tent.

He inquired if the colors were safe, and, being informed that all that was left of this tattered flag was brought off the field, he emotionally stated, "Thank God for that; I am so glad that they are safe; keep them as long as there is a thread left." He was sent home on a steamer but the journey was exhausting and possibly hastened his death, which came at his home in Oxford. The memory of this noble leader will always remain in the thoughts and prayers of our Sixth Connecticut Volunteers.

After the battle, I was not only busy with our own casualties, but equally with some Confederate prisoners. Happily a rebel captain was able to make some arrangements with our General Vogdes for exchange of prisoners. This was to be done at sea. I, with my stewards, loaded the Confederate wounded onto the decks of the *Cosmopolitan*. This was on July 24, just six days after our "grand assault" on Fort Wagner. A large steamer (probably a blockade runner) came alongside one of our monitors. The sea was calm and the lines were tossed and secured to their ship. The transfer went well, with many hands assisting, and we received 225 of our own wounded back. Despite their extensive wounds, tears of joy were in their eyes and many inquiries were made by all as to the outcome of their battlefield friends. A report was received stating that 25 amputations were done on our prisoner troops and 50 percent of our troops died in their hands. Our concerns over the welfare of our black comrades of the Fifty-fourth were only partially answered. The report of the disgraceful treatment of Colonel Shaw's body was also confirmed.

## Ellington Boarding School.

Rev. F. W. CHAPMAN, A. M., Principal.

*Ellington Preparatory School (as depicted on an envelope)*

*Robinson Homestead, Colchester, CT*

*Cartoon (General Gilmore Firing Cannon at President Davis)*

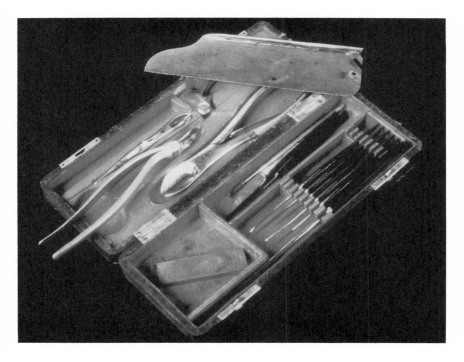

*Surgical Instruments of Dr. Robinson*

Ft. McHenry—Baltimore
Courtesy of National Park Service

*Civil War Memorabillia*

*G.A.R. Medals*

## CHARLESTON HARBOR DEFENSES

*Map of Morris Island and Charleston Defenses*

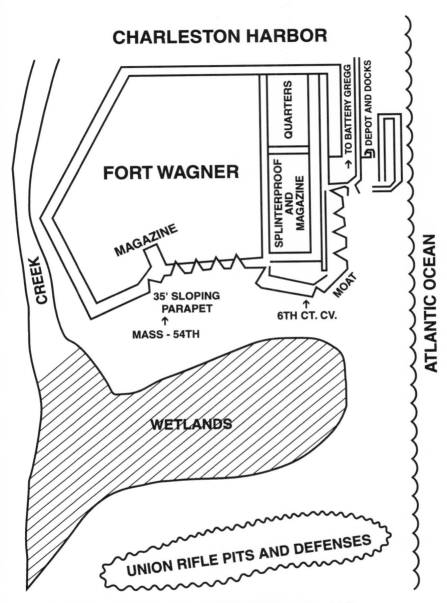

*Depiction of Fort Wagner, SC*

*Dr. Myron Robinson*

*Dr. Robinson's Medication Kit*

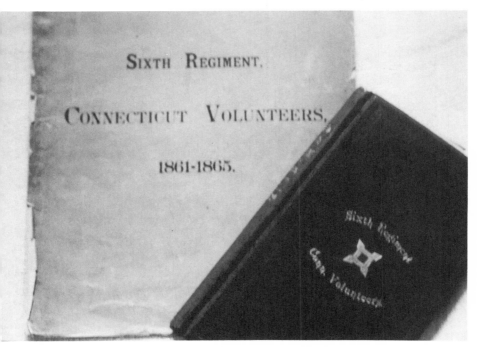

*Depiction of Book Sources of the 6th Connecticut Regiment Activities*

*Dr. Robinson in his "Horse and Buggy"*

*Fitch Home for Soldiers, Noroton CT*

*Dr. Robinson and Two Members of this Staff at the
Fitch Home for Soldiers*

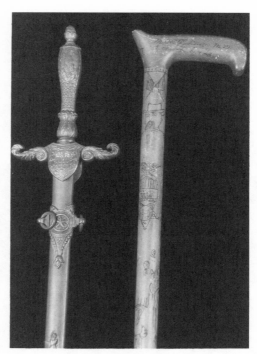

*Carved Wooden Cane and Dress Sword*

*Robinson Gravestone, Colchester, CT*

# CHAPTER SEVENTEEN:

# Battle Account of Lieutenant Kost

A little-known history of that never to be forgotten battle was reported by Lieutenant Rudolph Kost in a Bridgeport, Connecticut newspaper on March 27, 1905.

The following story of personal experience could not be given out at the time for the reason that the writer was captured and remained prisoner until the close of the war.

This is a story of the siege by Lieutenant Rudolph Kost. It would thrill every veteran of the Civil War. Memories of that awful black night of death can never be faced by the survivors. Failure to send reinforcements lost the fort.

This paper which we have been allowed to publish was read at the last reunion of the 6th Connecticut Volunteers for the first time, and as so many of our Bridgeport boys took a prominent part in that fearful charge, our people will doubtless be very much interested.

The late Lieutenant Rudolph Kost, the author of this paper, was widely known in this city, where he lived with his family for many years prior to his death. This record of what actually occurred during the memorable struggle should be preserved to the credit of the writer and his brave comrades.

During the many years that have elapsed, the writer has never seen a fair official account on our side of that unwritten history inside Fort Wagner from the time the charge was made until one o'clock the next morning, and the doings of that little band of soldiers which held a part of that fort which was taken at the point of the bayonet, until the hour of one o'clock in the morning as was previously stated. It might be of some interest to some of those who took part in it (if any are living) and it is also the object of the writer to convince the Reverend Mr. Palmer, formerly of the 48th New York YV which regiment also took an active part in the charge, that the part of this regimental history referring to Fort Wagner contains many errors.

Paul H. Hayne, a southern writer, upon the siege of Fort Wagner in the 1886 March number of the "Southern Bivouac" says, "then a grand deed, what the old north men would have called a deed of derring do, was performed by men of the ever dominant Caucasian race. The thought of which as I write a quarter of a century after its occurrence here in the tranquil Indian summer makes my heart beat and pulse throb simultaneously. Across the fatal and narrow stretch before the fort every inch of which was swept by a hurricane of fire, a besom of destruction, the 6th Connecticut Volunteers Colonel John L. Chatfield charged, with such undaunted resolution upon the southeast salient, that they succeeded in the very face of hell, one may say, in capturing it. What though their victory was a barren achievement when for hours they were penned in, 'no support daring to follow them.' Friend and foe alike now and then must honor them as the bravest of the brave."

"The history of the war rife with desperate conflicts can show no more terrific strife than this. It was in more than one particular a battle of giants."

Considerable could be added to Mr. Hayne's account but, considering that it was written by the enemy's side, credit is given with an impartiality to whom it belongs. The writer will simply state now what he saw and did himself that fatal night, as near as his memory will serve him and he would be greatly pleased if he could be favored with the names and the addresses of the survivors who were with him that night and especially with some of those who were captured with him, and such names as the writer remembers he will mention, as they might be able to corroborate this statement.

As the formation of the attacking troops took place just before dark, and after taking positions in the proper place in line with the regiment, it would have been impossible for the writer to say much about the formation of other troops that took part in it. All he could see was in front of them the object of attack. Our regiment, the Connecticut 6th Volunteers' Colonel Chatfield had to lead on the right on the waterfront or the sand beach; the 54th Massachusetts (colored) Colonel Shaw had the lead of the center, and the 3rd New Hampshire, if not mistaken Colonel Jackson and Lt. Colonel Bedell were leading the left column and the whole under the command of General Strong, all formed in close columns by company.

During the formation every available gun by land and water that could bear on Fort Wagner kept up a tremendous fire over our heads; it was so hot that the rebels as told by them while in prison were not able to venture out of their bombproofs and load their guns to respond to our fire. At a given signal all the guns stopped firing in the wink of an eye and silence reigned for a moment. Oh what an awful silence that was! The words "forward march" were given and were promptly obeyed. During this silence in our march, the rebels rushed out and manned their guns again, ready with doubled-shotted cannons and bristling bayonets to receive us, and when within about twenty-five or thirty rods of the fort, there was seen a sheet of fire the whole length of the fort, belching forth their destructive iron hail from every gun they had, large and small, into our advancing columns, intensified by the screeching and bursting shells over our heads from Forts Sumter, Moultrie, Gregg and others. It must have been a grand site for our friends in the rear of us in the army and navy and no doubt many sympathizing hearts among them beat faster at the moment that terrible iron hail was poured forth into our ranks. But in spite of this terrible destruction, our regiment rushed up to the fort in and through the ditch or moat which was half full of water and swept by sally port guns up the slope and over the parapet and drove the rebels out and from their guns at the point of the bayonet. The rebels may well call it a "daring deed." Here let the reader pause a moment and let his mind run over the space of ground in one half hour's time and let him imagine the change during that short space of time. Can the reader imagine the horrors of war? The excitement was intense. The dead and wounded (about 1500) lying in heaps inside and outside of the fort and in the ditch, the moaning of the dying and wounded, the continued firing on both sides, the thunder and lightning above and everything shrouded in darkness made weak men tremble and strong men clench their teeth. The writer doubts that there were many such scenes enacted during the war.

Several of the color bearers of our regiment were swept out of existence right in front of the writer and inside of the fort, as quick as one went down, another was ready to grasp that flag, only to follow his comrades gone before him. Colonel John L. Chatfield, while standing in the rear of the writer, and recognizing each other by our voices making a few complimentary remarks as to the splendid behavior of the boys and the success of gaining such a strong foothold inside the fort, and before the writer had time to answer the Colonel they mortally wounded by my side. The Colonel gone with a simultaneous report of the death of General Strong and a number of others; measuring the situation, jumping on the platform of a gun about the center of the salient and calling for the officers and men of the 6th Connecticut to rally was the work of an instant. General Kline, Lt. West, George Lewis, acting Lt. King and several non-commissioned officers and we responded, stating to them in a few words the condition of affairs as they appeared on the spot, requesting Captain Kline as superior in rank to take charge of the boys and hold the position by all means, and at the same time the writer offered his services to go for reinforcements. At this moment Major Fillar of the 55th Pennsylvania Volunteers and a volunteer aide on General Strong's staff requested the writer to stay. Captain Kline was urged to go at once for reinforcements and return with them without fail as soon as possible and we would hold the position if it could be done. He started and so did others without our knowledge but whose absence was learned soon after by our diminished numbers. That was the last seen of Captain Kline that night. The writer rallied the boys of his regiment, but a number of other regiments joined in with us; explaining the situation and expected reinforcements and the intention of holding our position to reinforce, calling on non-commissioned officers, remembering three that answered, one was Sgt. Andrew Wunuck, Company H, 6th Regiment, Connecticut Volunteers, Cpl. Jacob Schwoff, same company and regiment and a tall sergeant writer doesn't remember but no three braver men entered the fort that night and the names and addresses of the last two would be gladly hailed by the writer as they might be able to corroborate these statements. Sgt. Wunuck is dead; he died a miserable death being starved on Bell Island by the Rebels. This Sgt. Wunuck was an old Prussian artillery soldier and ordering him at once to swing that big gun in the salient to the rebel right, which they kept up a lively fire on our position, and give them some of their own shot and shell, if he could find any; the gun was in position in an instant, but the sergeant soon reported that no ammunition could be found. One sallyport gun of the rebels kept still sweeping their ditch from the right of our salient. Sgt. Wunuck and the New York sergeant with a dozen men (more or less) ordered in the embrasure of the big gun with instructions to silence that sallyport gun and keep the ditch clear for the expected reinforcements to enter the fort, but as it was dark and the gun could only be located by the flash of their fire, half of the men were posted behind the parapet to load the rifles and the other half in the embrasure to do the firing simultaneously to the spot, at the flash of the rebel gun.

At the same time two other parties were posted, one behind the division wall dividing the salient from another part of the fort and in the corner where this wall meets the parapet; the other party was also posted behind this division wall and in the corner where the wall strikes or connects with the magazine, and some distance from the last mentioned party and between the two and nearest the magazine was an opening some four to five feet wide, leading to another section of the fort and no doubt to the entrance to the magazine.

Through this opening and over the walls the rebels kept up a lively fire from some light field pieces brought into position from the rebel right, sweeping our position and doing considerable damage. Thus fairly well protected, the writer directed the first two parties to keep up the rapid fire in the direction of the flashes of their guns, to make it appear as if we were a larger force than we actually were. The writer posted himself within hearing distance of the three parties and gave his directions and everything worked well. At the same time, while these operations were being carried out, under the instructions and directions of the writer, Major Filler, Lts.West, King and others with the rest of their able bodied men, and divided from us by a sweeping fire of the rebels through the center of our position, kept up a rapid fire from the top of the magazine and bomb-proof, which must have been some ten or fifteen feet higher than our position in the front or parapet part of the salient; thus separated by the rebel fire but in the same part of the fort and, as if by agreement, both parties kept up a lively fire in the same direction as the flashes of the rebel guns, and which must have been very effective and annoying to the enemy, as the party in the embrasure silenced the sallyport gun, and as Lt. Col. Bedell of the 3rd New York Volunteers, who in the early part of the attack, while leading his regiment, was captured and taken into the bomb-proof, told us that the soldiers in charge of the guns refused to come out anymore and work the gun any longer on account of our fire; it was a North Carolina Regiment.

Disgusted, but bound to dislodge this little band of "Yankee Devils" from their position, the strongest in the fort, they changed their tactics. We were first the attacking party but now they concluded to attack us and called for volunteers and under the leadership of Capt. Ryan of Charleston, with about seventy-five men, more or less, they made a furious attack on us but were handsomely repulsed, with Captain Ryan, their leader, and a number of others killed or wounded, according to their statement in the papers the next day. We, of course, could not tell in the dark how many we lost in the scrimmage.

Disappointed and maddened by this defeat, a second assault was made under the leadership of Lt. Col. Simkins and Major Ramsey. Bound to dislodge us, they made another furious onslaught with still a more disastrous result to them than the first assault. Lt. Col. Simkins was mortally wounded and Major Ramsey seriously wounded, besides other casualties, and the capture of Captain McDonald. This was the only prisoner captured that night and under the most peculiar circumstances, but the writer has never seen any account of it nor credit given to the boys that accomplished it under such difficulties.

When "Mac," the plucky little Irishman of Co. G, 6 Conn. Vols. of New Britain, Conn. reported the capture of this prisoner to the writer, he said "Lieut. what shall we do with rebel!" Taking the prisoner in hand he was found mute on every question he was asked except that his name was McDonald, and his rank a Captain. Turning to the soldier and facing the prisoner at the same time, the writer turned the prisoner over again to this brave soldier with the following words in a clear commanding voice. It was intended for the prisoner as well as the soldier, "Mac. You bring this officer safely into our lines; shoot him if he tries to escape, otherwise you will see that he is unharmed. Report and deliver him to headquarters and tell the General to send reinforcements at once." The soldier saluted his officer and started proudly with his prisoner for our lines, and the writer more hopeful of a final success, turned his attention again to other important duties on hand, hurriedly telling the boys of the capture of an officer and the dispatching of the prisoner into our lines and the instructions to hurry reinforcements, and that the sending of a prisoner into our lines, taken from the enemy at about eleven o'clock at night, must convince them that we were not all dead yet and that the General would surely send reinforcements. All this had a magical effect on the boys and gave them new vigor in life.

As already stated, it must have been about eleven o'clock and time enough to come into the Fort in front of our salient, as everything was kept clear in front of us; the guns that swept the ditch [were] silent. Five hundred fresh men entering and firing along the slope, drop a man every three to five paces, lay quietly on the slope and have them rest their guns on the parapet with eyes open, reinforce the men in the salient and supply the old ones with ammunition and have them keep up such a fire as circumstances might require.

Our rear of the salient being well protected by the waterfront of the Fort there was no danger for us from that part, the rear of the fort would have been our right in the fort and the rebel right of the fort our front from which point the rebels fired. These two sides could be easily swept by our fire and could be taken care of by the men in the salient assisted by the men resting their guns on the parapet in case of another attack being made upon us. Thus posted, any soldier can easily see that with five hundred men the fort could be held until daylight without the loss of a man. The movement was simple and would not have required any military skill, only pluck and a cool head, and at the same time as a matter of protection and to keep open our communication, the available troops on the island could be pushed up under the guns of the fort with the flank near the swamp well protected to prevent the enemy from coming around to the front of the fort, the only place from which they could come and did come, when they captured us inside the fort. By this simple movement and so few fresh men, the rebels would have never mounted, manned or fired another gun.

The prisoner sent out by the writer about eleven o'clock was safely delivered, which was proof that communication was open between us and our forces on the island, but the reinforcements did not come, and if the soldier that delivered that prisoner should still be living in his former home, New Britain, Connecticut, or anywhere else he would confer a favor by sending his full name and address to the writer. He can no doubt give more light as to the delivery of the prisoner and how the instructions given him that night by the writer were received.

Expecting reinforcements every moment, the boys were full of hopes and everything worked out satisfactorily until the non-commissioned officers reported ammunition was giving out. To supply this deficiency the writer crawled about the fort on hands and knees and emptied the cartridge boxes of the dead and requested the wounded that were able to do so, to empty their boxes and place the contents in easy reach of the writer for him to distribute them to the men. During these operations, the writer came upon Capt. Hurst of the 48th New York, a personal friend, who was mortally wounded, and First Sgt. Charles Grogan of Co. J 6th Conn. Vols., also mortally wounded; shook hands with both of them and exchanged a few encouraging words; they both in their feeble condition (both died shortly afterwards) urged the boys to hold on to our position till reinforcements would come, which we surely expected.

As ammunition was getting scarce and firing slacked off on both sides, the writer undertook a kind of reconnoiter on his own hook in the other part of the fort, looking for the magazine which was built of sandbags, and part in the salient and part in the other section of the fort, and, judging from the position of the fort and magazine, the door must have been in the other section of the fort next to the salient. Crawling out through the opening in the wall and along the wall of sandbags, being dark, and as an infantry soldier, not being well posted as to the construction of a magazine, it was a risky undertaking, but finally came to a spot supposed to be the entrance to the magazine, and the reckless idea struck the writer what a crash it would make to light some paper in the haversack and throw it into the magazine, but there were about 1500 dead and wounded; they would all be buried by the upheaval, the writer included.

A cold shudder ran through the bones of the writer and he returned the same way he came, but on trying to get through the opening again a wide-awake soldier of the 62d Ohio Regiment, came near running his bayonet through the heart of the intruder. Taking the writer for a rebel he demanded an immediate surrender but the countersign settled the mistake at once. This must have been near midnight but the boys were holding out and defending their position. The writer would like to know the name and address of the Ohio soldier, if living. He perhaps remembers the circumstance.

Firing was kept up until all the ammunition gave out, and, as no reinforcements came, the boys felt disappointed and discouraged and even at that hour of midnight it would have been time, and without any danger in entering the fort in front of our position, and we might all have got out about that time had the order been given, but when victory is in the grasp of your hands, gained at such terrible sacrifice, it would be cowardice to desert it as long as there was a ray of hope to keep it in your grasp. We were undecided whether to remain or to run the risk through another fire. All was silent and dark, only the moaning of the wounded and dying could be heard; not a shot was fired on either side. This silence was a foreboding of good or evil for us; we had not long to wait. While whispering over the situation with that true hearted soldier, Sgt. Wunuck, men came rushing up the slope and over the parapet and our first thought was that some of our men were coming, but when we heard the word "Surrender" we knew at once with whom we had to deal.

The writer and the sergeant made a dash for the parapet; we separated at once. The writer ran against a rebel sergeant who, at the point of the bayonet, demanded a surrender, seeing a pistol in one hand, a sword in the other, he demanded both, but was informed that these articles would only be surrendered to an officer, and that fellow, no doubt, was under the impression that he had captured a Yankee officer of note. Had General Gilmore done his duty as well as those men in the fort, the surrender would have been on the other side.

Brought before Col. Graham of South Carolina, who asked very politely what rank and demanded sword and revolver (both were presents from friends at home) the parting was done with a feeling which cannot be well described by the owner of the articles and writer of these lines; he felt as if he wanted to sink into the ground under his feet.

After getting all those able to walk into line we were marched single file to the top of the bomb-proof, the highest in the salient, and the highest in the fort, and from which the flag of the 6th Conn. proudly waved, and more than one of its bearers was struck down and met death in its defense.

# CHAPTER EIGHTEEN:

# Battlefield Medical Matters

Even though six weeks had gone by since the Fort Wagner assault, I would often wake up at night in a cold sweat. This was apparently related to bad dreams associated with that grisly night. I well remember that I thought the earlier attacks by small boats on the inland side of Morris Island were frightful, not knowing what was to come shortly.

Through no fault of our own, the ultimate victory at Fort Wagner and Charleston was denied us. It was common gossip that the assistant secretary of the navy, Gustavus Fox, wanted Charleston destroyed, not only because of its value as a seaport supplying major needs of the Confederacy, but also because the firing on Fort Sumter by the rebels was a symbol of defiance. Furthermore, Secretary of the Navy Welles needed justification for his outlay of funds for an ironclad fleet.

Our new Colonel Duryee was less popular because he insisted on rigid training and drilling of the troops, even during this period of convalescence. This might have been justified for some newer members of the Sixth, as they were conscripted and not volunteers. The morale amongst the veteran troops was quite low for all the reasons mentioned before, but also because of concern as to how well the draftees would fight. A higher rate of desertion and dereliction of duty was commonplace. My job was made infinitely greater since many claimed sickness to get excused from duty. This lengthened my already long hours and kept me from attending the truly sick and recuperating troops. Some of our new recruits left much to be desired as far as their readiness for combat was concerned. To gain credit for high enlistment rates, recruiting personnel would indeed pass unqualified persons—especially those with preexisting conditions such as hernias, convulsive disorders, lameness, syphilis, and advanced age.

Because of conscription and paying bounties to substitutes, persons accepting such "bribes" would hide disabilities from the examiner. I was made aware of General Order 51 of December, 1861, which called attention to the alarming "losses" due to disability. Medical Director Tripler was concerned that the army was "becoming a wastebasket for castoffs of society." I knew of him because of his improvement in getting casualties off the field after battles and because he more recently became surgeon general of the Army of the Potomac.

In discussing fitness of our troops with other medical personnel, I came to agree that the so-called "children's diseases" wreaked havoc with our military, especially when living in close quarters. Measles, mumps, scarlet fever, etc. struck down country boys because they never traveled far from home and therefore had not developed immunity, I suppose. Add to these travails the factors of poor diet, exposure, insufficient training, and fatigue and it became easier for me to understand how time-consuming sick call was becoming.

Since whiskey was in the regular line of dispensing to our troops, it was easily available also to the doctors. I could see that drinking was thus a problem at all levels (our medical shelves were always well stocked with spiritus frumenti).

Hospital stewards were most helpful to all of us. Most had a background knowledge and training in pharmacy, minor surgery, dressing bandages, and dental extraction. Therefore such stewards included druggists, medical and pre-medical students in many cases.

In the heat of battle and with so much to do and so much confusion, the help of the hospital stewards and the nurses was of inestimable value. Although at times Clara Barton seemed to be somewhat of a social butterfly, her greatest value was in bringing national attention to both the need for more nurses and to the great value of bedside care.

### *Historical Note*

Hospital Staff: hospital stewards were Charles Dorman of New Haven, Joseph Colton, Almon D. Powers. Assistant surgeons were Edward Bulkly and Henry Hoyt. Surgeons were Myron W. Robinson and Frederick Dibble (the latter relinquished the title to Dr. Robinson in 1863).

* * *

### *Historical Note from the Diary and Letters of Hannah Ropes*

There was no formal nurse training in the United States until the mid nineteenth century. Some religious organizations stressed it however as an avocation.

Because of concerns over women in crowded conditions with "strange male patients," a suggestion made by Dorothea Dix was approved by the War Department to have general supervision for women nurses. Dorothea Dix said that for a nurse to be considered for duty in Army hospitals she must have certificates from two doctors and two clergymen of standing; be over thirty years of age; have good moral character; be modest in dress; be unattractive; and be able to cook, read, and write, thus to help with the pharmacy and orders as well as to help the soldiers with letters.

Hospital surgeons had the right to summarily discharge any nurse they considered incompetent or insubordinate. Some conflicts grew when the nurses felt that the doctors were too lacking in compassion with their military "no nonsense" approach toward medical care, recovery, and concern over malingering.

Before 1861, there were no general army hospitals, only post hospitals, which were usually small. After the first battle of Bull Run, July 21, 1861, there were about six hospitals in the Washington area, and they were grossly inadequate. Ventilation and food preparation were bad, and there was no morgue. There were decaying walls due to poor construction and lighting. The senior surgeon was the boss and the assistant surgeons and ward physicians had many other chief responsibilities. Chaplains were also on staff, one for each permanent hospital. Duties ranged from religious services to keeping death and burial accounts.

Also present were contract surgeons (civilians), of whom fifty-five hundred served during the war. Medical students dressed wounds and did general secondary medical duties around the hospital while the stewards (enlisted personnel) were responsible for the patients' clothing, ward hygiene, food, and the pharmacy. Ward masters (usually convalescent soldiers) assisted in patient care and cleaning.

Contract nurses, usually male, attended the sick also. The head surgeon was hampered in his medical duties because of his administrative duties, and because of the need to make his funds go as far as they could toward supplies and food. (Some misuse of funds was identified.) Any extra money was often used to buy extra food and newspapers; even waterbeds are mentioned in the articles. A ration of eight cents per day for food by the stewards was noted. More aggressive treatment of the wounded was requested but often did not happen.

* Hannah Ropes was a Civil War nurse who popularized the idea of compassionate care for the wounded. The doctors channeled their efforts into strictly medical/surgical care and often felt that such "T.L.C." was superfluous. Hannah Ropes was the matron of the Union Hotel Hospital in Georgetown D.C. from July 1862 to January 1863—when she died of tuberculous pneumonia.

* * *

Our new medical helpers from the north were quite amazed at how difficult it was to both live and care for serious wounds under such primitive conditions. The Sixth probably received the deadliest fire of all at Fort Wagner, and had one hundred and forty-one killed and many others missing in action. Despite all efforts, many wounded died the next day.

I learned that despite our failure at Fort Wagner, continued harassment of the Charlestonians persisted. A large Parrott gun (16,700 pounds) was brought into James Island and added to the battery there. The battery, minus the Parrott gun, continued to serve its purpose in the fall of 1863 and early 1864. The parapet alone weighed eight hundred tons. This eight-inch gun was called the Swamp

Angel. It fired at regular intervals on the town of Charleston. The people of Charleston could not understand that civilians would come under fire in this way, but it served as somewhat of a reminder of the presence of the Union forces within cannon distance of their city. It was hoped that it would force the city to surrender, because it could fire a two-hundred-pound projectile over four miles into the center of Charleston. Admittedly, Charleston was never taken by force by the Union, but only by the withdrawal of the Confederate troops to avoid capture by General Sherman. The shelling ceased when the Parrott gun blew up and destroyed itself on August 23, 1863. This gun was bought by Trenton, N.J. after the war for scrap iron purposes, but it was later displayed there in a city park.

The weeks following the final assault on July 18 found me busy in every way possible. A general glum feeling pervaded all of us. This was not only because of last minute failure of all of our plans with ultimate defeat, but because of constant insect and heat problems along with sicknesses of all kinds. I didn't feel too well myself, with some shaking fevers and bony aches and pains, but there was no time to give in to this. Postoperative care in the fly-filled tents was most difficult. Wounds required further suturing and dressing and even some amputations needed revising. Fortunately some of the more seriously wounded were taken back to Hilton Head (and I learned that from there some even got to go back north). Sickness problems again far outnumbered the battle injuries. My daily sickness reports took more time to make out than I really had.

Fresh water was ever a problem, there being no springs or streams on Folly Island. Even digging deep holes did not remove some of the brackish element in the water. Soldiers improvised two methods that were of great help in procuring water. They used their rubber ponchos to catch and divert the rain from the frequent thunder storms. This was contained in buckets and barrels, where it didn't last long. Another method was to place a barrel with no ends deep in a hole in the ground. Water filtered into it which made it somewhat more drinkable. Fluid loss from sweating and hard work in this climate led to great thirst problems. I repeatedly warned the troops that whiskey, which with quinine was used as prophylaxis, should not be used to quench their ever-present thirst.

We medical officers received a bulletin from the Department of the South, outlining regulations that could minimize sicknesses. It emphasized finding tent sites on higher ground and away from the swampy areas and latrine areas. A detail of soldiers was organized on a daily basis; they walked along the edge of the campsite picking up debris on the way toward the opposite side of the camp. Garbage and kitchen waste was to be buried in pits and covered over each day. Latrines were kept far away from the camp and water sites. My job included inspecting and enforcing this, as well as the regular airing out of tents. The details of proper housing and tent construction were also included in this directive. Attention to proper diet was finally being given emphasis, with the supervision of the types of foods and their preparation. Bathing, proper protection from the sun, and laundry changes were matters that I strongly supported and had always emphasized to the troops. Rat control was a necessity, and it offered some diversion to the troops as a chance to show off their sharpshooting abilities.

All of these important programs helped the soldiers maintain their health, but still did not seem to finish the lengthy sick calls. Many of these sick calls were annoying but trivial problems such as heat rash, fleas, and mosquito bites.

A few casualties still trickled in from Morris Island. Our soldiers had dug "zig-zags" to inch their way closer to Fort Wagner. None of us knew whether this was to maintain a strong holding action on the well-entrenched rebels, or to create a springboard for a future assault. In any case, rebel sharpshooters took occasional shots at our soldiers as they advanced. One discovery, both pitiful and disgusting, was of a multitude of our dead comrades' decomposing bodies when their shallow graves were intercepted by this digging.

I encouraged the men to swim in the nearby ocean, as I had done near Savannah some time ago. Fresh water for bathing would be a great luxury, but this worked out well; the Connecticut boys made good use of their past knowledge of fishing and clamming. A few sharks appeared off Stono Inlet but only one shark injury occurred.

Some depression and general languor became commonplace among the troops. To help avoid the boredom of this camp life, several diversions were planned by myself with the help of my staff. Some of our more learned soldiers shared a limited supply of books with one another. Even a debating society attracted many members. Construction of many elaborate churches was carried out (surprisingly good, given the paucity of building materials). Worship services and bible classes were held at regular intervals. I myself found card playing to be a diversion and noted that this interest spread rapidly amongst the enlisted men. Some collected unusual shells and sent them to their homes. Others sent home for fishing tackle items, which were forwarded to them (a soldier from the Norwich area who did well in this regard). Occasionally we arranged a picnic-type banquet, which featured some primitive orchestral attempts. We played games, including sack races, three-legged races, and wheelbarrow races. Heat prevented any such games from lasting long. Different platoons tried to "show their stuff" by means of fancy close order drill. Again, the heated evenings limited such showmanship, but at least the morale was greatly improved.

Since many of my men from the Sixth were back at Hilton Head (several because of injuries and illness), the time came for me to rejoin them. I could attend them better and in fact the large amount of paperwork for the sick calls on Folly Island was beginning to overwhelm me.

With the sun behind me, I could sit in the shade of my tent, light my pipe to help keep the mosquitoes away, and look out at the ever-changing yet monotonous moaning and crashing of the beautiful sea. This was the only calm part of my day. I longed for and prayed each night that some conclusion could be made to the war.

# CHAPTER NINETEEN:

# *Licking Our Wounds*

As I stood on the deck of the *Cosmopolitan*, I was happy she had been fitted out as a hospital ship. As the hot afternoon sun set over the offshore islands, on which so much blood had been spilled, I became sadly aware of the need for our troops to stand down. As the bard once said, "To lie awhile and bleed awhile, to rise and fight again."

The steamer trip back to Hilton Head was a sad time as we headed south along the wetlands, swamps, and islands. A melancholy seemed to settle over all. There was little in the way of talking or singing or joking among the war-weary troops. Despite hearing of major victories at Vicksburg and Gettysburg, I wondered when the war would ever end. The Vicksburg "victory" was not one of overwhelming assault; an assault did not give victory, but rather a prolonged siege and starvation of the inhabitants. While I felt that eventually we would take Charleston, perhaps our efforts at Fort Wagner could at least be considered a Pyrrhic victory that denied Charleston as an important base for Confederate supply.

The Gettysburg battle was considered a victory but many field officers and even newspapers commented on two aspects of the victory: the great loss of life (on both sides), and the failure of General Meade to pursue the retreating Confederate army's long baggage train. President Lincoln was said to be perturbed by this failure to convert a major victory into a rout that might have ended the war. Despite our greatly reduced fighting potential, our presence back at Hilton Head could prove a discouragement to the rebels to consider a counterattack against what had become a central base for our campaign.

[Letter from Hilton Head, S.C. dated September 1, 1863, and mailed from Port Royal, S.C. It is mailed to Miss Julia Abell, Colchester, CT, care of S. P. Abell, Esq.]

*Dear Niece:*

*I have been hunting through your letter this afternoon in order that I might answer it promptly. Why, how the time has passed it don't seem so long. It is dated June 18th—you said in it you was going "to write me a few words and then wait patiently to see if it affected me as it did everyone else."*

*I do not believe it does— Does it? Well Julia, I ought to have written before but I have not written hardly anyone for the last two months and have not felt as though I could write. Since your letter "Life has passed with me but roughly." Hard working, hard marching—for so short a march—sleeping out of doors in the sand, bothered worse by mosquitoes than on "Folly's Island" and what is worse, someone shooting at me day and night for three weeks every single day and sometimes they fired pretty near to me especially the first day.*

*I did not think they were very good marksmen so I let them blaze away. I never fired at them once because I used different weapons from what they did and could not get near enough. If I had, I think my weapons would have been quite as effective as theirs—Don't you?*

*But now I am far away from all these frightful horrid sights and only hear now and then the long deep roar of the artillery.*

*I have now a nice house to live in, it is a cloth house though. I have two large "Mole Tents" and a "Fly" between under which I can sit and look out upon and enjoy the breezes from old "Neptune." One tent I use for a bedroom and parlour, the other for a sitting room. It is real comfortable but I want to get back to Morris Island once more. The flowers you sent me I have saved just as you sent them. I am going to send you a "cotton blossom" and a leaf from a "magnolia flower." They are white on the trees and look splendidly when in full bloom. I wish you could be here and see the wild flowers and see the orange groves. They are perfectly splendid now and nearly ripe. I have had several. I ride out everyday to a plantation to see a little sick girl (white girl) where there are several trees. Julia, I want you to take good care of the "Little Corporal" and make him grow fast and learn how to drill as I want him promoted before long to be Colonel. I am afraid he will be old enough to be Maj. General before the war ends by the appearance of things now.*

*Now Julia write me soon and I will be more punctual in the future. Give my love to all and kiss baby for me.*

*Your Aff. Uncle*

*Myron*

Our orders directed five companies of the Sixth to provost guard duty— relieving the Eighth of Maine. Guard duty kept the Sixth occupied to a good degree (guarding not only rebel prisoners, but also malefactors of our own troops). I was ordered to witness the execution of a few of our own soldiers who were court-martialed and convicted of desertion in the face of the enemy. The horrors of this war were to multiply as years went by.

Hilton Head, S.C.
Sept. 4th, 1863

Dear Frona:

Your letter was received a long time ago and I suppose an answer at this late date will be better than none at all. I am now enjoying comfortable health, better than a few weeks ago. I was sick for some time so I did not sit up long enough to do what work I was compelled to do. I was alone with the Reg't all the time it was on Morris Island and sometime before and since that and I got perfectly tired out when we first started for Morris Island July 8th, to make a night attack. We started in row boats and after being out all night in the water we returned and arrived wet, weary and hungry about daylight. The next night we started again the same way and after rowing all night we arrived in sight of the rebel batteries. The bombardment commenced about sunrise and for a while it was terrific and to the eye of a soldier, splendid. The rebel fire was directed entirely at us in the little boats and fortunately only one boat of the whole was struck wounding one so that he died and injured two others. I landed with the wounded and after caring for them as well as circumstances would permit I put them in the boat and directed my men to take them across the river as soon as the firing ceased. I then started on the beach for where the Reg't was about to land and soon came whistling by my ears, balls from the sharpshooters and rifle regiments. But they were so soon drove from there where I found quite a number of wounded. After caring for our wounded I went to picking up the Sickest. It was a very hot day, I fell once from the heat and do not think I have been well since that time. I was sick the rest of our stay on the island but had just as much to do as if I had been well. The night of the attack on Wagner I had lain in bed all day and eaten hardly anything and when the Col. told me what was going to be done I got up and went without any supper and worked until daylight. Next day when I got back to camp, I could hardly stand. That night before the charge the bombardment was the most beautiful sight I ever beheld and after the fight the most terrible and heart rending I ever saw or imagined and I never wish to see another such a sight of human beings mangled some screaming, others moaning and groaning and dying and struggling, it was dreadful. I had to keep my lantern shaded for as soon as they saw it they would fire at me. I worked on the field till all were carried off. I sat down on the stretcher after we got them all away. The light was just breaking in the east (Sunday morning) and as I thought of the scenes of the past night, I was perfectly overcome. I could not help it but now I am rested, I wish again I was on the island it is so lonely here and dull. We are going to have Charleston pretty soon but have not got it yet. We are within 18 yards of Fort Wagner at last accounts. Write soon. Love to all

Your Brother

Myron

I hear we are again under marching orders or are about to be.

Please write how Father and Mother are. Father does not write me anymore. Weather today is comfortable for this climate. Thermometer has been at 113 degrees in the shade one day and a good many over one hundred.

In Haste—Myron

As the fall season wore on, I gave up some of my longer watches on the beach and even the occasional try at fishing. (I did put some of our small boats to use with two soldiers, with moderate success on these few occasions.)

One day became pretty much like another but I remember a particular day in which I took care of a most cantankerous prisoner (only a minor illness, fortunately). He was the son of the mayor of Charleston. This Captain Monroe and myself had interesting conversations in which he voiced total rejection of any aims of the Federal government. He completely rejected shaking hands over this "bloody chasm." He was especially embarrassed to be a captive from the Charleston area because of the symbolic position of Charleston as a mainstay of the Confederacy.

We all had mixed feelings upon returning again to Hilton Head. It was the second time we had to return under conditions of exhaustion, painful wounds, and low morale. The war had been under way for more than two years, and we seemed to keep finding new ways to "snatch defeat from the jaws of victory." This pervading despair was worsened by the appointment of the not-too-popular Colonel Duryee. All of these matters led to a low re-enlistment rate once ashore. Many expressed to me the feeling that had Colonel Chatfield survived, this would not have been the case.

Now, three months after our bloody, horrible night at Fort Wagner, I said good-bye to many of the fine soldiers as they completed their three-year tour of duty and headed back home. I envied them and wished each one success. I gave instructions to some as to wound care and dressing changes. Some would require artificial limb fitting in the future; canes and crutches were the plan for the near future.

I myself longed to see the fields of Hebron ready for harvest in the fall of 1863. Seeing the glorious fall foliage change to yellow, red, and gold over the mountain sides in Connecticut would have been wonderful. To sleep in a comfortable bed with good home cooking seemed to be asking for a bit of heaven. Living in the field and the rigors of warfare were starting to tell on me. Frequent coughs and weakness seemed to be bothering me more and more.

Fortunately, my health eventually improved to a degree. The episodes of severe coughing, shaking chills, and general malaise lessened week by week during garrison duty at Hilton Head. To further improve our care of battle casualties, and to train some of my new men, we spent time reviewing and practicing these methods of care. In other battles elsewhere, houses, churches, cow barns, and any similar structures were used for care of the wounded after major battles. These were less available to us in the mostly deserted islands that were the scene of our recent attacks.

As mentioned before, the hospital tent was a white-walled tent, fifteen by fourteen feet, the side walls being four and one-half feet high. Each regiment had three tents, but these did not often lend themselves to our terrain. The "Sibley tent" was a large conical tent, and smaller ones of inverted "V" of canvas were very practical. We discussed among our medical group the factors leading to the placement of a depot or a field hospital beyond the range of enemy artillery (one to one and one-half miles we often considered a reasonable distance). We no longer had band members or stretcher bearers for ambulance use, so we divided our own medical section into two groups. One group would stay and prepare the hospital and casualty treatment area, the other accompanied the troops as stretcher men and to give first aid.

The climate was cool and I welcomed it after the sweltering heat of our summer campaign. Besides reading, my other main relaxation was riding my horse along great stretches of beaches. The days became a little shorter each day and the cooler nights led to more campfires and stoves being used. The soldiers on picket duty required heavier clothing as the weeks went by.

# CHAPTER TWENTY:

# *Recovery Proceeding Well*

At Hilton Head, a sense of forlorn depression set in upon me. Sleep seemed impossible, not only because of sand fleas and mosquitoes, but also because my mind could not shut off the recounting of that tragic night of July 18 at Fort Wagner. Sometimes I recounted in my dreams the scenes of that night—badly wounded soldiers trying to escape the withering fire from the Fort Wagner rifle pits as they headed into the surf, disabled and weakened by blood loss, and often dying as they called for help. I could still feel the frustration of our medical team when we could not stop the bleeding and the shock that led many of our comrades directly from our operating tents to the burial site.

My spirit slowly was restored, thanks to long horseback rides along the beach—and even directing myself to more kindly medical practices such as caring for some nearby civilians and children. As our regiment gradually recovered, I found more time for myself, and I began to feel more like my old self.

I sent home for some of my medical books due to a renewed interest in studying and maintaining my medical knowledge. My quarters were suitable but reading by lantern light definitely slowed me down.

*Hilton Head, S.C.*
*October 7, 1863*

*Dear Brother S.P.\**
  *I received your kind letter a short time since and perused it with a great deal of pleasure. I received a letter from Theron\*\*, he appeared before the board and was exempted and has gone to Albany. I am glad he does not have to go for he would not be equal to these hardships. It takes a pretty good man in active ser-*

*vice for a soldier. There is no war or news here of importance and I doubt if there will be until Admiral Dahlgren is removed. He may make good guns but he can't take Charleston and I do not think Gilmore intends to do anymore till the Navy do as they agreed to, that is if he would take Morris Island they would move up the channel to the city.*

*I have visited some of the ironclads of late that are here for repairs. The Papaie is so damaged as to have to go north for repairs. I think they are a glorious humbug. One like the new Ironsides is worth them all they allow themselves. I hear she was injured a few nights ago by a torpedo. There is the mostly bitter feeling here and in the Navy toward Dahlgren. The Navy officers say if they can have their own way they would take the city and the engineer of the Monitor Passaic told me he offered to run all the obstructions and clear the way for the others and he would not let them until the Navy work there will be but little done here.*

*It is now getting quite cool in fact cold nights. Some like our northern autumn nights and as it is cold and late I will close with my love to all and a kiss for the Corporal. I bid you goodnight hoping you will write soon.*

*Your Brother*

*Myron*

\* S.P. refers to his brother-in-law Silas P. Abell

\*\* Theron was one of his half brothers.

Garrison duty was not all boring. There were occasional attempts by rebel infiltrators to spy on us. The meandering streams through the wetlands between Hilton Head and Port Royal made it fairly easy for them to remain concealed. We caught them every so often, quizzed them and interned them in prison camps.

In the nice weather in the late summer of 1863, and while garrisoned at Hilton Head, I had a rare opportunity to take a short trip and visit the nearby town of Beaufort. The sick calls lessened and the members of the Sixth showed some return to their old spirit and improved military attitude. Taking two of my hospital stewards with me and a two-man team in a small boat, we crossed the waters to the Beaufort docks. The blacks who remained there were most happy to help us tie up the boat as we left the scene of sparkling waters behind us and walked toward the center of town. We couldn't make out what the Negroes said as they gave us directions. A spoken language called "gullah," which is somehow a combination of English and their native African language (I later learned it was from the area of Sierra Leone, on the African coast. I also was told that their cleverness in planting the cotton, rice, and indigo in the area was a result of the land's resemblance to their native land in Africa.)

I was pleased to note the excellent condition of the town and its shaded walkways. The houses with their fine columns and upper porches provided good ventilation and views of the surroundings. It was said that this entire area capitulated so quickly during the first few months of the war that this town thereby escaped being destroyed and burned, as were many other towns that showed resistance to the Union forces. In any case, it was well within Union lines and not in any danger of attempts to retake it by the Confederate forces. An extremely large number of slaves must have been required to work the large plantations in this lowland country; other than the great heat from the summer sun, it must have been an entirely beautiful scene to look upon in past times.

We wended our way down the quiet side streets to visit the very old arsenal that had existed for some years before the war. There were actually some partially destroyed Blakely cannons and other armaments there and nearby. The U.S. gunboat Seneca destroyed these guns and gun carriages at the Beaufort arsenal in November, 1861. I read a plaque at the old armory indicating that it was authorized by the state of South Carolina to be a laboratory for making shot and explosives as long ago as 1795. The walls of the old powder magazines were easily identified. A General Steven Elliot was in charge of this armory, and I later learned that he became commander of the Confederate force occupying Fort Sumter.

As I mentioned before, there was very little resistance at that time and the town seemed almost hospitable to our visiting troops. We were also told that some people from the Massachusetts area, with a missionary zeal, set about an educational program for the Negroes. After a very pleasant afternoon of such visiting, and being shaded by the canopies of large oaks and Spanish moss, we returned to our boats and to our encampment at Hilton Head. Such pleasant moments in this war helped to ease our tensions and gave hope that someday we could return there in peace. The stalemated situation around the fortifications at Richmond and Petersburg gave us little hope that such peace would come soon.

From *The Civil War in Song and Story* by Frank Moore,
"Last Man Of Beaufort."

On the day that the town of Beaufort, S.C. was entered by the national troops, all the inhabitants were found to have fled, except one white man, who, being too much intoxicated to join his compatriots in flight, had been forced to remain behind.

Tis the last man at Beaufort
Left sitting alone
All his valiant companions had "vamoosed"
No secesh of his kindred
To comfort is nigh,
And his liquors expended,
The bottle is dry!
We will not have thee, thou lone one
Or harshly condemned—
Since your friends have all "mizzled,"
You can't sleep with them;
And it's no joking matter

To sleep with the dead;
So we take you back with us—
Jim lifts up his head!
He muttered some words
As they bore him away,
And the breeze thus repeated,
The words he did say:
When the liquor's all out,
And your friends they have flown,
Oh who would inhabit
This Beaufort alone?

*Hilton Head, S.C.*
*October 17th, 1863*

*Dear Father:*

*I received your kind letter a short time ago which I must say was quite unexpected as I had given up all hopes of hearing from you.*

*I was glad to hear from home, though, and hope you will do so again. I am now quite well and hope this will find all my friends the same. You must not expect much news this time for we are lying in the sand (as usual) where news would hardly reach us if there was any and I do not think there is—and even if there was, I would not be allowed to give it under penalty of "cashiering" and "dismissal from service" which I do not care about.*

*I bought me a pony last week (about the size of Mr. Cheeseboros) and paid with saddle and bridle $160 and sold it two days after for $180 to a man who expects to take it north tomorrow. So you see horses are somewhat high here. If I had the mare I sold Orville here I could get over $200 for her.*

*I bought me a horse this week that came from Florida for $110 he is very poor but is gaining flesh rapidly. He is six years old, a stallion dark by and will weigh I should judge 700 pounds and will outrun anything in South Carolina. I think I could get $150 for him when I get him ready for sale. Did you get any money from Theron? If so please give me credit for it. I hope soon to pay my debts and I do not care how soon. N. B. I want you to send my trunk as soon as you receive this letter. The key is secured to the handle and send by express with these articles:*

*3 linen shirts if I have them*
*1 Carpenter's Physiology*
*1 Webster Dict. quarto edition*
*1 Latin Grammar*
*1 Latin Reader*
*1 Olendorf's French*
*1 Spiers & Surrennes Dictionary*
*1 blank book with pencil notes*
*1 Package private matter sealed with wax, be sure to send it.*

*1 Package Official Letters*
*my pocket medicine case and my Bible.*

*Please attend to it immediately as I am in want of a trunk for my clothes and write when you send it and take a receipt for it. Pack securely, don't fail to send it soon.*

*To give you an idea what it costs to live here and for clothes living does not cost as much as one on Morris or Folly Island. I suppose it costs me one time over one dollar a day and poor living for me at that, but it was the best I could do. I bought, after I came here 1 pr. Shirts $8. 1 hat and trimmings $12, 1 pr pants with cord $16.75, 1 pr shoes $4. Isn't that rough or rather isn't that robbery.*

*I must close to send by this mail. My love to all. Write soon and believe me as ever*

*Your Aff. Son*
*Myron*

Toward the end of the year, some of the soldiers received Christmas gifts, and this offered a break in the tedious camp-life that we were trying to become accustomed to. Drilling in the nasty weather was a painful chore, but at least it got some activity into our men, who otherwise would only have been playing cards and carousing.

[Letter from Hilton Head, with the envelope depicting the American flag in the corner with Dr. Robinson's handwriting underneath stating, "Long May It Wave."]

*Wednesday Night*
*November 13th, 1863*

*Dear Father*

*I received my trunk yesterday—Am under great obligation for sending it. You did not write what the Ex. Bill was. Did you try to send anything besides what I wrote for, nothing else came.*

*It looked as though something leaked out but there was nothing there to show. The weather here not very cold, yet I have no stove yet but some are getting them. Received a letter last week from Charles. He is quite poorly, I wish I was nearer to him so I could see him but I am afraid we will have a chance to re-enlist at the end of three years, but do not know.*

*We caught two Rebs on picket night before last. They said they were looking for a place to land a force to make an attack here. I hope they will not come for now. I am better than I had been, had the shakes but once yet. I send you a likeness of Jeff\* when Gilmore threw the "villonous compound" at him. I hope he will keep throwing it at Jeff till his "last ditches" till everything is used up and then stop and let us out of this scrape. Do not forget you have a boy in "Dixie" but write often and believe me as ever*

*Your Son*

*Myron W. Robinson*
*Assist. Surgeon 6th C.V.*
*Hilton Head, S.C.*

[This letter had an enclosed cartoon card showing Jefferson Davis being shot at by General Gilmore with an artillery shell.]

The wind off the ocean made it difficult to keep the tents warm and to keep the stoves drawing normally. Backdraft and smokiness aggravated my chronic cough problems, but at least boredom and discomfort were an improvement (I guess) over being shot at. The rhythmic booming and "gravelly" ebbing of each wave lulled me to sleep nightly, and my bad dreams lessened. It would not be a gay Christmas on that wind-flayed point of land.

*Hilton Head, S.C.*
*December 12th, 1863*

*My dear niece*

*It is now Saturday night. The rain is pouring down in torrents and the wind is blowing like the mischief. Wouldn't you like to live in a cloth house with such weather? My stove smokes so that I have taken down the pipe and run it under the front door to my house or tent. I put it out the front door because it is the only door I got. I see tonight the other officers are following my example. Some of them got smoked out of their tents and had to come to mine.*

*It has been raining two days and it makes it extremely unpleasant. The wind shakes my tent and jiggles me so I don't write good you must excuse me. You had ought to hear the ocean roar now and see its foam capped billows. It sounds like the long deep roar of thunder. I have gotten tired of hearing the constant moaning of its waves.*

*My tent is only a few rods from its beach—O! such a splendid beach—for twelve miles as smooth and hard as pavements. I often take a ride down it for pleasure.*

*I was going to scold you for not answering my letter sooner but I suppose you are busy at school so I guess I will spend the rest of my time in scolding somebody else and so hoping you will answer soon as possible and with love to all I remain as ever*
*Your Uncle*
*Myron*
*P.S. Tell "Frona" I will answer hers very soon. Take good care of the little "Corporal"*
*Myron*

I felt as patriotic as ever, but it did seem that a firm hand in control of our army could have brought about better results in this dreary, bloody chess game.

I had a feeling of pride and felt my chest swell to see our glorious flag go up at sunrise, but this was countered by my pessimism over our leadership and by the endless casualties that demanded my attention.

[Letter postmarked Port Royal, S.C., to sister Frona Abell.]

*Hilton Head, S.C.*
*December 29th, 1863*

*Dear Sister*

*I now take my pen to answer your letter which was received some time since and read with much pleasure.*

*We are having very pleasant weather now, a little cool but not enough to be uncomfortable. If I had a good house for quarters I would sooner it be cold than not for I always like the cold weather.*

*I received a letter from Charles a short time ago, he was well and in good spirits. Also one from Theron, he was at Flushing with Mr. Downings. I have been advising him to join the Army but it does not seem to do much good. I think that if he could get a position he is qualified for he would do better. I do not advise him because he might think so much of service, for I do not. I am thoroughly cured of "War Fever" I ever had and if I was out, I would stay out. I am tired of the treachery and selfishness or as Mr. Morford calls it "shoddiness" which is every day evident. Besides, I think I can do better elsewhere. I asked the Colonel the night before last to approve my resignation, but he was not willing to. It is so dull here if I stay I hope we will be away from here and be accomplishing something towards crushing the rebellion.*

*Our men this past week have been re-enlisting as Veterans, about 200 of the Reg't have re-enlisted and got their bounty of $475 and $400 more coming. They enlisted for three years, same as before and I think there is no doubt but that they will be required the whole time.*

*It does not appear to me as though the war is half over yet nor do I think it is. Gen. Seymour says it is a ten years war and possibly this is correct. I must close. My love to all "Little Corporal" in particular. Tell Julia when she writes to send one of her pictures to me for I would like one very much. Write soon.*

*Your Aff. Brother*
*Myron*

*Hilton Head, S.C.*
*December 30th, 1863*

*Dear Father*

*You will receive a map of S.C. per express in your name please keep it for me. If there is any charge, it would be between Andover & Hebron as I paid Ex. charges here.*

*I have been unwell for a few days but guess I shall weather it through. I have a severe cough that troubles me considerably.*

*If you have to pay anything on the map charge it to me.*

*This from your son*

*Myron*

I wished I could get home in the hope of straightening out the squabbling in the family. At least winning this "battle" might make father's remaining years more pleasant, but I was quite distracted from this by considerations of the war; I felt that even a short trip up north, while it might improve my health, would not solve all other problems.

# CHAPTER TWENTY-ONE:

# *Home on Leave*

*Hilton Head, S.C.*
*April 16, 1864*

Dear Father,

*I received your kind letter this morning and hasten to reply to it.*

*I need not tell you how glad was I to hear from you. For you know that I am always glad to hear from home.*

*By the time you receive this, I expect to be what the Soldiers call—roughing it. We are under "marching orders" and expect to embark soon for either Army of the Potomac or the Peninsular, the last I hope for I have a horror of the Potomac Army—the other is hard enough.*

*All the White troops are being taken out of the Dept. as fast as possible and their places supplied by our "Sable Brethren." I expect there is going to be fighting somewhere, I expect Richmond is going to be taken—I expect they could not get the better Regt. to help take it than the glorious Old Veteran Sixth C.V. If they will fight before "Richmond" as they fought before "Wagner"—and they will, the city will be ours. That was terrible fighting—desperate.*

*I shall never forget that night. Let me live as long as I may, the roar of Cannon—the rattle of musketry—the groans of the wounded and dying—the heaps of slain—are so deeply engraven in the minds of those who were there that they never speak of it but with a Shudder of horror.*

*But new scenes now await us— new fields are to be covered by the fallen— other homes which have not yet tasted the bitter fruits of this war have yet to be made sad—other hearts have yet to be made desolate.*

*We have quite an excitement here tonight. The 100th NY Reg't. have had an engagement with the 9th U.S. Colored, a few shots were exchanged, one or two wounded, one leg broken, and the affair was stopped by sending down two of our Companies. The White soldiers commenced clubbing the Colored ones who were on Patrol duty—and beating them and the "darks" as any Soldier should give cold lead in return.*

*The 100th is one of the Reg't. that broke and ran at the assault on Fort Wagner. Such men are just brave enough to attack a man at their own advantage because he belongs to an unfortunate downtrodden race.*

*Our troops have just returned 1 1/2 o'clock in the morning. Do you wonder why I am up so late or so early? I am watching with a man who has been sick some time with the Small Pox—one of our Captains. He is very sick—is better than he was—I have been very much exposed every day since he was taken sick, but do not think I shall take it. I hope not, for I have seen enough of it.*

*Tell Orville if Minnie has not been vaccinated to have it take, to have it done the first opportunity. I have seen enough of Small Pox .*

*About going to Hebron, I don't know what to say, for I am not free. If Pomeroy leaves I think I would go if I could.*

*If E. P. says any more about my getting high wages now or any one else, you can tell them it doesn't amount to Shucks or rather a young man like me ought to be getting money faster. Our pay has been reduced since the commencement of the war, articles of merchandise, as an average have raised 20 percent and we are paid in currency that has depreciated 60 percent. That's how we make money. Now we have got to lose a good many things to go to Virginia.*

*I shall probably send my trunk home but will write before doing so. I must close. Give love to all and write soon direct to Washington DC and it will reach the Reg't. Tell O and L to write. Good night from your Aff. and unworthy Son,*
*Myron W. Robinson*
*Assistant Surgeon 6th Con Vol*
*Washington, D.C.*
*(To follow Regiment)*

It came as no great surprise to me that the commanding officers would find better use for our troops; they moved us to the siege line of Petersburg and Richmond. Although our ranks were thinned, there was no doubt that we must be put to better use than simply garrison duty. In April, 1864, I began to anticipate extending my duties and services to an even greater extent with the probable battles of the forthcoming warm season. Each springtime, I hoped that this would lead to a conclusion in the next few months. In the preceding winter months, I was able to go through more medical training and battle casualty training with my small medical staff. We began our job of packing up the gear in preparation for shipping northward to the campaign areas near Richmond.

### * Historical Note *

The summer of 1863 became known as the turning point of the war. Victories such as at Vicksburg and Gettysburg led the north to be quite optimistic about an early ending of the "War of the Rebellion," nevertheless final victory eluded the Union armies. Lincoln, sensing the dissatisfaction with the prosecution of the war and the rising influence of the "Copperheads," sought a new leader for he federal forces. His attention was directed to a General Grant whose aggressiveness and leadership in the western campaigns was noteworthy.

In his new role as commander of The Army of the Potomac, Grant crossed the Rapidan just after midnight on May 4th 1864 to begin his campaign to take Richmond and thus end the war. However, despite the poor condition and supplies of the Confederates, their morale remained high. This led to a series of battles as he moved southward on a parallel course to Lee's forces to the west in an effort to interpose the federal forces between Lee's forces and Richmond.

A General Benjamin Butler was the commander of the Department of Virginia and North Carolina. He was given this command as a political expedient because of the need in the field and furthermore had previously been dismissed from his position as Military Governor of New Orleans in December 1862, where the citizens roundly hated him because of his harsh rule there. Grant placed him in charge of the 10th Corps to aid in the action toward Richmond.

The 10th Corps, including the 6th Connecticut, sailed up the James River and encamped in a loop of the James River called Bermuda Hundred. It became known as the Army of the James.

They fought a series of inconclusive battles there, including a severe one at Drewry's Bluff, but Butler at least kept the Confederates at bay. Grant was mostly satisfied with this holding action but took the occasion to transfer 10,000 troops to the more active theater of action at the Petersburg-Richmond siege line. This transfer included the 6th Connecticut Volunteers.

\* \* \*

Another year, 1864, was well underway. The sick call lists were small and welcome signs of spring were in the air. Some other "signs" were also in the air. Dispatches from ships and other messages presaged that some action was being planned for us. We certainly didn't serve much purpose there, since the strength of our garrison was more than enough to discourage any attempt by the rebels to dislodge us.

I was rewarded with an extended leave to return home. I understood that orders were given for an April 27, 1864 departure for our regiment to head north and take up battle positions in the James river area, outside Richmond.

With leave orders all in proper fashion, I sailed out of Port Royal harbor to Philadelphia. I transferred my luggage to a train in Philadelphia; thence by a seemingly endless ride to New Haven. I sat on the train with a passenger who got aboard in New York. By a pleasant coincidence, he was a young doctor and was about to take up duties at Knight's Hospital in New Haven. He informed me that on June 9, 1962, the War Department made arrangements for this hospital (named after Dr. Jonathan Knight, professor of surgery at the medical department of Yale) to receive the sick and wounded of the Union forces. I viewed the temporary barracks and tents that were constructed at this hospital, thus increasing the capacity to 1500 patients. My train mate showed hospitality to the degree of inviting me to stay at his quarters near the hospital. The following day I worked my way north toward Hebron. The last few miles along the high ground along the Connecticut River were a welcome site. I could hardly wait to get home. A tearful and joyful welcome awaited me not only from my beloved family, but from many of our neighbors.

[From *The Civil War in Song and Story*] A humorous poem from an invalid soldier in a New Haven, Connecticut hospital, who was wounded at the battle of Fair Oaks.

L-E-G- On My Leg (An "Elegy")

Good leg, thou wast a faithful friend,
Truly hast thy duty done;
I thank thee most that to the end
Thou didst not let this body run.
Strange paradox! That in the fight
That I of thee was thus bereft,
I lost my leg for "the Right"
And yet the right's the one that's left!
But while the sturdy stump remains,
I may be able yet to patch it,
Even now I've taken pains
To make an L-E-G to match it.

The highlight of my month's leave came when I went with some brothers and sister Sophronia to a church social. There my eye was caught by a lovely young lady named Emma Stewart, whom I had met long ago while at Berkshire Medical School. I reintroduced myself and learned of her visit in this area from the nearby town of Portland. We met at a few other dances and picnics at the shores of Lake Compounce.

The time fled by all too fast. I left some heavier clothes at home and packed up some medical books in preparation for my return to the war. As I repacked to visit New York and then return to the war, I decided to leave my journal at home, thus to preserve it in the event that I did not return. Possibly the family might find some solace in reading of my actions—all the way from Ellington, Berkshire Medical School, and through my duties at Fort McHenry and our campaigns at Hilton Head, Fort Pulaski, Jacksonville, and our deadly battle at Fort Wagner. I began a new journal after the end my stay in Hebron. I hoped it would not take too many more pages before I could write about the ending of the war.

Emma had plans to visit near New York City, so when my leave time was running short, we combined our plans and I accompanied her and her brother to her friend's house in Yonkers, just outside New York City. This hospitable family was the well known Warwicks of Yonkers who had done well in the shipping business, notwithstanding the war. They insisted that I be their house guest and I later escorted Emma to Hillsdale, New York, where she met with her old school friends. There were still more dances, picnics, boat rides, and many other diversions surrounded by beautiful spring scenery.

Leaving all this, as well as my new friend Emma, was difficult indeed. We promised to meet again when (and if) I returned from the seemingly unending war.

I was able to catch a small steamer on the Hudson River down to New York City. Beyond a depressingly long list of killed in action and missing in action, did anyone seem concerned over the war to which I now returned? This pleasant life was a world apart from what I had been through and was now returning to. Our organization landed in Gloucester Point, opposite Yorktown at Hampton Roads to begin our Virginia campaign. I joined them there following my leave.

> *Saturday Night, May 23, 1864*

*Dear Father and Mother:*

*I now seat myself at a late hour of the night to write you a few lines to let you know that I am back again in my old quarters. I should have written before but I have been engaged in putting things to right again.*

*I sailed from N.Y. the 5th of this present month . After leaving home, went to N.Y. and from there to Hillsdale, N.Y. with my "best friend" to visit some of her relatives and after a visit of 4 or 5 days returned to N.Y. Had a very fine time indeed, I enjoyed myself much.*

*Excuse scratching for I am nervous tonight as I can be—yes I will write it. You never asked me to come home with her for a visit so supposed you did not care to see her—but you shall see her someday and then I know you can but feel proud of her as well as your youngest son. Her health is very poor but I think is gradually improving.*

*Pa what makes you go Humph! when you read this? Don't you believe it ?*

*If you don't I will prove it to your entire satisfaction some day—No news here at all only what we get from the North. When will this war end? If it don't pretty soon they may count me out, for I am tired, tired, tired of it unless Gov.\* raises our salary I must look for other business for I am on the make.*

*How are things in Hebron now, what Dr. is there? Has Pomeroy left? Will you write soon and often and let me know that I am not forgotten. Write soon Write often Write! Write!! Write!!!*

*Send me a paper when you have a chance. Tell them to write. Don't you think I have written enough nonsense for once? I do, so will resign myself to the arms of Morpheus hoping that in the morning I shall be less tired than I am now.*

*Your Aff. son*
*Myron W. Robinson*
*Asst Surg 6th C.V.*

*Refers to Connecticut Governor William Buckingham.

# CHAPTER TWENTY-TWO:

# *James River Campaign Begins*

The pleasant memories of my recent visit home to Connecticut, and my feelings of longing for my now beloved Emma Stewart, were painfully displaced by the deafening roar of muskets and cannons. With difficulty I found my way to report in to my superiors at the Connecticut Sixth headquarters. This difficulty was caused by the dense forest and tangled briars and bushes. Especially with the early spring foliage, it was impossible to see more than a few yards in any direction.

Spring planting would have been underway at this time on our Hebron farm, and Sophronia's son (my little nephew) was getting older without my being able to see this "little corporal" again soon. I hoped someone was there to teach him how to fly a kite, the names of the wildflowers, and maybe even look for frog's eggs in the many ponds near our farm. I also hoped the squabbling over farm matters and ownership had all been settled since my visit home.

The many wounded we began to receive told of desperate battle conditions. A skirmish line and use of cannons were not feasible because of the dense forestation. This was even worse than the jungle growth which allowed surprise attacks to succeed against us near the battles of Savannah and James Island long ago. While caring for a corporal with a severe shoulder wound, he related to me that casualties occurred because friendly troops were being mistaken by their own comrades and that this was a frequent occurrence.

As if all these injuries and casualties weren't enough from this savage close combat, a new horrible group of injuries arrived, namely severe burns caused by forest fires from all the gunfire and gunpowder. Casualties that could move slowly or not at all were entrapped in this hellish scene and received life-threatening burns. We used our entire supply of salve in forty-eight hours. I will never forget the cries of agony from the injured men trying to escape those fires.

When in the barrier islands off the Carolina coast, we never had a chance to see more than several hundred or a thousand soldiers at a time. Now, on the long battle line between Petersburg and Richmond, one could not help but be impressed by the size of our forces. Large cavalry units and artillery units were most impressive as they dashed here and there in making plans for the forth-coming campaign. The rule of the day seemed to be an attack here and a with-drawal there, all adding up to a loss of time and men in this May heat. Attack against entrenched positions proved costly and kept me busy with my always woeful job of trying to repair the damages of shot and shell to the young men. At least at Hilton Head and Folly Island we had the occasional sea breeze.

With the greater industrialization and greater population in the North, all felt that it would be a brief war with only a few skirmishes, after which peace plans could be drawn up. The first battle of Bull Run was an indication of how wrong our optimistic planners were. We all sensed a spirit of lack of support from our northern friends. It was almost as though we delighted in this painful "war-game." How we longed for a significant breakthrough and victory in the thirty-five-mile siege line between Richmond and Petersburg.

Early in the war, Union Forces had been unsuccessful in a rapid advance to take Richmond. Richmond was the nerve center of the Confederacy and its chief point of all operations. The important city of Petersburg was twenty miles to the south. Being unable to take this also, the Union placed the entire area under siege. The rebels had thus built an entire defense line, in reality thirty-five miles long, in a north-south direction all the way from Richmond to Petersburg, block-ing any approach from the east.

If the Richmond-Petersburg area had been taken, it would have brought a rapid end to the war. The terrain showed the James River circuitously wandering gradually northward toward the Potomac just south of Richmond. The Appomattox river ran off a loop of the James River called Bermuda Hundred. It headed southwest and west just above Petersburg. The Confederate forces estab-lished outerworks defenses around Richmond from Drury's Bluff through Chapin's Farm and northward toward the Chickahominy River. An innerworks lay several miles behind us and almost completely encircled Richmond. The Richmond and Petersburg railroad ran directly south from Richmond and was several miles west of the defense lines the north-south configuration.

The defenses circled around south of Petersburg, crossed the Jerusalem Plank Road and anchored at the Boynton Plank Road (both of which figured prominently in the conflict). Globe Tavern, south of Petersburg, also figured in this conflict.

General Grant became convinced that he would never take the Confederate capital by storm, partly because of the coordination of the Confederate com-manders along this line. Important to the Connecticut Sixth was the fact that Longstreet had reunited his First Corps, which occupied the defenses at Appomattox River, including those across Bermuda Neck. Because of Lincoln's reelection at this time in history, the Confederate hierarchy came to know that an early end to the war by negotiation was most unlikely, despite the time gained by Lee to improve his resistance planning. Therefore, a war of attrition necessarily set in. The vigorous headlong attacks cost Meade and Butler many casualties (eleven thousand in the initial June assault, five thousand in the many skirmishes since).

From rebel captives in the Petersburg area, we learned that the prolonged siege had not entirely dampened the spirits of the local citizenry. It was reported that they even held "starvation balls" (a dance in which the glasses and dishes were turned upside down as a symbol of the necessary austerity, as no drinks or bits of food were available for serving).

[Letter to his father from Old Point Comfort. The envelope has two keys enclosed. The weight of which required two three cent stamps.]

*Gloucester Point, Va.*
*May 25th, 1864*

*Dear Father:*

*Seated on the ground under the fly of a tent I take my pencil to write a few lines before we move expecting every moment to hear or being liable to hear the "Long Roll Beating."*

*We are now soldiering in earnest, bivouacking in an open field. My personal baggage I had to reduce to almost nothing and sent the rest home. It has gone today to Fortress Monroe to be Expressed home. There is one trunk and one chest. I paid no express money on them as I could not here and did not know what it would be there. My friends are equipped for an active campaign but sufficient if it is not too long a one.*

*If you will pay it and let me know what it is I will send you what I can and as soon as I can.*

*I had to buy a horse and equipment with cost to the Government of about $175 (not quite). I had to borrow $150 here to pay. I have a dapple grey stallion which I value at $250 but do not know whether he would bring that price or not, he is a noble animal—*

*When you get the trunks—the keys I will enclose in this letter— please unlock them at once and air the books & clothes so they will not mould.*

*If I live through the campaign I shall want them. I suppose I know in fact that there is to be hard work and hard fighting, the hardest of the war. I wish you would write soon and often.*

*Direct it to 6th Reg't C.V., 3rd Brigade, 1st Division, 10th Army Corp, Via Fortress Monroe, Va—The Reg'ts in our Brigade are 6th and 7th Conn. and 3rd & 7th N.H. Watch the papers and you will soon hear of us. I expect to have the Reg't to take care of alone again. Write soon—Goodnight*

*Your Aff. Son*
*M.W. Robinson*
*Asst. Surg. 6th Conn. Vols.*
*3rd Brig 1st Division, 10th Army Corps*
*Via Fort Monroe, Va.*

Preceded by several gunboats, the army of Benjamin Butler moved up the James River. This river had many bends and turns as it traversed the area south of Richmond. General Butler was supposed to have brought his troops to this area to help with the attack on Richmond. Nonetheless, he was bottled up in a loop of the James River called Bermuda Hundred. In the meantime, Grant was frozen in front of Petersburg by a long line of fortifications that extended all the way from Richmond south to this area around Petersburg.

[Letter addressed to his sister, Mrs. S. P. Abell, Colchester, CT postmarked Old Point Comfort, VA.]

*Near Point of Rocks, Va.*
*June 5th, 1864*

*My Dear Sister:*
*I have been expecting a long while a letter from you and have been thinking for a long while I would write and this being a favorable opportunity I now employ hoping that this may find you enjoying life's choicest blessing, "health."*

*My correspondence is being reduced so that it takes but little time to tend to it for as no one writes, I have none to reply to. I have but one or two frequent correspondents who favor me often with letters. Perhaps I had better take some of the blame to myself as I have not written for so long a time—but I have not been where I could as if I could or had the time to do it.*

*We are and have been having ever since we landed a very severe Campaign. How soon it will end no one pretends to surmise but I hope before long for the men are becoming tired out and sickness is often on the increase. I had over one hundred to attend to this morning. I am now alone with the Reg't and I think a good prospect of being for some time to come. The Reg't is in camp behind an earthwork where Rebs keep up a crossfire with artillery occasionally, for diversion I suppose. For the last two days they have been very quiet but from appearances I think the engagement will be a general one in a short time, perhaps in two or three days. We hear the firing in Grant's Army very distinctly and signal officers report that they saw shells explode over Richmond. I hope this will prove true. I suppose we will soon hear from it. I do not expect to be any nearer Richmond than I was three weeks ago today. I was then 7 miles from the city in a very uncomfortable situation. I must close, please write soon how Father is and all the news. Poor Father I wish I could see him and cheer him in his sorrow. I came very near resigning last week and may before long unless his honorable excellency Gov. B. makes purer promises and pays more attention to the fulfillment of those he has already made.*

*Give my love to all and will write soon. Tell hello to kids and the "Little Corporal" for me. Direct as usual*
*1st Division, 10th Army Corps*
*Via Fortress Monroe, Va.*
*and between us as ever*
*Your Aff. Bro*
*Myron*

It appeared that the Union Forces of twenty-five thousand men were to be transported up the James River since the gunboats went up a day earlier. After two days along this beautiful river, we disembarked at Bermuda Hundred. Our medical group was the last to leave the transport but we had no trouble filing our way inland at the rear of our troops. Our ease of advance was made possible because of the large size of the corps preceding us. Trees had been felled to allow passage through the heavier forested areas and there were "corduroy roads" over some swamp land. Hit-and-run attacks by Confederate units caused but little hesitancy to our advance, although it gave us work to do with our medical care. In our desire to disrupt communications and supplies for the rebels, telegraph wires and more than three miles of railroad track were torn up in the Petersburg-Richmond area. On May 9, 1864, the 18th Army Corps engaged the rebels near Richmond.

Several casualties occurred on the 10th of May, when a large Confederate force under D. H. Hill left their bastion at Richmond, and a heated two-hour battle ensued. The rebels withdrew from the field while we strengthened our positions (and my work became heavier with our war wounded). Capt. J. E. Wilcox of Waterbury, Connecticut was killed; there were twenty wounded and four missing in this skirmish. All this was noted in the morning report the following day.

> Bermuda Hundred Va.
> May 12th, 1864

*Dearest Father*

*I received a letter from Orville yesterday bearing the painful intelligence of the death of our beloved mother.*

*I received the news—though not wholly unexpected, with the deepest sorrow and in the situation I am now in feel lonely and almost friendless. But she has gone to her rest—to her heavenly home where I hope we shall all meet her after the cares and toils of this weary life shall have ended.*

*But in the hour of sorrow and affliction we have one Friend "of whom we may seek consolation and to whom I feel that I can look with confidence knowing that He doeth all things well."*

*Oh if I could only have seen her once more and been there when she died to have said "the last farewell"—but it was otherwise ordered.*

*I sometimes feel that I have seen my friends all for the last time being hourly amid dangers both seen and unseen. While I am writing this Reg't is forming again to march and I feel unable to do anything were I in any place but this—now is the time of greatest need and everyone's duty is plainly that of energy and perseverance. We march Monday to the Railroad from Petersburg to Richmond and to within 13 1/2 miles from R. Then down within 4 of Petersburg. Our Reg't then Tuesday morn tore up the track for some distance and met the enemy on the turnpike road and in the woods and after a bloody fight of 3 or 4 hours we drove them back and came back to our camp here in the woods, hungry and tired. Yesterday I had an attack of Dysentery but feel better today and shall go out with the Reg't.*

*Rations here are scarce, we march two days and fought, and hardly a man had over one decent meal in the time. I had nothing the 2nd day till I got into camp that night except a piece of hard tack. The firing has continued through the night and intervals this morning. The Reg't is starting so I must close. My love to all, and believe me Dear Father to be as ever*

*Your Aff. Son*
*Myron*
*P.S. I will write again soon, write me often direct to*
*1st Division 10th Army Corps*
*Via Fortress Monroe Va.*

On May 14, following along behind our Sixth, we were headed to Proctor's Creek near Drury's Bluff. It seemed to me to be somewhat of an optimistic gamble for General Butler to establish the base headquarters in such a precarious place, however, he was a general and hopefully had good reconnaissance basis for this plan.

On the evening of May 15, our regiment occupied the center of the picket line. All seemed quiet until about dawn, when that blood curdling rebel yell from a thousand throats foretold the massive attack upon us. I was close enough to see the "fire and withdraw" method of our troops as myself and a corpsman rapidly gathered up our supplies and made haste toward the rear. By this time the entire corps was involved and one could hear the Minie balls whistling through the spring foliage as we withdrew. Our speed was greatly slowed by trying to get enough stretcher carriers through the somewhat dense forest, although we were greatly helped by soldiers and some of the "walking wounded." There was no severe panic, but bedlam nevertheless prevailed.

We withdrew six miles back, and my job of coordinating the ambulance removal of the injured was badly complicated by the road being choked with rebel prisoners, Negro men and women, walking wounded, cattle, and all manner of things. Our regiments fired from wooded defensive positions and from ravines. Also the firing of our batteries stabilized our positions and the battle ended. Of course this was not an end for me, inasmuch as the Sixth lost seven killed and fifty-three wounded. Other wounded (including rebels, civilians, and soldiers from other outfits) kept us busy into the night. A ship came up the James the next day and happily improved the roster of our regiment by the return of some of our troops from furlough. (Many of these men had been given furloughs as a reward by virtue of their reenlistment).

*10th Army Corps Field Hospital*
*Virginia May 29th 1864*

*My Dear Father*
*This is the "day of Rest" and as my usual daily duties are accomplished I take my pen to write you a few lines before devoting my time to anything else.*
*I am now in the enjoyment of life's greatest blessings—health—and may this find you the same. You will see by this that I am not now with my Reg't but am*

detailed at the Field Hospital of the 10th Army Corps receiving the sick and wounded from the whole Corps.

We have now about 100 patients, but have two surgeons besides myself which makes one's work very hard and confining. But I have this advantage from being with my Reg't that I have a house to sleep in and a good table to sit at which I find makes a great difference with my health and general condition. Until I came here I slept out of doors in fair weather, and raining under trees and fences in open fields and forests with Hard tack and Pork when I could get it when I could not go without with marching and fighting and working both in season and out of season. We had eight days fighting, five of which I participated in. Two weeks ago today, I was so busily employed that it was not till near night that I learned it was Sunday. If I had it could have made no difference for the wounded were brought in as fast as we could attend to them.

Last night a week the Rebels charged on our entrenchments but were quickly and I think fearfully repulsed. Our firing was terrific and lasted till after midnight. Our troops are leaving today except our division and the artillery. It is expected they go to reinforce Grant.

May God give him a full and glorious victory and bring to an end the wickedest and most causeless of all Civil Wars. I wish it might soon end that I might return to my home and friends. But O how changed will home be. A vacant seat by the fireside and at the festive board.

But were it in my power I would not call her back for she has gone to that Rest prepared for those who love the Lord, where there is no more sickness or pain or sorrow but eternal peace and love and joy reigns supreme.

Father write me often please for I feel despondent at times at not hearing often from all my friends. Tell Eliza—give my love to her and tell her I have written her several times and gotten no reply. My love to all friends. Tell Warren to write me a good long letter.

I must close this for want of time and believe me dear Father to be as ever,
Your Aff. Son
Myron
Direct
MW Robinson
Asst Surgeon 6th CV
Terrys Division
10th Army Corps
Bermuda Hundred, Va

[Mailed from Old Comfort Point, VA. The envelope says Official Business—U.S.A. Med. Department—Addressed to Mr. Wm. Robinson, Hebron, CT—"In Haste" handwritten on it.]

Bermuda Hundred
June 19th, 1864

Dear Father:
Enclosed please find ($20) twenty dollars. It is all I can possibly spare now. I am better than I have been but I am kept quite busy. I have had a very good

*chance to operate the last week and improved it to my advantage. I would write more but I have not time.*

*Please acknowledge the receipt of this as soon as possible. It is very busy times here now.*

*Your Aff. Son*
*M.W. Robinson*
*Asst Surg 6th C.V.*
*10th Army Corps*
*Bermuda Hundred, Va.*

I found myself again becoming overwhelmingly tired, but with no time to rest because of the continuous nature of the campaign. I felt the troops deserved great credit for their tenacious resistance to the ever-lurking, death-dealing enemy. The heat, insects, and poor rations were starting to show their effects.

*Bermuda Hundred, Va.*
*July 3rd, 1864*

*My Dear Sister:*
*This beautiful sabbath morning finds me on duty for the picket line between our own and the enemy entrenchments.*

*I am now residing in a cave or "Bomb Proof" on a stretcher with seven men lying around on the ground to assist me in case of any necessity. I think that with my little company I can defend and hold the "Bomb Proof" unless we are attacked, in which case they all assure me that they are very good runners and of my own fleetness of foot, I need no more demonstration than when I was some ways away from my "hole." I think my speed would have equaled if not excelled that of the ancient "Spartans" as I ran into my nest so cozily built under ground. But today, they are very quiet save an occasional crack of a musket from the advance line—reminds one of that calm that precedes the gathering storm.*

*Tomorrow being the anniversary of our independence, I expect that there will be some disturbance from what I can observe—but I may be mistaken in my expectations and hope. I shall see. It is very hot here and dry—every breath feels as if heated by a flame. How long this campaign will last, no one knows but it does not seem as if it could hold out much longer as the men are all tired and worn out. I think this has been the hardest and, I am sorry to say thus far the most unsuccessful campaign of the war. It is thus far been an absolute failure I think and with a loss of 70 to 100,000 men. It may and I hope will end in a complete victory but from what I fear I was grieved to hear of affairs home. What a wicked show—Let who will be to blame I believe that either of the three might have avoided it if they disgraced themselves only, I would not think so much of it. I don't think I ever want to see them again or our own relationship—I can never forget it, of course poor Father insists that instead of being in the midst of such troubles, he should have someone to comfort him and to clear his pathway to that world to which we are all traveling. I fear this will kill him that I shall never see him again. I could endure anything but this. I wish that he would sell his farm at once and go to where he could spend the rest of his days in peace and quietude.*

*It is too bad—too bad. Give my love to all and write soon. It is very seldom that I hear from Conn and I hope you write often soon.*

    *Your Aff Brother*
    *Myron*
    *Direct it to 6th C.V.*
    *2nd Brigade*
    *1st Division*
    *10th Army Corps*

I was busy with my medical staff in an impromptu lean-to surgical tent on a nice day in early June, 1864. Our losses were proportionately greater, considering the size of the opposing forces. The seven killed included my close friends Lieutenant Colonel Meaker, Captains Charles Nichols and John N. Tracy, Lieutenants Bennett S. Lewis, Charles Buckbee, and Norman Provost. Captain Horatio Eaton of Hartford was killed while giving evidence of his bravery by encouraging his men in the attack. I knew him well because he served with the Third Company and went afterwards to serve as a Lieutenant in the Sixth. He had a large circle of friends, especially among his own troops. Our forces were further diminished by the capture of Captain Beeble, and twenty of his command.

After these many years, I am still unable to be hardened to the fact of losing such excellent Connecticut friends to the grim reaper, or to their capture. Transfers to the hospitals back north were also personal losses. In my close relationship to these Connecticut soldiers and officers, we learned of mutual acquaintances back in Connecticut, and made firm resolves to visit one another once the war was brought to an end.

By June of 1864, a few months since we left the pleasant climes of South Carolina, we were dispersed as part of a battle line said to be thirty-five miles in length (all the way from above Richmond to the entrenchments extending to and around Petersburg to the south). In contrast with the hesitancy noted in past Union generals, General Grant certainly showed a very aggressive spirit in his zeal to defeat the forces under General Lee. The news reports we received were discussed at officer's mess; they indicated a rising concern in the North over the war. The never-ending war had made lengthening lists of dead and wounded to be published daily. In less than a month, Union losses were put at twenty-eight thousand.

The casualties brought in by ambulance told me in the course of their treatment that the enemy had arrived at the Cold Harbor area several days before our troops arrived. (To penetrate anywhere in this line would have helped us gain Richmond, which seemed easily in our grasp back in 1862.) They set up a defensive line in a crescent, with the flanks anchored in a swamp at each end. Though at the beginning we had almost empty hospital tents, we were later deluged with injured and dying. We lost seven thousand in the first deadly eight minutes of the battle. The rebels lost far fewer from their well-entrenched positions.

Sadly, many of our brave injured told me of trying to bring back wounded with them, but rebel sharpshooters denied them this. General Grant must have been mad to order still another advance.

# CHAPTER TWENTY-THREE:

# The "Crater"
# and Bermuda Hundred

**\*Historical Note\***

In July of 1864, an attempt to breach the walls of Petersburg was undertaken. A proposal came from the regimental commander (Lieutenant Colonel Henry Pleasants of the Forty-eighth Pennsylvania). Being skilled miners, they tunneled under the defending wall of Petersburg and in the course of several weeks completed a 511-foot shaft. Ten thousand pounds of dynamite were placed under this outwork. A heroic soldier was required to relight the fuse and run for his life as the gigantic explosion was set off. While it succeeded in razing the defensive works, the overall attack plan failed. The Union troops, instead of filing around the crater and through the wall, went down into the crater where they became victims of a deadly fusillade and ultimately withdrew with extensive casualties. Burnside was obliged to step down and the siege at Petersburg resumed.

\* \* \*

*Bermuda Hundred, Va.*
*July 13th, 1864*

*Dear Father:*
*I have waited and waited to receive answers to my last two letters, one of which was four weeks ago. I enclosed $20 twenty dollars but hearing nothing of it I presume it has not reached you and according to my usual luck it is lost. My prospects for a fortune I do not consider very flattering if I continue on this way but I shall not despair if I remain in the Army. I think the world will owe me a living when I leave it, for I am already growing gray.*

*My health for two or three weeks has not been very good. I feel sometimes as if I could not hold out. I dread the "Dog Days" here—it is bad enough now. I am not so uncomfortable as to omit my usual duties but I lay down as soon as completed.*

*The weather is extremely hot. All is quiet on our front but Grant is still blazing away—last night the rattle of musketry was fearful. I think he must hold in his old position nearby, but do not know. The news of the Rebel's advance into Md. is received with universal satisfaction among the soldiers. All feel as though now is the time above of all others when the North should unite as one man, not only to repel raids, but to come down and help us. It may seem at home as if we have men enough but if they would come down to help us, we could show where we lack. Then let the Rebels overrun our northern towns and cities until they feel that interest they have not yet felt.*

*I must close. My love to all—Believing me as ever*
*Myron Robinson*
*Assist Surgeon 6th C.V.*
*Bermuda Hundred, Va.*

The battle lines seemed stabilized and only minimal forays and picket line action occurred for several weeks. There was intermittent shelling day and night, but some of our soldiers told me that there was time for peaceful "swapping" with the rebels while on picket duty (indeed our lines were only a short distance apart). Newspapers, tobacco, and coffee were the most frequent items of barter. This must have seemed strange to the soldiers who only a few days before and a few days afterward could become mortal enemies.

*6th Regt C.V. 1st Div 10th A.C.*
*Bermuda Hundred, Va.*
*July 27th, 1864*

*My Dear Father:*

*I received your letter Saturday and should have answered Sunday but I received a letter from Charlie\* Sunday morning and immediately saddled my horse and started to see him. I did not know he was so near me. He is near Petersburg about ten miles from me. He is looking well but rather poor. His health is perhaps as good as it could be expected in this climate. I saw G. R. Bill also Adgate Loomis. They were well and looking very healthy. The ground there is all dug into. Pits and graves it is all dug over, every inch was contended for from appearances.*

*I suppose that Grant will blow them up before long as it is said he has mined one of their batteries and placed six tons of powder under it to blow it up when everything is ready.*

*We were expecting a "Sortie" from the Rebs here but they came not, if they had, their army would have been decimated by hundreds and perhaps thousands. They dare not come. We are ready for them at any time.*

*I have not felt very well for a few days and had a stormy night and my tent which is exclusive for dry warm weather did not protect me well. I got wet and took cold.*

*I so wish I could come home and see you if only for a day or two but times are so busy now.*

*I would send more money in this letter but have got but 20 cts. and do not know when we shall receive pay again. I have three months due me and I will send some as soon as received. You did not write whether you received my Commission or not. Please let me know. Write soon and believe me to be*

*Your Aff Son*
*Myron*

\* Charles was a half-brother, born Dec. 1, 1830

By late July of 1864, we were awaiting some "magic blow" that would crack the siege line, thus taking control of Petersburg and hopefully Richmond soon thereafter. It was a nice "escape" from the warring to visit brother Charlie. In the ride to see him I noted that the ground was completely pockmarked with shell holes and "rat holes" that we hid in and sometimes had to bury our comrades in. We shared the news from home and I rode off feeling somewhat better in spirits. This was the last time that I would ever see him.

*Bermuda Hundred, Va.*
*July 30th, 1864*

*Dear Sister:*

*Your letter was received in due time and you do not know how glad I was to receive it, containing as it did your "Phiz."\* Many thanks for it, I think it is a splendid one, it looks just like you.*

*I received a letter last Sunday morning from Charlie and so after breakfast saddled my noble steed and started for the Ninth Army Corps which I found with but little trouble. He is about ten or twelve miles from here. I saw Geo. and he was very well. Charlie looks rather thin and has not, I believe, been very well.*

*I want to see him again and shall try to if he does not move. It has been rumored here that they have been fighting today but rumor is not always reliable. It is also rumored the Rebs are evacuating and are moving off to the South, tearing up the tracks of the P&R RR, but I do not credit it—our Brigade is under arms today, it is reported we are to assault the enemy works in our front. If so, we should probably move at dusk.*

*That vivid description by Moore of—"The sight entrancing when morning's beams are glancing and plumes in the gay and dancing. When hearts are all high beating and the trumpet's voice repeating that song whose breath may lead to death but never to retreating" has lost all its charm for me. There was a time when there was a certain degree of pleasure in witnessing a battle—there was a kind of grandness of witnessing the movements of great bodies of men and to see the display of military skill of generalship. But I have seen enough—I think distance limits enchantment to the view.*

*Won't I be glad when this war is over, but there is no knowing when that will be. I fear not this year or the next. I cannot, with all our successes, see the beginning of the end,*

*I must close hoping you will write soon and with remembrance to friends in general and the little Corp. in particular.*

*I remain*
*Your Aff Brother*
*Myron*
*P.S. Tell Julia I have looked for her picture for a long while.*

* "Phiz" refers to a photo.

In the battle of Deep Run, although brief, we suffered five killed in action, sixty-nine wounded, and eleven missing in action. I spent my days close to the battle lines and a seemingly endless procession of "broken soldiers" to repair. I gained much expertise in probing wounds, with removal of bullets and metal fragments. I got my medical aids to become expert in applying and regularly releasing tourniquets. The blood loss was still so great that it was amazing that many lived through the procedures. Debriding destroyed tissue and suturing up a wide variety of wounds gave me great confidence that I one time lacked.

I was interrupted in these surgical "tactics" by the sad announcement that my brother Charles had been lost (possibly a captive, but probably fatally injured).

I came to feel a true brotherly feeling for all my men of the Sixth, but experienced a personal melancholy over the loss of a true brother and family member. The uncertainty of his fate depressed me even more.

The reality of this was brought home to me by the delivery of his possessions to me, accompanied by a young lad who served as some type of orderly for Charles. He stated that he ran away from home in Maryland in hopes of being a drummer-boy or flag-bearer for Charles' outfit. He would have liked to stay with me, but my tedious irregular hours would not allow it. I gave him a letter of recommendation and sent him off to City Point to return home. I promised this lad that if there were some way possible, I would arrange travel to visit us in Connecticut. He had learned much about Connecticut from Charles and was most anxious to visit there.

*In the Field, Bermuda Hundred, Va.*
*August 9th, 1864*

*Dear Brother:*
*Having a few leisure moments I will improve them in writing to you.*
*You have heard before this of the fate of Charley, doubtless heard of it before I did as I did not learn it till Sunday last when I went expecting to see him and then learned that he was missing. I believe most of the officers think he was killed while leading the Reg't—in command of it in the charge. Captain Loomis thought he was a prisoner, unhurt, but the flag of truce could not learn he was their prisoner. His "little contraband" came yesterday to live with me and I am going to*

*keep him. He says he went out on the battlefield with the truce flag as far as they would allow him to but could not find him. He thinks from the statement of one of our Sgts. that he was wounded on the arm and taken prisoner, if so—which I doubt—I fear a worse fate awaits him.*

*The boy is quite intelligent and seemed much attracted to him. He says he told him he should come and live with me if he got killed. He got his things valise etc. all together ready to send home before he came to me. I found a letter from you and one from Mattie. I found ten dollars in yours which I now have but will send you as soon as I get paid off if you wish me to. I would send it now but I am so short, have got to sell one horse to live on. I directed his things all to be sent to you by express fearing they might be lost with no one to look to them in the field. Tell Mattie that her wish in his letter that he might be spared from "Rebel darts" is hopeless. Tell her Uncle Myron has not forgotten her and wonders why she does not write to him. I hope Charles will yet prove to be a prisoner but I fear for the worst. I am afraid the war is never going to end until there is a perfect and an entire change in policy. Would that we might have peace. Blessed Peace.*

*My love to all. Write soon, often and long letters and believe me to be*

*Your Aff Brother*

*Myron—2nd Brigade 1st Div. 10th A.C.*

With "death" being my regular accompaniment each day, I hoped that I would somehow become hardened to it. Not so. Mother had gone to a better land and also Charles. I had such happy memories of being at home with them, and I had always hoped to return home and renew these times of happiness. After all the hard years of war and the tragedies around me, I had the feeling that I really hadn't much to live for.

Despite the hardships of the soldiers of the Sixth in this Bermuda Hundred area, it was of great help in the minds of our soldiers to know that a significant amount of good came from the battle of Fort Wagner and all of the battles leading up to it. The Confederate troops felt it necessary to evacuate Charleston rather than be surrounded and captured by the forces of General Sherman, now returning north from his great path of destruction through Atlanta, Savannah, and on a return trip back up through the Carolinas.

This swath of laying waste to the countryside was reported to be of a two-pronged nature. Many cities, especially Columbia, learned the fury of this devastating policy. On withdrawing from Charleston, the Confederates set fire to the city. The Union forces were reported to have tried to put out these fires, but did much looting in the process. In this way, it was felt that Charleston was "punished" for starting this war. The symbolic destruction of this city also seemed important in the minds of the soldiers on both sides of this conflict. We learned that our General Gilmore was given credit for capturing the city. Sherman also came to Charleston and said if Charleston was seen by anyone, they would say "no more war."

It seemed to me that General Sherman epitomized the type of leadership we needed. The overly cautious approach to battles by generals such as General McClellan and more recently our General Gilmore led to a bleeding out of our strength rather than taking the audacious steps needed to win. One of the lieutenants in our regiment quoted to me the philosophy of Clausewitz regarding the making of war. This philosophy was "L'audace, L'audace, toujours L'audace."

# CHAPTER TWENTY-FOUR:

# *Skirmishes Along the Siege Line*

Septic fevers and respiratory infections gradually became more of a problem in the colder and wet climate. I had the pleasure of the acquaintance of a Captain Lewis Allen, Jr., of New Haven during the sad weeks in which he rallied only to fail again in his recuperation. He was the former drill officer of the New Haven Blues, having held several important ranks in his rise to this grade. He participated closely in all our battles and again we had the melancholy feeling that accompanied loss of one of our fine officers.

Three-year enlistments had expired for many of our men. As they were to be mustered out, I spent a great deal of time with these fine soldiers. Many required advice as to medicines needed (we still had many gastrointestinal problems, skin infections, jaundice, etc.). Others required dressing changes and instructions as to further wound care once out of our battle zone. A few even showed some mental problems (perhaps from the continual exposure to violent death and the elements), but perhaps some from overuse of whiskey.

The flag waving, parading band music and all the huzzahs and posturing seemed to be wearing thin on myself and many of the troops. We were three years into the war, and despite some victories (and a few Pyrrhic victories), much seemed stalemated. Dissension in the North over drafting led to bloody encounters according to the few newspapers we received. Even some members of the Sixth were sent north to prevent civil strife. (Troops were kept in reserve on shipboard, and despite the proximity to home and loved ones, sadly they were not allowed to meet with them.) It was reported that there was an element of workers, specifically Irish workers, concerned that liberated Negroes would come north and take jobs. We had had "draft riots" before; now the rioting was caused by concern over the honesty of the ballot box.

A few of the soldiers rejoined us and reported several things of interest and great concern. Many felt that unfair draft laws caused much resentment in the North, as well as the fact that white workers felt that their jobs would be jeopardized with a large free black population, as mentioned before. Newspapers and other distributed literature noted that they were "willing to fight for Uncle Sam but not for 'Uncle Sambo.'" Organized resistance to the draft was commonplace, especially among the hard-liners who felt that the working class Irish in New York would be unfairly treated by a large pool of cheaper labor coming in. The burning of the draft offices occurred and a mob of rioters burned and pillaged their way down Third Avenue and on to an armory, where they swarmed inside and stole many rifles stored there. At no time was it necessary to bring the Federal troops ashore from where they were stationed on shipboard off Staten Island.

Happily, the skirmishing, fighting, and associated illnesses and injuries diminished to the point that my sick calls and needs for hospital care were lessened greatly. My comrades of the Sixth noted a "bittersweet" turn of events. It seemed that the Federal government was concerned that stuffing of the ballot boxes could occur up north and the voting of war measures might be lost. For this reason, General Butler, General Hawley, and Colonel Rockwell went north to the New York Harbor area. I learned that some of these troops disembarked at Staten Island, but most of them stayed on the ship. There was no need for the authorities to use any military action as apparently the election process went off without too much rancor. Needless to say, the morale of these troops as they returned to the Virginia battlegrounds was quite low, because they were not allowed to see home or loved ones, even though close by.

General Butler was at that time in charge of what appeared to be a large assault force. With the oncoming warm weather and the need to travel light in the forthcoming campaign, much of our goods and clothing were sent off to Norfolk for storage. I learned later that the ship sank on its return trip. In the urgency of cutting back on supplies, I had some difficulty in preventing my meager medical supplies and tents from being reduced as well. Full rations of quinine and whiskey were easily allowed but beef, beans, and potatoes were excluded in favor of rations of saltpork, and bacon. While on Hilton Head, only good army food and supplies came to us, but foraging gave us fresh fruit, fowl, fish, and occasional livestock. This probably had much to do with the fairly good recovery of our embattled troops.

Other reports told us that the "Copperheads" were becoming more vocal in their opposition to the war. Newspapers reached us by packet ship and told us of the desire of this group to consider allowing secession and forgetting about emancipation. This position seemed to draw more followers as the war dragged on and the casualty lists posted ever more tragedies. Pictures appeared showing bereaved families of soldiers reading the casualty lists at village posts, town halls, and railroad depots.

On those hot Virginia days, the sun rose early. Even before the first pink outlines of dawn appeared behind our tents of the medical section, an orderly with a lamp would arouse me from my fitful sleep. I was joined frequently by Henry

Hoyt (an assistant-surgeon from New Haven) and would drink down some hot coffee while nibbling away at some hardtack. We divided up our duties to visit the ill and wounded. This, and giving new orders to the stewards, rarely gave us time before the sounds of warfare were in the air and our new crop of casualties arrived.

Our hospital tents and facilities were set up just east of Proctor's Creek, near the Drury's Bluff battle site. The battles of Chester Station, Drury's Bluff, and other skirmishes kept our medical group continuously busy during the hot days of 1864. Battles near Bermuda Hundred between May 20 and June 2 were furious and eroding to our strength.

The direct assault and taking of Richmond had been stymied for the time being. Our area of the battle line had been brought to the south near Petersburg. The disposition of casualties under our immediate care, as well the packing and unpacking of medical supplies, was a headache, but nothing compared to the voluminous medical reports and paperwork.

In the evenings, I was happy when the booming sounds and bright flashes were only those of still another thunder and lightning storm, and not that of further rebel bombardment. I could fully see that the well-entrenched Confederate position gave them some advantage, but we knew that they were sustaining losses as well. We learned this through our frequent probing forays into their lines and also from word-of-mouth reports from their injured prisoners under our care. This was further confirmed by a steady dribble of deserters from the Confederate cause.

In past times, I had taken a spy glass to look at the surface of the moon. That was all I could think of when I saw my shell-holed surroundings, under the hot sun. Every one of the "craters" along the siege line had its own story to tell.

Two days passed after the disastrous charge at Cold Harbor before permission was finally given to try to recover the wounded. This delay seemed to be due to great wrangling between Lee and Grant, but ultimately, with a flag of truce, collection of our dead and injured occurred. This proved to be too late for our boys, who died horrible deaths from thirst and with no relief of pain.

No matter how remote and desolate my quarters, official mail seemed to get through. I received special orders number seventy in the field on July 14, 1864. It read, "Asst. Surgeon Myron W. Robinson, Sixth Conn. Volunteers, will, in addition to his other duties attend the sick of the garrison of Battery number one. By order of Brig. General A. M. Terry."

I was not sure these orders would do the greatest good for the greatest number of soldiers, but I was certainly willing to follow such orders. My only two problems were that it would increase my fatigue, being with the picket line for many hours of the day and night; also, sharpshooters could not tell a doctor from anybody else (even if they wanted to). Since we readily attended the injured and dying of both Union and Confederate forces, it would make sense that we would be exempt from threat of injury, but I readily perceived that battle conditions, especially at night, precluded any such consideration. Many accounts reached my ears of the shortsighted ruling by medical authorities of some states, that state medical facilities should take care of their own casualties and no others.

We came to learn that downheartedness was at least equally present among the rebels. We learned this especially after the June 2 attack on our lines accompanied by a hot artillery duel. The Third New Hampshire threw the enemy back. At that time, there were a large number of desertions from the Confederate forces, including even a lieutenant. Fortunately, I had very few wounded of our own to care for.

We were not so lucky a few days later. I traveled with our medical component close behind the lines as we crossed the Appomattox River. The rebels covered their withdrawal from their rifle pits with heavy shelling. Reports I received from the wounded I attended told of sharpshooting from camouflaged areas in the trees and bushes. This later led to a general rebel advance, loss of our previously taken ground, and heavy casualties. Trying to move back our medical care tents and attempt to treat our most severely wounded were hellish tasks under the conditions. The walking wounded helped us, but very many had head, chest, and abdominal injuries, which led to an agonizing death for many of our fine soldiers.

I awoke on the morning of June 22nd, to an extremely hot day registering 103 degrees. Apparently President Abraham Lincoln had sailed down to City Point and came inland. Rumor had it that a meeting was held by our president and high-ranking persons with their counterparts from the Confederate side on a ship nearby. The terms offered the Confederates were essentially those of unconditional surrender, and nothing was agreed upon, unfortunately. There may well have been some exchange of ideas between these leaders, but naturally I was not privy to any of such information. We were ordered to appear at regimental quarters and a limited version of a dress parade was given in his honor. President Lincoln came on horseback attended by General Butler and staff. His troubled and careworn appearance did not improve much despite the loud cheers from our troops.

We were close enough to the rebel lines that they also heard this cheering and surmised from such cheers that we had received news of some important Union victory. They greatly despised General Butler and called him "that beefy bloated Massachusetts Yankee," and thus felt that this was some type of trickery on his part. To the credit of President Lincoln, it was a widely held belief that, while having no particular military training, he made many important strategic decisions that led to good outcomes.

As I sat on an ammunition box at mess call, the talk among our officers was of the forthcoming strategy. This was a covering action to allow the withdrawal of General Phil Sheridan's cavalry as they joined General Grant at the siege of Petersburg. Our medical group was held in a reserve area and thus any casualties had a long and painful evacuation to reach us. The long early summer evenings gave us some advantage in such evacuations.

I reacquainted myself with Sergeant (later Lieutenant) Grogan. A severe thigh injury led to the necessity of getting out the bone saw and amputation instruments for this unavoidable treatment. He had already distinguished himself in that short-lived successful attack on Fort Wagner about a year ago, when he carried the severely wounded Colonel Chatfield down the steeply sloping escarpment and across the moat that was filled with the bodies of many of our comrades. He reached our lines despite the withering fire which was hailed upon us and which the troops of the Sixth will never forget.

While the main struggle of these two great armies seemed to be in the Petersburg-Richmond area, I noted continuous repositioning of supporting forces in the area east of these two important cities. Being curious over the rationale for the standoff all along this line, I asked many questions of my fellow officers at mess call and especially around our evening campfire talks. Richmond being the actual seat of government for the Confederacy, its capture seemed to be the key to ending the war. Failing to capture it easily, attention was directed at taking Petersburg.

A common rumor was that General A. P. Hill, of the Confederacy, was moving south of Richmond toward Petersburg. As in any chess game, we had to counter this move and thus we left the intermittent battles near the James River and Bermuda Hundred and undertook a forced march. By making some of this march by midnight on August 14, 1864, we were spared the blistering heat as we crossed the James River on a pontoon bridge.

Our troops dropped much of their military gear to charge rebel breastworks at a place called Strawberry Plains, near Malvern Hill. Our three days' rations were beginning to run low. Chronic fatigue from these long forced marches led to many "sickness complaints," some real, some imaginary. On such long marches I was privileged to ride occasionally on our horse-drawn ambulances. However, I noted that when it came to "fall out" on these long marches, the soldiers practically dropped in their tracks at the side of the road. They seemed instantly to be asleep only to be jarred awake by the sergeant's bugle and the "fall in" command. I know not where they garnered such inner strength to keep going on this signal.

As the rebels fell back, they nevertheless kept up the drumfire of Minie balls in our direction. I almost became used to the sound of such bullets tearing through the leaves and forestation around me. My ears rang from the continuous roar of howitzers and musketry, and the smell of gunpowder hung everywhere in the air.

I received reports from our soldiers who were foremost in the advance, stating the steadfast progress of the Sixth despite heavy rebel firing from behind their breastworks and dug-in positions. Seeing the overwhelming force confronting them, they withdrew, but only to regroup and call upon their reserves; the battle surged back and forth but ultimately led to our withdrawal.

My stewards and others of the staff attended to sixty-nine of our wounded (and also a few rebel prisoners). The Minie balls destroyed so much bone when they hit an extremity that splinting or other temporizing measures were of no avail. The Minie ball was actually .58 caliber in size and made of soft lead. It was more than one-half inch in diameter. It was easy for me to see that, with the velocity of a rifle shot, severe damage would be done where ever it hit. So-called "conservative" measures were actually not conservative but radical, because impaired circulation and infection led not only to amputation but also to fevers, suppuration, and death. I painfully had to explain all this to Captain Dwight Woodruff before performing his amputation. Nevertheless, he died a few weeks later of blood loss and general debility. Would this tragedy never play itself out and end?

Sensing the gradual encroachment on their Richmond-Petersburg line, the rebels attacked all along the line two days later. The two great armies inflicted heavy casualties on each other, with the Confederate forces eventually withdrawing back to their defensive perimeters. Heavy rains and swollen streams added to our misery caused by the tenacious mud and inability to ever get ourselves and our equipment dry. The Sixth was now advancing to take up positions to the rear of Petersburg. The heavy mud not only delayed our heavy armament and field equipment from moving up, but it also proved to be a great hindrance to ambulances and transport of our medical tents and equipment. One of my chronic problems was the difficulty of where to set up our medical care area. This was of concern because there was a constant trickle of casualties coming in as we proceeded across this battle line.

Having arrived at our destination, the problem of setting up our tents was discussed at our small staff meeting. We deemed it inadvisable to set up tents because they seemed to serve as a magnet drawing enemy fire. Our veteran troops of the Sixth taught the newer members the advantages of digging fortifications into the ground. These "zig-zags" were dug in front of the fortifications long ago at Fort Wagner and saved many soldiers from rebel fire. The troops called these small redoubts "rat-holes." It seemed they had either a shovel or a rifle in their hand at all times. The entire line of General Grant's Army confronting Petersburg dug in this fashion. The holes were shallow enough to allow rapid evacuation and yet deep enough to afford protection from enemy musketry. I had a fairly fancy dugout made for myself but it still collected water.

It was difficult if not impossible to keep my journal up to date. Whenever I had a chance, I tried to write down what had happened in the recent past. Problems arose because my "rat hole" was so damp that I had to dry out the pages before I could even write on them. I was glad I left my past journal writings at home when on leave three months ago. The heat, insects, early "lights out" bugle calls, as well as my evening rounds on our casualty tents, all seemed to frustrate my attempts to record all these actions.

Throughout the hot summer of 1864 in Virginia, the battle lines seethed back and forth, with no obvious victor on either side. We had no permanent positions to fall back to and lived pretty much in the open. Our commanders keep probing the rebel defense line between Petersburg and Richmond, but with no notable success.

# CHAPTER TWENTY-FIVE:

# *Success and Sadness*

One dramatic change from our daily skirmishing occurred at a place called Deep Run. General Terry again showed his military brilliance by developing plans for a surprise attack on the enemy. I was posted far enough forward, with the medical staff, that I could perceive how this battle plan developed. Heavily supported skirmish lines moved silently and secretly through the woods until, at a certain point, bugles sounded and General Terry gave the command to attack. As I attended to some of my wounded, I learned that this attack carried our forces across a huge abatis that would otherwise have been an insurmountable problem.

Despite heavy enemy fire, our troops sprang upon them in their rifle pits and forced them to withdraw a considerable distance. Having destroyed a good bit of their defenses, and taken many prisoners, our forces withdrew to regroup again. I was sorry to see a close companion of mine, Captain Woodruff, had had his upper arm shattered in the attack. Reluctantly, and with his full understanding, I had to get out the surgical equipment and bone saw to remove this arm. I was saddened even further to learn that a few weeks later his injuries led to his death. Captains Bennett Lewis and John Slottlar were also wounded, as were Lieutenants John Waters, Joseph Miller, and George Bellows. It was surprising to me that the injuries and fatalities were not greater in number, in view of the hand-to-hand combat and the heavy hail of bullets flying through the trees in front of the enemy's position.

On August 15th, I followed closely behind the troops (with some of my medical personnel and equipment). As the sun went down, the heat lessened but the insects worsened. However the hornets nest we walked into was man made! Their howitzers and musketry were well entrenched, but we needed to move on toward our Petersburg goal. The action seethed back and forth over his redoubt, ultimately in our favor.

We suffered losses of five killed, sixty-nine wounded and also eleven missing. The troops learned what it meant to "put your shoulders to the wheel" because of our often struck artillery and supply trains. I had to find a suitable area in this "rat hole" covered terrain for my medical tents and personnel.

I received Special Order Number Thirty-eight which showed interest by our leaders to have medical officers further forward in the picket lines. Delivered from Headquarters, First Division, Tenth Army Corps in the field near Curtis, Virginia by order of Brigadier General Alfred Terry, signed Adrian Terry, and dated June 10, 1864, it read as follows: "In the event of any engagement in which the command shall participate, the medical officers named below will immediately report at the division hospital for duty as follows. [A large list of doctors followed, including myself.] One-half of the hospital attendants of each regiment of this command will also report at division hospital in this event.

"The brigades of this command will successively furnish one medical officer for duty in the picket line commencing this day with the First Brigade. The others following in the order of their numbers. This officer will be stationed at the headquarters of the picket under the orders of the general officer of the day and will be the only medical officer with the picket."

> *6th Reg't Conn Vols*
> *1st Div 10th A.C.*
> *"Army of the James"*
> *Sept 19th 1864*

*My Dear Sister*

*I now seat myself at this late hour of night to answer your welcome letter which was received on the battlefield of "Deep Run" and read with much interest as do all letters from my friends which (letters) "like angels visits are few and far between."*

*Suffer the apologies of the severity and activity of this campaign to plead for my delinquencies and I will spend my time and paper in scribbling what I fear will be uninteresting to you. Here I am in the habit of pouring forth my griefs and abuses I might fill this sheet and many others and among other complaints stand prominent that of no letters from my friends. I do not mean you for you have always been good to answer my letters even more prompt than myself.*

*Well, I suppose they think if perchance some stray ball should be stopped by me an official notice of my "Requiescat in pace" would be duly given and until that does occur, there is no necessity of writing.*

*Well I know I am nothing but a Soldier, a mere thing "pro tem" which in short is of little account as one draft furnishes a great many—but then it is to me a satisfaction to know I am thought of at all and besides my love for that once dear home which I left two years ago to peril life, health, and if need be everything is not all gone, although my dear mother is no longer there to make it home.*

*When I shall again return to it I know not, sometimes I think never—if my life is required for my country, I yield it without a murmur trusting that "the God of Mercies" will fold the arms of his love and protection around me. Many many have fallen in this campaign, and many more must fall before the war ends. Sometimes I feel all worn out—a few days ago I had an attack of "Erysipelas" so I could not open one eye, but that now has left me.*

*Today there has been active cannonading—no harm done. Two shots went over my tent, and the last I saw of them they were going towards Wilmington NC. I afterwards learned that they did not reach there but halted some ways this side. Musket balls are whistling over me every little while. That is what I want to have them do—go over. But I must close, hoping you will answer soon I subscribe myself*
    *Your Aff. brother*
    *Myron*
    *P.S. Many thanks for Will's "photo."*

The end of the war seemed tantalizingly near, yet the casualties of Cold Harbor and our battles at Chapin's Farm in September, 1864 and on the New Market and Derbytown and Charles City Roads in October kept me from any early optimism. Still another winter loomed before me and, despite the many rumors of armistice, nothing happened. General Grant had proven his tenacity, but what a price in blood!

The nights were becoming a little cooler, (although the days remained hot) as September came along. I was happy to have more time to inventory supplies, to train my personnel, and to review government regulations regarding battle care.

I came to feel that I would give anything to be able to rest up, bathe, and get a good meal. Shelling day and night served its purpose of worsening the morale and disposition of our soldiers. Sick call revealed many anxiety problems attested to by the pale and haggard appearance of the soldiers. At this time Colonel Redfield Duryea resigned, claiming ill health. Indeed he had appealed to me several times to advise him on his recurrent intestinal infection problems. Weight loss and poor appetite, as well as depression, all seemed to be weighing on him. I believe he sensed the lack of confidence his men felt in him, and this was still another factor leading to his decision to retire. My good friend, Colonel Rockwell, of the First Connecticut Battery was named in his place. The troops knew of his steadfastness in battle and his dedication to our Connecticut soldiers. It certainly met with my personal approval.

    *Hd-Qrs Sixth Conn. Vols*
    *In the field December 20th, 1864*

*Dear Father:*

*It is now Sunday night and I will try to answer your kind letter which was received yesterday morning.*

*I had received a letter from Theron a day or two before announcing the death of Orville which was so sudden and unexpected. It was not such news as I was prepared to receive.*

*Oh! how altered will be my home when I return from the war. I cannot realize that Death has visited the family circle since I was there and taken such a much loved brother and mother from thence. But it is so, and no one knows who's turn will come next. I sometimes feel as though I have seen home for the last time but I need not feel so, it is only when I get lonely. I have enjoyed very good health of late except an occasional ill day.*

*Wednesday night I will send this the first opportunity I have. We are expecting an attack today. My love to all. In haste*

*Your Aff Son*
*Myron W. Robinson*
*Surgeon 6th Conn Vols*
*1st Div 24th A.C., Va.*

### *Historical Note*

Electioneering was actually carried out in the military camps during the fall of 1864, especially by some "Copperheads." The election was between Lincoln and McClellan. There was a difference between the states as to which soldiers were allowed to vote and which soldiers were not allowed to vote. In Indiana, the soldier was not allowed to vote in the field, however a form was developed allowing for New York soldiers and many others to vote in their army camps. Many in the north favored the "Copperheads." This was more of a peace party, which felt that the war had gone on long enough and that there was little to gain from further loss of life. Furthermore, they were not so sure that the emancipation of Negroes was all that urgent at this time.

I received letters from some of the mustered-out troops expressing gratitude toward me and thankfulness for being out of the terrible war. They also wrote about the fine reception they received on arrival in New York, on board the steamer United States.

A parade down Canal Street to Broadway greeted them followed by banquets; this happened again later on in New Haven. They arrived in New Haven aboard the *Nassau* and were surprised by a large fireworks display as they pulled into the dock that they had left years earlier.

\* \* \*

For them it had been a long and dreadful three years, but on September 13, 1864 they were mustered out. In my heart I was quite happy for them, but I still felt a degree of despair wondering when I myself would again see the Connecticut shores. The leaves were turning and some falling and drifting with the colder fall winds. The war stagnated into limited cannon duels and picket duty.

It is difficult if not impossible to keep my journal up to date. Whenever I have a chance, I try to write down what has happend in the recent past. My problems occur because my "rat hole" has been damp (and even wet) to the degree that I have to dry out pages of my journal before I can even write on them. I am glad I left my past journal writings at home when on leave three months ago. The heat, insects, early "lights out" bugle calls, as well as my evening rounds on our casualty tents all seem to frustrate my attempts to record all these actions.

The Sixth had solidified its position outside Petersburg. We were fighting on the north end of the siege line and were rewarded with the sight of the spires of Richmond in the distance. I presumed that General Lee sensed not only the symbolic effect over the possible loss of Richmond, but also the loss of his own home and wife, as both were in the city. He dispatched troops from Petersburg to relieve pressure on Richmond.

Nearby Fort Harrison was of some tactical importance and was finally taken. I went over to help the doctors with the Seventh and Tenth Connecticut because they had received very heavy casualties. Our troops had lived under deplorable conditions for seven months without tents or overcoats for most of the men. As if things weren't bad enough, on October 7 a widespread general attack was made on the Tenth Corps. The Sixth was in the forefront. Fortunately we were taking only a few injuries and the rebels were receiving very heavy losses (despite having the advantage of the terrain). They ultimately gave up the assault near the earthworks called Chapin's Farm. It was at this spot that the letter of promotion came to me and at least this did lighten my spirits—I became an assistant surgeon in the regular army.

Winter is now approaching as 1864 draws to a close and the war drags on. Troops from Pennsylvania informed us how well the small wooden huts set up long ago by our revolutionary forces at Valley Forge had stood up. These existed long after that war was over. The huts we built kept the troops warm and improved morale unbelievably. The only thing I noticed that lowered morale was the fact that there was still a lack of support for our cause by our northern citizens. Added to this was the loss of sense of unity of the fighting unit because of reorganization and resignations. Enduring all of these hardships of the elements and privation combined with continuous exposure to a possibly horrible death led to a great sense of camaraderie, which now might be lost. It was hard for me to always cheer up the troops, when many times I did not feel at all well myself. My promotion was one occurrence that did indeed brighten my outlook.

# CHAPTER TWENTY-SIX:

# *The Final Assault—Fort Fisher*

*In the field*
*December 20th, 1864*

*Dear father:*

*It is now Sunday night and I will try to answer your kind letter which was received yesterday morning.*

*I had receivd a letter from Theron a day or two before announcing the death of Orvill which was so sudden and unexpected. It was not such news as I was prepared to receive.*

*Oh! how altered will be my home when I return from the war. I cannot realize that Death has visited the family circle since I was there and taken such a much loved brother and mother from thence. But it is so, and no one knows who's turn will come next. I somtimes feel as though I have seen home for the last time but I need not feel so, it is only when I get lonely. I have enjoyed very good health of late except an occasional ill day.*

*Wednesday night I wil send this the first opportunity I have. We are expecting an attack today. My love to all. In haste*

*Your Aff Son*
*Myron W. Robinson*
*Surgen 6th Conn Vols*
*1st Div 24th A.C., Va.*

Orders arrived to strike tents and move the entire regiment to the Cape Fear and Wilmington area.

The main Confederate army was now bottled up in the siege line between Petersburg and Richmond. While we had thus far not broken through to these towns, the Confederates remained pinned down and low in supplies in this defense.

Perhaps because of our good record in oceanside and amphibious campaigns, we were included in plans to leave this stalemated position and move east in attempts to take Fort Fisher and Wilmington, N.C.

It was well known that Wilmington, on the Cape Fear River, was the last remaining port by which the Confederacy could gain its needful supplies; we knew it must be taken and closed. The Sixth had already seen so much action and received such severe losses, I wondered why it couldn't be somebody else this time. General Grant had ordered the denial of this port since he strongly felt that the Confederacy would wither and die on the vine with the closure of this last artery of supplies. Our wagon trains and transports moved us off to the east in preparation for the struggle. I had concerns regarding health matters because of the history of many deaths from Yellow Fever, which indeed wiped out some areas of Wilmington entirely.

It is now early on a dark and cold December morning and the sound of the "Longroll" indicated developments are underway for us to move still again to another field of battle. Since it was well known that Wilmington, on the Cape Fear River, was the last remaining port through which the Confederacy could gain its needful supplies we knew it must be taken and closed. The Sixth had already seen so much action and received such severe losses, I wondered why it couldn't be somebody else this time. General Grant ordered the denial of this port since he strongly felt that the Confederacy would wither and die on wagon trains and transports moved us off to the east in preparation for the struggle. I had concerns regarding health matters because of the history of Yellow Fever which had indeed overwhelmed several areas of Wilmington.

After being relieved from the siege line outside Petersburg, we went into camp at Samuel Hill. On the January 3 we struck camp and marched twelve miles to Bermuda Hundred. We set up our tents about a half mile from the landing. It snowed nearly all night and then cleared off. Despite being cold, the men were all in good spirits. The snow was so heavy that upon awakening in the morning hardly any light could filter through the tent cloth itself. We remained in camp all day on Wednesday, January 4, and we started for the landing at three o'clock in the morning on January 5. We embarked on a smaller boat and then disembarked. Later in the day we embarked on the *Manhattan*. We arrived at Hampton Roads at half past nine at night and cast anchor. Nineteen days' rations were distributed.

### *Historical Note*

The strategy of pinning down Lee's army and blockading ports of entry for the needed war materiel was paying off. While a few Caribbean ports remained open, all of the Atlantic ports of entry had been effectively blockaded with the exception of Wilmington, North Carolina. Blockade running had shifted to Wilmington following the battles at Fort Wagner and the ever-present blockading fleet offshore. Wilmington had a railroad and two widely separated passages from the ocean to the Cape Fear River. This caused the Union blockading boats to split their forces to cover such entrances.

Wilmington itself was by then not a very desirable town. It had been ravaged by yellow fever brought to it earlier by the blockade runners. Some attempts at quarantine had proved of only small value. The staid citizens of Wilmington had largely moved out some time before as it became a notorious, rough seacoast town. The main defense of Wilmington was Fort Fisher on a peninsula at the very northern approach to the harbor. The defenses there were very elaborate, having been built by General Whiting (first in his class at West Point). Prior to this construction job, he had served at the first battle of Bull Run and also under Stonewall Jackson in the "Seven Days Battle." With his great engineering skills, by 1863 he had developed extensive batteries. These were commanded by Whiting and they kept the Union fleet from entering the river, at the same time giving covering fire for the blockade runners. By April of 1862, the only real Confederate cargo vessels were the *Gladiator* and the previously mentioned *Fingal*. The latter was later converted to the ironclad *Alabama*, which had remarkable success against the Union fleet. Newspaper accounts told of it "shooting its way" through the Union blockade fleet. For some time thereafter it sank other Union ships and was a most successful blockade runner. Later, it met up with the U.S.S. *Kearsarge* in a French port. It seemingly won this battle when one of its shells lodged in the steering mechanism of the *Kearsarge*. Having been at sea for some time, however, it was said that the fuse did not work. After this, the *Kearsarge* returned fire and sent the *Alabama* to the bottom.

A plan was approved by the Union leaders to take Fort Fisher with limited loss of Union lives. This was to be done by loading the Louisiana with a large amount of TNT. This was to be towed close to Fort Fisher and exploded. It was hoped this would demolish the fortifications and allow its capture. General Lee was said to have felt that if Fort Fisher fell, he would have to quit and the Confederacy would no longer endure.

The Confederacy imported at least four hundred thousand rifles or more through these ports. This was more than 60 percent of the Confederates' modern arms. Three million pounds of lead came through the blockade, one-half of the army's need. Saltpeter in large amounts, food, clothing, paper, and medicine all were supplied by these blockade runners.

In January, 1865, an earsplitting bombardment from our ships offshore, followed by sweeping infantry movement down the peninsula, with some aid from marines from the other side of Fort Fisher, took the fort.

\* \* \*

Despite the cold weather and the frozen wheel tracks in the mud, we were able to move our ambulances along with our supply trains successfully from the Petersburg area to the east, where we embarked for the Fort Fisher campaign. Even before our arrival, we could hear cannons being discharged in a "curtain raising" to this, our next battle. Although the placement of Fort Fisher was excellent for the purpose of guarding the entrance to the Cape Fear River, it looked to be a bad place to be in if the land behind you was not controlled by friendly forces. We had a large number of seasoned troops and we encamped at the north end of this peninsula to await further orders, which were not long in coming.

General Butler had proven himself to be less than desirable as a commanding officer. He seemed happy to remain bottled up in Bermuda Hundred, and his mismanagement led to a great lack of confidence and lower morale in his own troops. President Lincoln rapidly approved General Grant's dismissal of Butler from his command. Butler had earlier made an unexplained withdrawal from Fort Fisher. As explained elsewhere, the Louisiana explosion was aimed at destroying Fort Fisher, but with this failure Butler showed little inclination to proceed with any attack. Stanton, as secretary of war, also approved his dismissal because his bluster and lack of military ability led to the poor performance of his troops.

He was replaced by General Terry, a thirty-seven year old former clerk of the New Haven superior court. He was admitted to the bar while still a student at Yale. He gained experience at the first battle of Bull Run and also at the Port Royal, Fort Pulaski and Charleston campaigns. He was a great favorite of the troops and rapidly restored their morale. My records show that Alfred H. Terry of New Haven had been colonel with Joseph R. Hawley, of Hartford, who had been captain of Rifle Company A of the first Regiment, as lieutenant colonel and George F. Gardiner of New Haven as major. The regiment, 1,018 strong, was moved early in September 1861 to the campgrounds at the Cedars. On September 17, 1861, the regiment was mustered into the U.S. service and the next day started for Washington, D.C., where it was brigaded with the Sixth and Third Connecticut and Seventh New Hampshire Regiments under the command of Brigadier General Horatio G. Wright.

Ironically, General Butler was still in Washington explaining away his inability to take Fort Fisher (the thick walls and the failure of Porter's fleet made his attack impossible, he stated). Amid his speeches and complaints, the news of Fort Fisher's fall came.

Sixty warships under Admiral Porter moved out from Beaufort and up the coast to Wilmington on January 12, 1865. This all-out effort was intended to seal off the Cape Fear River from the blockade runners, and hopefully hasten the end of the war.

Porter opened fire on the fort at close range with several of his ironclads. This had the purpose of drawing their fire; he was able to discover by the muzzle flashes the location of the rebel cannons. By Friday, January 13, less than one hundred defenders were manning the guns and less than one-half of the guns on the seaward side were in operation. No reinforcements would come because General Grant's swing up north eliminated such a possibility; General Bragg had to leave the fort to fend for itself.

Nonetheless some reinforcements (a brigade of South Carolinians) came down the Cape Fear river on orders of General Bragg. This force met heavy shelling from the Union boats that saw what was being attempted. They were very tired and demoralized and only one-third made it to the fort. At dawn the flotilla blazed away again, but until this time no troop threat was included.

Porter and Terry drew up well-coordinated plans for a combined ground and naval assault on board the ship Malvern. The heavy bombardment was to stop at three in the afternoon, when the ground assault would begin. They well understood that the cessation of the bombardment would also be interpreted by the rebels as the time to come out of their splinter proofs to meet the assault.

On Friday, January sixth, it was rainy and windy all day and we lay off Hampton Roads at anchor. On Saturday we sailed to Norfolk in the morning. We embarked on board the transport California under Captain Christopher Godfrey, of Providence, Rhode Island. We sailed at 2:00 P.M. and we opened our orders outside Cape Henry. We were ordered to join the fleet outside Beaufort, N.C. We passed Cape Hatteras at four o'clock in the morning and arrived off Beaufort, N.C. at half past two in the afternoon having made very good time despite a rough sea. I was very seasick.

Rough seas persisted all through Monday, the ninth, with myself and a large number of the troops experiencing great seasick problems. I was definitely convinced that life on the ocean was not the life for me. On Wednesday, the wind had shifted to the west with heavy thunder showers. This blew off from the shore and we commenced running in shore at one o'clock in the morning. We arrived off Beaufort at ten o'clock in the morning and seasickness problems diminished for all.

Thursday the twelfth was clear and pleasant. We arrived at Federal Point lighthouse about ten o'clock at night. The weather was fair with a gentle breeze. On Friday, we landed about ten o'clock in the morning, about four miles above Fort Fisher, N.C. with very heavy naval bombardment going on. Four men of the regiment deserted to the rebels at night. One man was killed. The surf remained very high when we landed. We bivouacked by Half-moon Battery. Unlike Fort Wagner, at least there was no easy way for the rebels to reinforce Fort Fisher. This was because it was at the south end of the peninsula guarding the entrance to the Cape Fear River. We were ever so slowly coming down this peninsula and were certainly planning to take this fort in the near future. On Saturday we remained in the same position until sunset and after we spiked the guns in the battery and burned their carriages and magazine, we moved down the beach still further a half mile and bivouacked again.

A prolonged and heavy bombardment from just offshore was deafening. The accuracy of these cannoneers was to be congratulated with the demolition of major parts of Fort Fisher. Admiral Porter and his 73 vessels had 655 guns available, but once the bombardment was over, the rebels resumed their defensive positions on the parapets. The soldiers of the Sixth moved down across the sand dunes and rushed the parapet. I had a sudden nightmarish feeling when I thought of that other attack across the sand in the dark assault of July 18, 1863, on Fort Wagner.

General Terry was well known to our unit and we had great affection for him, his Connecticut background, and his past campaigns. As our troops swept forward our hopes and prayers were aimed at the goal of taking this last supply port in order to bring an end to this ordeal. It seemed to me that this had mostly been a war chiefly to defeat, capture, or kill enemy armies rather than to gain or keep territories. Nonetheless, taking strategic strongholds such as Fort Fisher was obviously necessary. Amphibious assaults had become almost second nature for our troops but I felt sorry for them as the eight thousand men splashed through the cold January surf toward the fort. They had three days' rations and sixty rounds of ammunition each.

Finally the cannonading stopped and an awesome silence took over. Our troops rapidly moved along the beach, at first without any interference. As the rebels sensed the artillery barrage from Admiral Porter's fleet being lifted, they took up their position in the parapets to begin firing upon us. About two thousand navy and marine troops were landed along the shore and came along the beach area, while we stayed along the western edge of the peninsula as we moved toward the fort. From the positions of their guns and parapets, heavy losses were inflicted on the marine forces on the beach and close hand-to-hand fighting took place with ultimately our boys prevailing.

I cringed to see the row upon row of the advancing Marines being mowed down on the other side of the fort by the rebel firing, which became heavy now that the cannonading had ended. General Terry called upon Abbots Brigade with the old Sixth and Seventh Regiment, who finally completed this assault. My corpsmen stood by in small boats and we first took care of the wounded on shipboard. The rebels fell back and a great victory cheer signaled the end of hostilities on the evening of January 14, 1865.

I set up our tents and got busy rapidly with all the surgical care. I was happy we didn't carry out our initial plan to move into the fort itself, as later that night, a tremendous explosion shook the fort and added many more to our casualty list. It was later told me that some drunken troops of ours were searching through the fort with a torch. Whether they were looking for places to lie down or looking for loot or more liquor, it made no difference since they wandered into the main powder magazine with a torch that blew up themselves and their friends along with a large portion of the fort.

There were 139 killed and wounded and I immediately started working at the field hospital. I worked all day on the tragic soldiers from this event. I worked day and night on through Tuesday and Wednesday. Most of the casualties were evacuated, many by sea. I took this occasion to visit Fort Fisher in the forenoon and at Battery Buchanan I got a piece of the shattered flagstaff. I worked all afternoon at the hospital and heavy rain began at night.

A good part of the wounded were transferred to other hospitals. Heavy surf and rainy weather did not prevent the capture of two blockade runners. This was done by sending false signals at night. Saturday was dreary and cold, however Sunday morning the weather cleared and I attended church in the morning. In the afternoon I visited the U.S. Navy boat *Lasco* in the Cape Fear River and that night saw my dear old friend, Dr. K. H. Bancroft, who was an assistant surgeon in the U.S. Navy. I had not seen him for at least three years. I had a good time on board and returned at night in a dugout. On Monday, I visited a rebel hospital and met Mr. Taylor and delivered packages. There had been no mail for me as yet and I worked writing some letters myself. On Tuesday the twenty-fourth, I again visited Fort Fisher and Battery Buchanan. I was in camp with a Mr. Penfield, and we did an inspection of the fortifications of these places. Fort Fisher mounted forty-five guns and two mortars. Three guns had been disabled by our heavy bombardment. Battery Buchanan had four pivot guns and one brass howitzer.

I remained in camp all the next day, where a survey met and relieved me of the responsibility of medicines and medical equipment that had been lost and/or destroyed in our recent campaigns. The Pannier board consisted of Captain Marvel of the Seventieth Corps, Lt. Blakeslee of the Sixth Connecticut Volunteers and Bingham of the Thirty-second. I saved some of the papers related to this, since it seemed ridiculous that so much time and effort was spent in locating and trying to fix responsibility for the loss of such items. I was only surprised that more was not lost in the various amphibious assaults and the many disrupted wagon trains that we had to endure. On Thursday, I went to headquarters and obtained medicines, panniers, and other needed supplies. I wrote later in the evening to T. R.* in Norwich. The weather remained cold and wintry and some letter writing was done. I could hear gunboats firing on the ocean side. On Sunday, no religious services were held, although I remained in camp. I also remained in camp Monday; there was reconnaissance by our colored division.

Some rebel forces retreated toward Wilmington, and orders sent us up the northeast branch of the Cape Fear River in order to subdue them and take Wilmington. Fort Fisher was eliminated as a guardian of the Cape Fear River and its important port of Wilmington. The last Atlantic supply port for the Confederacy was now sealed, as was the fate of the Confederacy.

* T. R. refers to his brother Theron Robinson born 2/13/1835

[Letter to Miss Julia Abell, Colchester, CT. Postmarked Feb. 24, 1865, and with old three cent stamp.]

*Before Wilmington, N.C.*
*Feb 16th, 1865*

*My dear niece:*

*Shall I tell you how and when I received your letter? Last Sunday morning as I was lying in the sand on a massive beach between a small lake and the wide ocean (without any fire—without any tent) away down on the coast of North Carolina, I heard one say there was mail. So I went over to Hd Qrs by a big sand heap and they were sorting mail on a rubber blanket. I think there were 8 or 9 bags. I received my usual number of letters and among them was one from the "The Old House On The Corner" which it gave me great pleasure to peruse.*

*It had been months since I had heard from them and I had almost thought that sometimes they had forgotten that I was in the Army or where I was.*

*I wish you could see the place where I am now writing, the tide washes up nearly to the door of my tent. If it should rise two feet higher than it does it would go over our camp into the lake behind.*

*You have read of the capture of Fort Fisher and all about it so I will not say anything about it only that I was there and saw the whole and participated in a part and will tell you all about it when I see you. I will send you a perfect pic-*

*ture of the "Armstrong Gun" and some powder that was taken out of it. Also a leaf of "Ivy" from Smithville, near Fort Coswell.*

*I must close now to attend to other affairs. My health now is pretty good. I had been quite sick since the fight at Fort Fisher. I see Capt't Bill sometimes, he was well when I saw him last week. Give my love to all and write soon. I expect to go to Wilmington soon and hope then I shall have a better place to write.*

*From your Uncle Myron*
*Direct M.W.Robinson*
*Surgeon 6th C.V. Abbott Brigade*
*Fort Fisher, N.C.*

A pleasant break from this monotonous routine and weather occurred on February 1. I received a visit from Dr. Bancroft and Mr. Talbert, the chief engineer on board the *Lasco.* I had a great time and I walked down to the wharf with them afterwards. I remained sick for the next several days and at least had time to write up some of these notes, despite not feeling well. The usual chronic cough was only worsened by a large boil on my neck which was ultimately attended to. Dr. Kimball drew instruments for me from the operating case and teeth extracting instruments.

On Wednesday the 8th, despite still being sick, marching orders arrived. On February 9, there was some slight improvement in the weather. I drew medicines on a special requisition and also noted that Col. A. P. Rockwell was mustered out of service. Happily our marching orders were revoked.

# CHAPTER TWENTY-SEVEN:

# *Fort Fisher to Wilmington N.C.*

Despite the fact that we had successfully taken Fort Fisher as of mid January, there was still resistance that prevented us from taking our intended goal of Wilmington, N.C. I made out the weekly report on Friday, February 10. Marching orders showed us to be ready at six o'clock in the morning. I drew two stretchers and commenced the march upon the beach. This was begun about 9 A.M, with the attack at the same time on the left. The Second New Hampshire went out as skirmishers and captured fifty-two rebel pickets near Half-moon Battery. The loss was only ten or twelve wounded. We moved back and bivouacked on the beach and it was quite cold.

The next day was Sunday and we found ourselves entrenched between the lagoon and the ocean. This narrow and sandy spot housed three companies on picket duty. Our division of Schofields marched up the beach at night because they were searching for Mystic Sound (not found) and they returned.

On Tuesday the fourteenth, Butler was removed, and the Ames division marched up the beach at night with pontoons but returned. Marching orders ordered us to take three days' rations, all the ammunition that the men could carry, and all the forage that the horses could carry, and to be ready at sunrise. It commenced raining early at night. On Wednesday the fifteenth, the marching orders were revoked early in the day. It was raining hard and with heavy wind coming in from the southeast from the sea, although it cleared up at about eleven o'clock in the morning. A ration of whiskey was issued for the soldiers on the picket line (about two hundred were on the picket line). If the weather were only better this might have been almost pleasant duty.

On Thursday it was indeed nice weather and we had a regimental inspection. Fortunately the weather continued pleasant and convalescents came to us from

Virginia, with camp and garrison equipage. Despite our peaceful camp setting, firing could be heard on the left from the Cape Fear River. Although no definite pitched battle occurred, our gunboats beyond the river were firing at Fort Anderson. Also some picket line firing was heard. To my surprise it was noted that five men of the Sixth joined the Confederacy from our picket line. On Sunday we had no time for religious services as we continued our march on Wilmington about eight o'clock in the morning. This was clear and pleasant weather and Fort Anderson was taken from the Confederates as they evacuated from our front. Finding nothing to oppose our march, we made good progress and stayed all night nearby. I was fortunate enough to stay in the house of a Mr. Janto. I slept in a bed for the first time in a long time.

Our regiment was on picket duty about fifteen miles from Fort Fisher. On Monday we started at about half past eleven in the morning. In the advance, we seized the house of Mr. Thomas Craig, and moved by the flank on to the telegraph road. We bivouacked in a pine clearing four miles from Wilmington, as we were in reserve. This was a very cold and frosty night, however.

On Tuesday, we moved up to the breastworks thrown up by the Second Ames division. We sent back the horse taken yesterday. I noted dense black smoke on our front; it was about three miles to Wilmington.

Wednesday, February twenty-second, was a happy and jubilant day for us. We commenced our march at about eight in the morning and marched through Wilmington, with colors flying and bands playing. We chased the rebels to the northeast, ten miles from Wilmington. We had a fight at the pontoon bridge. They were trying to destroy it but were not successful, but ten of our men were wounded. This required some of my attention but most would be ready for duty again in the near future.

On Thursday the twenty-third, I was ordered back to the hospital in the field. I removed all the wounded and was able to join my regiment. Since there was no major rebel force, I took the adventure of going out with a scouting party three miles to the front, where I found the rebel cavalry pickets. We exchanged a few shots and we returned. The next day was Saturday, and again it was raining. I went out to forage with Bob Connell, but we got lost in a swamp. We ultimately decided that we would stay in close to the Wilmington area and be prepared for working in the hospital in that area. In this way we could attend to the sick and wounded from both sides.

# CHAPTER TWENTY-EIGHT:

# *The Heroine of Confederate Point*

**\*Historical Note\***

A viewpoint from the Confederate side is noted in The Southern Historical Papers, R. A. Brock, Esq., Editor, Richmond, Virginia:

The Heroine of Confederate Point
An Interesting Contemporaneous Account Of The Heroic Defense Of Fort Fisher, December 24th and 25th, 1864. By The Wife Of The Commandant, Colonel William Lamb.

(The patriotism and fortitude which animated and sustained the young matron, whose touching letter is here given, and is universally admitted, a typical exemplification of the Southern woman in the late war between the states.—Ed.)

In the fall of 1857 a lovely Puritan maiden, still in her teens, was married in Grace Church, Providence, Rhode Island, to a Virginia youth, just passed his majority, who brought her to his home in Norfolk, a typical ancestral homestead, where besides the "white folks" there was quite a colony of family servants, from the pickaninny just able to crawl to the old gray-headed mammy who had nursed "olemassa." She soon became enamored of her surroundings and charmed with the devotion of her colored maid, whose sole duty it was to wait upon her young missis. When the John Brown raid burst upon the South and her husband was ordered to Harper's Ferry, there was not a more indignant matron in all Virginia, and when at last secession came, the South did not contain a more enthusiastic little rebel.

On the 15th of May, 1862, a few days after the surrender of Norfolk to the Federals, by her father-in-law, then mayor, amid the excitement attending a captured city, her son Willie was born. Cut off from her husband and subjected to the privations and annoyances incident to a subjugated community, her father insisted upon her coming with her children to his home in Providence; but, notwithstanding she was in a luxurious home, with all that parental love could do for her, she preferred to leave all these comforts to share with her husband the dangers and privations of the South. She vainly tried to persuade Stanton, secretary of war, to let her and her three children with a nurse return to the South; finally he consented to let her go by flag of truce to Washington, to City Point, but without a nurse, and as she was unable to manage three little ones, she left the youngest with his grandparents, and with the two others bravely set out for Dixie. The generous outfit of every description which was prepared for the journey and which was carried to the place of embarkation was ruthlessly cast aside by the inspectors on the wharf, and no tears or entreaties or offers of reward by parents availed to pass anything save a scanty supply of clothing and other necessaries. Arriving in the South, the brave young mother refused the proffer of a beautiful home in Wilmington, the occupancy of the grand old mansion at "Orton," on the Cape Fear river, but insisted upon taking up her abode with her children and their colored nurse in the upper room of a pilot's house, where they lived until the soldiers of the garrison built her a cottage one mile north of Fort Fisher on the Atlantic beach. In both of these homes she was occasionally exposed to the shot and shell fired from blockaders at belated blockade runners.

It was a quaint abode, constructed in most primitive style with three rooms around one big chimney, in which North Carolina pine knots supplied heat and light on winter nights. This cottage became historic and was famed for the frugal but tempting meals which its charming hostess would prepare for her distinguished guests.

At first the little Confederate was satisfied with pork and potatoes, corn bread and rye coffee, with sorghum sweetening, but after the blockade runners made her acquaintance, the impoverished storeroom was soon filled to overflowing, notwithstanding her heavy requisitions on it for the post hospital, the sick and wounded soldiers and sailors always being a subject of her tenderest solicitude, and often the hard-worked and poorly-fed colored hands blessed the little lady of the cottage for a tempting treat.

Full of stirring events were the two years passed in the cottage on Confederate Point. The drowning of Mrs. Rose Greenough, the famous Confederate spy, off Fort Fisher, and the finding of her body, which was tenderly cared for, and the rescue from the waves, half dead, of Professor Holcombe and his restoration, were incidents never to be forgotten. Her fox hunting with horse and hounds, the narrow escapes of friendly vessels, the fights over blockade runners driven ashore, the execution of deserters, and the loss of an infant son, whose little spirit went out with the tide one sad summer night, all contributed to the reality of this romantic life.

When Porter's fleet appeared off Fort Fisher, December, 1864, it was storm-bound for several days, and the little family with their household goods were sent across the river to "Orton," before Butler's powder-ship blew up. After the Christmas victory over Porter and Butler, the little heroine insisted on coming back to her cottage, although her husband had procured a home of refuge in Cumberland county. General Whiting protested against her running the risk, for on dark nights her husband could not leave the fort, but she said, "if the firing became too hot she would run behind the sand hills as she had done before," and come she would.

The fleet appeared unexpectedly on the night of the 12th of January, 1865. It was a dark night, and when the lights of the fleet were reported, her husband sent a courier to the cottage to instruct her to pack up quickly and be prepared to leave with the children and nurse as soon as he could come and bid them good bye. The garrison barge with a trusted crew was stationed at Craig's Landing, near the cottage. After midnight, when all necessary orders were given for the coming attack, the colonel mounted his horse and rode to the cottage, but all was dark and silent. He found that the message had been delivered, but his brave wife had been so undisturbed by the news that she had fallen asleep and no preparations for a retreat had been made. Precious hours had been lost, and as the fleet would soon be shelling the beach, and her husband have to return to the fort, he hurried them to the boat as soon as dressed, with only with what could be gathered up hastily, leaving dresses, toys and household articles, to fall into the hands of the foe. Among the articles left was a writing desk, with the following unfinished letter, which after many years has been returned. It is such a touching picture of those old Confederate days that consent has been given to its publication:

"The Cottage," January 9th, 1865

My Own Dear Parents:

I know you have been anxious enough about us all, knowing what a terrible bombardment we have had, but I am glad that I can relieve your mind on our behalf and tell you we are all safe and well, through a most merciful and kind providence. God was with us from the first, and our trust was so firm in him that I can truly say that both Will and I "feared no evil."

I stayed in my comfortable little home until the fleet appeared, when I packed up and went across the river to a large but empty house, of which I took possession; a terrible gale came on, which delayed the attack for several days, but Saturday it came at last in all its fury; I could see it plainly from where I was, I have very powerful glasses, and sat on a stile outdoors all day watching it—an awful but magnificent sight.

I kept up very bravely (for you know I am brave, and would, if I thought I could, whip Porter and Butler myself), until the last gun had ceased and it began to get dark and still. I was overcome at last and laid my head on the fence and cried for the first and last time during it all. I then got my carriage and rode to a fort nearby to learn the news, but my heart failed as I approached it, and I returned to the house and waited for a dispatch, which I received about 11 o'clock, saying all was well. I was quite touched with a little incident which occurred during the day; the little ones looked very grave and thoughtful; at last Dick came to me in the midst of the roaring and awful thundering and said:

"Mamma, I want to pray to God for my Papa." He knelt down and said his little earnest prayer; then jumped up, exclaiming and dancing about: "Oh, sister, I am so glad! I am so glad! Now God will keep care of my Papa."

The shelling was even more terrific on Sunday, and I, not knowing how long it might continue, concluded to go to Fayetteville, and started Sunday noon in a small steamer, with the sick and wounded to Wilmington, where I was obliged to stay for several days in great suspense, not able to get away, and not able to hear directly from Will, as the enemy had cut the wire-and a martyr to all kinds of rumors-one day heard that Will had lost a leg, etc., but I steadfastly made up my mind to give no credit to anything bad. At last, I heard again that we had driven our persecutors off, and I returned again to the place where I went first, and the next day Will came over for me and took me to the fort, which I rode all over on horse back, but we did not move over for nearly a week. The fort was strewn with missiles of all kind, it seemed a perfect miracle how any escaped, the immense works were literally skinned of their turf, but not injured in the slightest; not a bomb proof or a magazine—and there are more than one—touched; the magazine the enemy thought they had destroyed was only caisson; the men had very comfortable quarters in the fort, pretty little whitewashed houses—but the shells soon set fire to them, making a large fire and dense smoke, but the works are good for a dozen of sieges—plenty of everything; particularly plenty of the greatest essential—brave hearts. Our beloved General Whiting was present, but gave up the whole command to Will, to whom he now gives, as is due, the whole credit of building and defending his post, and has urged his promotion to brigadier-general, which will doubtless be received soon, though neither of us really care for it.

We expect the Armada again, and will give him a "warmer" reception next time. The fort, expecting a longer time of it, was reserving their heaviest fire for nearer quarters. Butler's "gallant troops" came right under one side of the fort, but our grape and canister soon drove them off, and "not" Porter's shell, which did not happen to be falling that way at the time; they left their traces sufficiently next morning.

The "gallant fellow" who stole the horse from the inside the fort was doubtless so scared he didn't know much where he was. The true statement of the thing is that, an officer, unauthorized by Will or the general, sent a courier outside the fort with a message to some troops outside, and soon after he left the fort was attacked and killed by a Yankee sharpshooter hidden under a bridge. The poor body fell and the horse was taken, and the flag spoken of in the same way was shot from the parapet and blew outside when it was taken. When any of them see the inside of the fort, they will never live to tell the tale.

Ah, mother! You all, at home peacefully, do not know the misery of being driven from home by a miserable, cruel enemy! Tis a sad sight to see the sick and aged turn out in the cold to seek a shelter. I cannot speak feelingly because of any experience myself as God is so good to us, and has so favored us with life, health, and means, and my dear, good husband has provided me a comfortable home in the interior where I can be safe.

Will was worried so much about you, dear mother, thinking you would be so anxious about us. He often exclaims when reading some of the lying accounts: "How that will worry Ma!"

How is my daring Willie? We do so want to see our boy. I think Will will have to send for him in the spring. Kiss the dear one dozen of times for his father and mother.

Though it was a very unpleasant Christmas to me, still the little ones enjoyed theirs. Will had imported a crowd of toys for them and they are as happy as possible with them.

I have not heard from my dear home since last August, and you can imagine how very anxious I am to hear, particularly of sister Ria. Is she with George? Do write me of all the dear one I love so much, how I would love to see you all , so much, and home!

* * *

An idea of the ridiculous amount of paper shuffling that went on in higher headquarters is provided in some of the following notations. This addressed to me at Bermuda Hundred in an August 5, 1864, circular: "All officers are hereby notified that the Eighth Corps order in relation to the purchase of whiskey will be strictly adhered to thereafter. Orders properly approved will be allowed in the quantity of one gallon each month. The whole monthly allowance may be drawn at one time. This is by order of Col. Joseph R. Hawley, signed by Lt. Louis Moore."

There were also the very detailed triplicate Form Number 186 entitled "Return of Medical and Hospital Property," from the U.S. Medical Department for the Treasury Department to be transmitted through the surgeon-general's office. These reports were extremely lengthy and were in triplicate to make my job even more complex. On September 24, 1865, from the Surgeon-General's office in Washington, reads as follows: "Sir, in order to effect the settlement of your return of medical and hospital property for the period ending December 31, 1863, you will please forward to this office all the invoices and receipts relating to the property drawn upon said return as received and issued by you as per memorandum." Signed, "your obedient servant by order of the Surgeon-General, John S. Billings, Assistant-Surgeon, U.S. Army." This was addressed to me as surgeon-general, Connecticut Sixth Volunteers, Headquarters New Haven, Connecticut.

On December 13, 1864, again from the surgeon-general's office, reads, "Upon examination of your medical and hospital property return for the six months ending June 30,1863, a large amount of properties found dropped as 'lost' or 'destroyed by unavoidable accident, worn out, unfit for use,' your attention is directed to army regulation (paragraph number 1029, 1030 and 1033) which provide the ways and means of accounting for such properties.

"A great number of returns similar to yours received at this office, and a large amount of property involved renders it necessary to enforce a strict compliance with regulations in the settlement of all such items.

"Your account therefore remains suspended in this office until you comply with the regulations cited above. Very respectfully yours, your obedient servant, W. C. Spencer."

I received many outlandish requests similar to the samples noted above. I took time away from my appropriate medical duties to attend to this group of unreasonable requests. I was heartened to ultimately receive vindication for this. My explanation was that in many transfers of our unit from several battle line positions, many amphibious assaults, and many night marches led to difficulty in accounting for all equipment as managed by many members of my team. In any case, I received special orders number 5, from the headquarters 2nd Div. 24th Army Corps, Wilmington, N.C., on June 23, 1865, (this extract being from the report of the Board of Survey in attending the loss of one medical pannier for which Surgeon Myron W. Robinson, Conn. Sixth C.V. was responsible); it was approved by Joseph C. Abbott, brevet brigadier general, and read as follows: "The Board of Survey is hereby appointed to assemble at headquarters 2nd Conn. Volunteers at 10:20 A.M. tomorrow, January 24th, to inquire into and report upon circumstances regarding the loss of one medical pannier, property of the U.S. for which Surgeon Myron W. Robinson, Sixth Conn. Volunteers, is responsible and to fix the responsibility for the lost pannier. Detail for the board, Capt. William L Marble, 7th Ct., First Lt. Charles J. Buckbee, 6th Ct., First Lt. George B Bingham of 3rd New Hampshire Vols., by order of Brevet Brigadier General J.C. Abbott."

After opening remarks the inquiry of the board stated, "Surgeon Myron W. Robinson, 6th Ct. Vol. being duly sworn that the pannier was lost on board the steamer "Californian" when it came to the place where he landed from said steamer. It was left with his luggage in his stateroom on board the steamer, that it was left by order of Col. Rockwell, Ct. 6th Vol., that a guard was posted to take care of the property so left and that he has not seen the pannier since. Officer Wooster of the Conn. Sixth Vol. being duly sworn, that the pannier was left on board the steamer "Californian" and that a guard of thirty was left on board to protect baggage belonging to said regiment and on the night of June 13th, baggage was transferred from the steamer "Californian" to the steamer "Hancock" thence to the steamer "Idaho." On the fourteenth of June it was transferred from the "Idaho" to the steamer "General Lion" and on the night of January 15th, from the "General Lion" to the steamer "Hancock," next to the steamer "McClellan." As the baggage of the Sixth Ct. Vol. with that of three other regiments on the steamer "McClellan," that on the 16th of June, the baggage was landed from the "McClellan" in the surf in small boats and sometimes during these changes the pannier was lost, great care and diligence being exercised to guard against such an occurrence.

The board, after due deliberation on the testimony, adduced that the pannier was unavoidably lost and that Surgeon Robinson was in no way responsible for the same. Signed by the appropriate officers of this board, especially William S. Marble, Capt. 7th Ct. Vol."

I bothered to list all this in my journal so that I could remember how ridiculous things became with these trivia while we were in an active battle scene and lives of men hung in the balance. Time could much better have been spent in care of equipment and supply of our troops rather than in these trivial matters.

In early April, 1865, we received glorious news! Richmond had fallen. The tall buildings and spires of Richmond were in sight of our Union troops in 1862, and again within the eyesight of our Connecticut Sixth only a few months before in December, 1864. Initially our leaders were impressed (and even depressed) over the formidable fortifications protecting Richmond. We hungered for news for just how this capture came about.

Excerpts from *The Civil War In Song and Story*
First American Flag over Richmond

The crowning event of the rebellion was undoubtedly the capture of Richmond by the Federal Forces. The most striking incident of this achievement was the re-establishment of the United States of America flag in the rebel capitol. A division of the 25th, and one of the 24th Corps composed the portion of the Army of the James, which lay on the extreme right of Grant's Army of investment, occupied positions within seven miles of the beleaguered Rebel stronghold.

The night of April 2nd and 3rd was one of intense anxiety and expectation in the army of the James. Throughout the previous day they could hear the tremendous roar of the terrible battle in which their comrades were engaged, far away across the river upon the extreme left and around Petersburg, and they knew that the next morning, early, they were to play their dangerous part by assaulting the rebel works in their front in order to capture Richmond itself.

About 2:00 A.M., April the 3rd, a Lt. dePyster, hearing tremendous explosions and seeing a vast blaze in the direction of Richmond, mounted the wooden signal tower, about seventy feet high, at Gen. Weitzel's headquarters, and reported that he could discern a great fire toward Richmond. Through the aid of a prisoner and a deserter, it was ascertained that indeed Richmond was being evacuated. The troops were overjoyed and at 6:00 A.M. they took the path toward Richmond, which was strewn with all kinds of abandoned munitions of war, and amid the roar of bursting shells which was terrific. On either side small red flags indicated the position of buried torpedoes between the two lines of abatis and Weitzel's immediate front. These warning indications the rebels had not had time to remove. This fortunate incident preserved many lives as the space was very narrow between the explosives.

The rebel defenses seemed almost impregnable. Every elevation along the wall was defended by fieldworks, and very strong forts. Two lines of abatis and three lines of rifle pits and earthworks, one within the other, defended every avenue of attack and point of advantage. The first and second lines were connected by regular lines of redans (a V-shaped outcropping on a fortification that allows muskets to be fired at an angle, thus increasing the field of fire and its effectiveness) and works—the third, near the city, and commanding it, disconnected. If our troops should have had carried the defenses by storm, the loss would have been fearful since the contest would have been constantly renewed, because the rebels, as fast as one line of defenses was occupied, would only have to fall back into another to recommence the butchery of the assailants under every advantage to themselves.

That flag was carried by Lt. dePyster, buckled to his saddle and had floated, in like triumph, over the Crescent City of the south, the first real flag hoisted over the rebel capitol. As it rose aloft, displayed itself, and steadily streamed out in the strong gale, which was filling the air with fiery flakes from the adjacent conflagration, it was hailed with deafening shouts by the redeemed populace, who swarmed the open space below and around.

The powers that be of the Confederacy must have seen the helplessness of their situation. Their port cities were denied them and their armies were completely checkmated and outnumbered. This war that was so unbelievably brutal was drawing to a close. Bulletins we received told us that Lee withdrew west from the Richmond area and surrendered at the house of a Mr. McLean, near Appomattox Courthouse. Ironically, the McLeans left the battle zone north (near Manassas) to avoid the destruction of the war and yet the final battles occurred on their doorstep.

A bulletin we received contained items of unusual interest to me regarding General Grant's kindly actions at Lee's surrender. He allowed the "farm boy" soldiers who had horses to keep them in order to get their spring planting underway. Also, his administrative staff worked all night printing "safe passage" papers for every Confederate soldier, thereby allowing them to cross Union lines safely on their return home. Lastly, he arranged for thousands of rations for these hungry, tattered, and often barefooted troops from the South. It was further reported that General Lee later told his troops that "I did the best I could for you" as he left the sad troops to head home on his horse, Traveler. Our own battle weary but victorious Union forces would now head home.

The "Old Sixth" moved to Goldsboro and then to Raleigh to muster out. Before they left, I shook hands and bid a well-meant farewell to this wonderful and gallant group of men. Nobody could put into words all the things they had gone through in these many years and more than a few glistening eyes were noted with the emotions of the separation. I myself felt heavy at heart upon separation from these men I'd known and lived with so closely during these past desperate and dangerous years. I could dispel this gloom only by thoughts of the victory now ours and by the thought that they would be returning to health and loved ones. Needless to say, I also deeply yearned to return to Connecticut and especially to see my lovely fiancé Emma.

# CHAPTER TWENTY-NINE:

# Sad Farewells, Then Hillhouse Hospital

I have never felt such mixed emotions as I felt when the last soldiers of the "Old Sixth" waved goodbye as I stood there on the railroad platform. The depression and sorrow that I felt was like a deaden coat weighing on me. I stood for a long time in the depot until the noise and smoke of the cars disappeared into the distance. My confusion as to which direction to take was caused by my knowledge of the great need for medical care for the soldiers of both the north and the south, and the needs of the local populace of Wilmington. I really wished that I could go home!

It is now early April, 1865 and even more glorious news comes our way. It is hard to believe, but the war is now over. Bulletins we receive tell us that Lee withdrew west from the Richmond area and surrendered at the house of a Mr. McLean, new Appomattox Courthouse.

The bulletin contained items of unusual interest to me regarding General Grants kindly actions at the surrender. He allowed the "farm boy" soldiers that had horses to keep them in order to get their spring planting underway. Secondly his administrative staff worked all night printing "safe passage" papers for every Confederate soldier thereby allowing them to cross Union lives safely on their return home. Lastly he arranged for thousands of rations for these hungry, tattered and often barefooted troops from the south. It was further reported that General Lee later told his troops that "I did the best I could for you" as he left the sad troops to head home on his horse "Traveler." I now believe our own battle weary but victorious Union forces will now head home.

Senior officers and higher echelon people in the military profession urged me to take a position at Hillhouse Hospital in Wilmington. I hoped that someone else might fill this position, but it was not to be. In my heart of hearts I knew I couldn't leave with so much to be done for the health care of these valiant troops from both sides. In Wilmington, I was given quarters in a very proper building on hospital grounds. Think of that ! I am actually going to live in a building with a floor, solid walls and a roof and, wonders of wonders, there is heat and even a bath.

Things did not come easy because a severe typhus epidemic broke out, which complicated all aspects of hospital care and supply. The job was overwhelming at first. I was given an extensive tour of the hospital building by the very small staff, many of whom would soon be departing for their homes—mostly to the South.

Several days and even weeks were spent in inventorying our supplies—at least we had supplies. A great shortcoming was the limited staff; assigning them to areas of the hospital, listing shift duties, and seeing how much help could be gotten from recovering soldiers took much time. Much of the staff was well experienced, having suffered through yellow fever outbreaks and the chronic flow of sick and injured from the Army of Northern Virginia and elsewhere. With a good spirit of cooperation, the war was put behind us and the medical needs supervened over all other considerations. However, I was forced to admit it would likely take several generations before the animosity expressed in this harrowing war would finally disappear.

On the other hand, what made me happy was that after several months, I noticed my hospital population declining for happier reasons. Many were getting well enough to go home (although many stayed on simply to help their comrades, which in turn helped me of course).

To lighten the general drabness of the place, church groups came in to sing hymns and choruses for the men on Sunday evening. I also arranged for church services on Sunday morning for the ambulatory patients. Other volunteers came in to read to the men and even write letters home for them.

What I found most pleasant was walks along the quay side of the Cape Fear River and looking over the ships that brought in goods from many far away places. The seagulls wheeling and diving off shore and the fishermen and fishing stories helped to lighten the day as well. The other event that I looked forward to was the weekly discussion groups I had arranged amongst our medical staff. These doctors brought forth animated discussions about not only their present patients, but also about medical matters they had learned of not only in the past but in present medical documents. Having my medical books enclosed in my trunk, I was often able to contribute.

The terrors of the war began to fade from me (and from my dreams). Even the terrible news of the assassination of President Lincoln was diluted by the happier events of the country pulling itself together.

As I sat on a bench in front of my quarters and watched the splendid summer sunset, I felt a torpor lulling me into reminiscences of the past years. The exciting and often horrible experiences of the past few years, including my medical experiences, flew before me like leaves before the wind. It was always been pleasant to receive letters from home. They seemed few and far between during the conflict but now they came even more often and indicated that the farm was doing well and that my return home was looked forward to. All seemed under good control at the hospital and I put in my request in to be mustered out of the service. My recent leave in early May last year gave me a great appetite to return home.

In the summer, my orders sent me to Raleigh, North Carolina, where I was mustered out on August 24, 1865. Mustering out again entailed a remarkable degree of paperwork and accounting for medical equipment.

Although I felt the nearly four years of intense, seemingly around the clock medical care and emergencies had equipped me well to return to private practice, I planned to take a post-graduate course at Bellevue Hospital in New York once discharged. I hoped this would bring me up to date on any medical advances and acquaint me with any fields of medicine that could have escaped me while I served in the field.

It was a bittersweet departure from my hospital staff and patients as I prepared to leave for home. The patients were uniformly sad to see me go and even a small impromptu party was given in my honor! The typhus epidemic problems had gone for the time being, and the organization of duties and services of the hospital were well arranged. All this allowed me to leave with no misgivings.

I sailed down the Cape Fear river as I left. I took a last look at the battered Fort Fisher as I sailed north to Philadelphia. I didn't even mind the many train connections as I went north to good old Hebron, Connecticut.

# CHAPTER THIRTY:

# *Home at Last*

What a wonderful respite from the war! Unless one has endured separation under such dangerous conditions, he cannot imagine what a tearful and joyful reunion this was! I was told I appeared gaunt, but tanned and healthy otherwise. Sister Sophronia and her husband, and especially the "little corporal," greeted me. He jumped up into my arms and hugged me. He had grown so big in my absence that I hardly recognized him. He felt well rewarded when I presented him with some spare brass buttons from my uniform.

My reception upon returning home that day in August, 1865 was gratifying and tremendous. For that happy moment I felt as though the suffering I had seen and been through was worth it. The Union was restored, and as a news item put it, we no longer used the phrase, "The United States are," but rather "The United States is." The crops were ripening and I felt that there was true peace in the world.

I met my dear Emma several times in the few weeks before I went to New York for my further education at Bellevue. Her father was kindly toward me when I visited their place overlooking the Connecticut River in Portland. On one such occasion I met her brother Tom Stewart, a ship captain. He had many a lively tale to tell regarding his sea adventures. On one such adventure his ship was crippled by a devastating storm. Despite the loss of the mast and gear, he piloted the ship safely to the harbor. He showed me the lovely gold pen (with a jewel embedded at one end) that was inscribed by the passengers in thankfulness to him, along with the dates of this event.

The time at Bellevue passed quickly and there were indeed many new things to learn. Some reports from Europe about invisible items called bacteria as causation of disease were especially noted. The stethoscope was developed, by which one could listen to the heart and lungs by auscultation. Much of the medical substances that I'd learned of long ago at Berkshire Medical School were from herbal sources. While these were still commonplace, they were being augmented by other chemicals. Indeed, this education was a "two-way street," because many students as well as professors were interested to learn of how we handled major battlefield injuries, as well as the many debilitating medical conditions. It has been noted that other medical conditions were a far greater cause of illness and death than were battlefield injuries during this four-year conflict. Regular rounds were made on patients with the attending doctors and professors instructing us. Physical medicine became a very important tool and the previously mentioned stethoscope gained great esteem in our minds. We learned this was first promulgated by a Dr. Laennec, who helped describe many conditions of the heart and lung that were previously only guessed at.

After my pleasant and instructive stay at Bellevue, I received a diploma of sorts and left to take up my life again in Connecticut. The program I completed at Bellevue gave me great confidence in being up to date in all manner of modern medicine.

Having grown up as a "country boy" and having lived in the "wide open" for several years in the army, I felt "hemmed in" in the large city. I knew I would always be happier living and working in a place where wide views and landscapes would be a regular part of my life.

*Colchester, Conn Jan 4th/66*

*Dear Father*

*I have not yet heard from the man in Bridgeport who has my mare, whether he will buy her or not.*

*If you can find where I can borrow one hundred dollars for six months or longer it would help me out I think. I would like it by Tuesday at least. If you can, I wish you would find out and let me know by mail Monday night.*

*I think prospects are good enough for success if I can live through the first starting in business.*

*If you can attend to this Saturday, you will accommodate me very much and help me through.*

*Your Aff Son*
*M.W.Robinson, M.D.*
*Colchester, Ct.*
*Wm. Robinson Esq*
*Columbia, Ct.*

You can't imagine how luxurious it felt to wash up and climb into a comfortable clean bed. No bugle calls or emergency trips to the recovery tents to interrupt sleep. The only problem was that it took a little time to get used to comfortable beds. Early rising on the farm and in the hospital was no problem, since the days also started early in the army.

I must admit to lolling about for a short time in bed. I looked at the ceiling and thought of my plans to get back into the practice of medicine. With some of my mustering-out pay, I bought some civilian clothes and also a horse. Some weight loss during the years in the service made other clothes left at home even more unusable (my new clothes fit well, but I was afraid I would outgrow them soon if I kept eating as well as I had been since my return).

As I returned to the farm in Hebron, following my New York stint, I was not only happy to see everyone again but also to learn that the conflicts over the operation of the farm remained settled.

Living in New York, buying new clothes and books, and educational expenses did not leave me much from my army and mustering-out pay. I had previously decided that Colchester, Connecticut would be the most satisfactory place to set up practice. A rubber factory and a new railroad running through it would improve my prospects in this small town. I could also be near my Hebron home and to my friend Emma and her Portland home. The time went by so slowly during the war years, yet the days, weeks, and months flew by so rapidly during my post-graduate time at Bellevue. To help me keep track of all these new surroundings and occurrences in my life, I scrupulously continued notes in my journal.

# CHAPTER THIRTY-ONE:

# *Resuming Medical Practice and a New Life*

I felt sorry and embarrassed to ask my father for a loan to help me get started in practice. Even with all his other responsibilities and limited finances, he seemed quite happy to do this. I guess now that Mother had passed on, he wanted even more to have family nearby. In long evenings by the fireplace in Portland, Emma was delighted by these plans (I had finally gotten up enough nerve to ask her for her hand in marriage). We were quite happy in each other's company and dreadfully lonely during my time at Wilmington and at Bellevue.

I am afraid I really tired my poor horse out by the many trips needed to finally select a house right in central Colchester. There was quite enough room for my office and for my quarters (we were already looking over proposed dates for our wedding). There was also a comfortable large barn, which not only housed some chickens but had a separate area for me to put my buggy and faithful horse. It was close enough to allow me to get out to it, rig up my buggy, and be on my way to wherever I was needed.

I finally moved my limited possessions to the new house in Colchester. I went to bed that night with mixed but mostly happy feelings. I'd waited all these years—as a preceptor under Dr. Craig, years at medical school, the war years, and post-graduate time at Bellevue—and now my notice of intent to practice was in the local papers. As the wind whistled down the chimney, I was beset only by the worries and apprehension that I was deeply in debt, with a house to maintain and plans to marry in the offing. I was happy that I at least had been given admitting privileges at nearby William Backus Hospital, in Norwich. My letter of appointment also stated that they regretted to inform me that the rates charged for in-patients had now been increased from ten to twelve dollars per week.

These were busy times for me. I felt needed in this community and starting practice was most fulfilling. These were also romantic times for me as Emma and I talked about wedding plans and all the details to be considered as we set out on our life together. (Her father had consented to this union some time ago.)

Frona agreed with Emma that it would be nice if I personally sent out wedding invitations to my local friends and also to any nearby comrades from the war years. Emma and I had previously agreed upon a wedding date of April 27, 1867, and she carried out plans to invite her many social friends and especially her relatives from Portland.

Frona and her husband had kindly offered the Abell house for the wedding ceremony. As the day came, I felt as nervous as I did on the morning of a major battle in the war. Not from any misgivings over the marriage, but only my concerns over being able to provide a happy home and life for my beloved.

All these concerns vanished when I saw how beautiful my bride-to-be appeared as the coach drove up to my sister's house. The Abells had done a wonderful job of filling the house with spring flowers and garlands. The scent from the spring flowers was most pleasant as we met at a table arranged as an altar. The lonesomeness of all the war years evaporated like the morning dew on this beautiful spring morning. What could be more superior than to be surrounded by my many sisters, brothers, nieces, nephews, my father, and especially the "little corporal?"

The ceremony and repast afterwards all went by too fast. With the sounds of the well-wishers calling after us, we departed for our new "home" in Colchester. I had already made plans for care of my practice so that Emma and I could take a short time to drive north to my old "stamping grounds" in the Pittsfield area. These idyllic days also passed by all too quickly, and we returned to the many tasks needed to start housekeeping and medical practice in our Colchester home. April 27, 1867 will be long remembered as the happiest day of my life.

I joined the New London Medical Society and participated in their many meetings and scientific sessions.

Thunderstorms in the middle of the night still conjured up battle scenes in my dreams, but the horrible carnage of these past events became progressively more blurred, and fortunately, further apart in my dreams.

From the depression and sadness and loss of friends in the war, I now was elated at the pleasant turn of events in my present life. There were many social events and chances to escort Emma, but also I went to many GAR reunions both in Connecticut and elsewhere. I was determined to save the elaborate badges from these conventions as mementos. Our fifth reunion was in Waterbury, Connecticut. This was in honor of our great commander Colonel Chatfield. His home actually served as our headquarters for the many events planned around the ceremony honoring both the living and the dead. The events surrounding his great leadership and unfortunate but heroic death were recounted several times by many of us.

While at this GAR meeting, Amanda Chatfield (widow of our gallant leader at Fort Wagner), had questions for me. She was anxious to know, on a firsthand basis, the details of his critical injury while leading the Sixth in the storming of the parapets at Fort Wagner. Although this may have been distressing to her, I gave her a detailed account of his reception at our medical area and of the care given him. At the least, she was pleased to know of the major attempts to treat him and of the valor he showed even at a time when he must have guessed that he was mortally wounded.

At a subsequent GAR meeting in New Britain, Connecticut, a Mr. Leonard came up to me and gave me a resounding clap on the back. He was most kind to me and told all within earshot how I dealt with his injuries and possibly saved his life many years ago.

Although I had witnessed many scenes of carnage on the battlefield, I particularly remembered an incident following a battle at Deep Run on August 16, 1864. In this Virginia campaign, some delays prevented the recovery of wounded from the battlefield. Ultimately, we were allowed to use the white flag to go out into the battle area where the cries for help were gradually turning into groans and later into soft mewling from soldiers at the doorstep of death.

We were searching for any soldiers who had a chance for life if evacuated. Some had their heads and faces half torn off; others had gaping abdominal wounds with their intestines spilling onto the ground. Although passed up as "hopeless" by some of the medical staff, I recognized a familiar Connecticut face, in great distress from a severe wound on the upper thigh. Even though this scene from Hades was dimming in the setting sun, I was able to clamp off a large artery and extract the bullet. I then arranged for his transport to the rear.

Mr. Leonard reminded me of all these details at his home in Litchfield, Connecticut, to which Emma and I were invited. We had a great visit with the Leonards and returned home to Colchester the next day. Mr. Leonard was kind enough to send me a newspaper item regarding all this and our visit there.

While looking for some older medical books, I came across a dusty old trunk in the barn. In it were some papers from the war of several years past. I decided to preserve the official orders, my sword, and other memorabilia, but in particular I decided to make further entries into my journals, which I thought were lost, but now discovered. I will now bring this old "War Journal" up to date with my life's path since the conflict. I had left the older journal in Hebron when home on leave in April, 1864. The second journal looked in even worse condition, probably because I couldn't protect it well from the elements in the Petersburg-Richmond siege.

Several years of caring for the nice people in this small Connecticut town had its rewards but, even though I was given strict cardiac advice years ago while at Bellevue Hospital, I developed a condition which left me short winded with but little exertion. After living with this condition for a few years, I thought that my breathing and general health would be improved by a trial of living in the west for a while. At a GAR convention, I learned of an opportunity to be a medical supervisor and superintendent of a gold and silver mining operation, near Sacramento, California (the Monte Cristo Gold and Silver Mining Co.). I don't know whether the climate or a less-demanding life were responsible, but I did improve.

Needless to say, I missed my family too much, and, with this mining operation doing poorly, I returned home.

Sadly, our firstborn son had severe respiratory trouble at birth. Little Harry died after only a few days on this earth. While this sadness will always have a place in our hearts, we became happy again with the birth of a son (Ralph Stewart Robinson) and a daughter (Annie May Robinson).

# CHAPTER THIRTY-TWO:

# Old Soldiers Never Die

After many years of practice in Colchester, I was offered the position as superintendent of the Fitch Soldiers' Home, in Noroton, Connecticut, possibly because of my deep admiration and affection for my former brothers-in-arms.

Challenging as the many years of ministering to the sick in the Colchester surroundings had been, more and more I began to feel a certain emptiness in my life, and accepting such a position would also be less demanding on my health. I thought perhaps accepting this position would solve these problems for me.

As a horse and buggy drove me and my family up the hill from the Noroton railroad station to the brick quadrangle and associated houses of the Fitch Home, I saw the blue-suited old soldiers lingering around the grounds. They were smoking, whittling, and occasionally looking up at the flag snapping in the June breeze.

Many rushed forward to greet me and at the same time tried to hide their emotions at seeing me. None of us were quite successful in this venture, as betrayed by the need to blow our noses or wipe our eyes.

A small group presented me with a cane upon which designs were burned into the wood showing emblems, insignias, and other reminders of this War of Rebellion. I felt quite a lump in my throat as I took a deep breath; my heart swelled with pride and at that time I felt an indescribable sense of joy as I was truly "home."

# BIBLIOGRAPHY

Adams, G.W. *Doctors in Blue*, New York, NY: Henry Schuman, 1952.

Angle, Paul. *The Civil War Years* (A Pictorial History), Sterling Press, 1992.

Bill, L. *Military and Civil History of Connecticut During the War 1861-1865.*
Croffut,1868.

Cadwell, C.K. *The Old Sixth Regiment, Its War Record 1861-1865.* Tuttle, New Haven,
CT: Morehouse and Taylor, 1875.

Cadwell, C.K. *The Sixth Regiment Connecticut Volunteers in the War of the Rebellion*
1861-1865. Hartford, CT: Press of the Case, Lockwood, and Brainard Co., 1889.

Commager, H.S. *The Blue and the Gray.* Fairfax Press, 1982.

Foote, Shelby. *The Civil War*, a Narrative (Fredericksburg to Meridian.) New York, NY:
Vintage Books, 1986.

McPherson, J.M. *Battle Cry Of Freedom-The Civil War Years.* Oxford University Press,
1988.

Moore, Frank. *The Civil War in Song and Story.* Collier, 1889.

Ropes, Hannah. *Civil War Nurse.* University of Tennessee Press,1988.

Ward, G.C. *The Civil War-An Illustrated History.* Knopf, 1990.

Wise, S.W. *Gate of Hell.* University of South Carolina Press, 1994.